Trying to escape his tortured past, Sergeant Liam Jacks travels aboard the transport vessel, the Santa Claus, as the security chief alongside his best friend and captain, Marc Danverse. Having survived the Civil War, they shuttle amongst the Proxima Centauri planetary cluster, trying to find some modicum of peace. Something of which Liam is in short supply.

During a stopover on the planet Luxoria, they take on a mysterious passenger. Hadrian Jamison's history is questionable and his effect on Liam is undeniable. The more they learn, the more questions they have. As they are drawn together, Hadrian's presence threatens to disrupt the quiet.

When Hadrian's past catches up to claim him, the ensuing conflict is more than any of them expected.

A NineStar Press Publication

Published by NineStar Press
P.O. Box 91792,
Albuquerque, New Mexico, 87199 USA.
www.ninestarpress.com

# The Luxorian Fugitive



Printed in the USA
First Edition
March, 2018

Print ISBN: 978-1-948608-31-2

Also available in eBook, ISBN: 978-1-948608-25-1

Warning: This book contains sexually explicit content and graphic violence, which may only be suitable for mature readers.

# THE LUXORIAN FUGITIVE

Centauri Survivors Second Chance Chronicles, Book One

*J. Alan Veerkamp*

# Chapter One

*"HAVE YOU FOUND him yet?"*

*"We're looking…"*

*"Hurry! We don't have much time!"*

*"Scanner picked up the target in the crowd."*

*"I have him in my sights."*

*"Sergeant, terminate with extreme prejudice!"*

*"I…I can't. You can't ask me…"*

*"Take the shot! That's an order!"*

*"Captain, you can't be serious."*

*"Pull the trigger, damn it, or we all die!"*

*"Oh God, forgive me…"*

Cold sweat rolled off Liam's body as he sat upright in bed, sheets tangled around his legs. His deafening pulse drowned out the soft whir of the environmental systems and the mechanical hum of the ship's movement. There was a hollow quality to the titanium hull of his private quarters that seemed to amplify the resonance of the dream.

"Pull it together, Marine. You're not a child." The horror refused to recede even now that he was awake.

Liam looked around his room as his reality began to settle. The windowless space was nearly pitch-black; the only illumination came from the data screen on the wall, its soft cyber-green time code proof that he was not lost in the abyss. Yes, he was aboard the cargo vessel the *Santa Claus*. Yes, they were en route to Luxoria from Alpha Centauri Prime for a supply delivery and pickup. Yes, he was security chief of the thirty or so men employed on the ship. Yes, the dream was of a harsh memory, but still just a dream.

"Mrs. Claus. Status report please." Liam spoke in quiet, shaken tones while threading his unsteady hands through his hair. A synthetic voice, sounding like a middle-aged woman, hummed back in response.

"It is zero three seventeen, Sergeant Jacks. We will be docking at Luxoria Spaceport Alpha at approximately eleven fifteen. System sync to the Luxorian environment is in progress and will be complete in two hours and twenty-five minutes. Is there anything else I can do for you?"

"No." His reply was brusque, but Mrs. Claus's feelings couldn't be hurt; she was artificial, after all. Normally, Liam found Captain Danverse's penchant for ancient Earth history—including the ship's name and the computer's voice identity—endearing. Marc was his best friend, after all. But that night, there was no comfort in it.

Even without the nightmares, it was hard to sleep well when forced to acclimate to a new planet's environment and timeline every time you came into port. The ship's systems were designed to gradually shift the sleep cycles of everyone on board to match up to the active hours for each destination. Add the dreams into the equation, and his rest was as fractured as his self-esteem.

"Lights. Low." Twin light panels on opposite sides of the small room began to glow. The undecorated metal walls were nothing more than panels hiding the storage spaces within. The large bed looked out of place in the three-by-four-meter space but at his size was required for any chance of a comfortable night's sleep. Not that he'd seen many of those in a long time. A lone desk sat in the corner with a basic chair on wheels covered in dirty clothes. Several recessed shelves held stacks of paperwork, but the entire room was devoid of anything personal.

Liam peeled himself from the dampened sheets, the fabric refusing to release due to the tackiness of his salty skin. He knew he couldn't sleep anymore, even if the bed weren't already cooling and saturated. The ship ran warm, but he couldn't suppress a slight shiver as the air hit his bare body. Even the dense pelt of hair that covered his chest, arms, and legs provided little warmth at the moment. He slid into a pair of cargo shorts and sleeveless shirt that were piled in the corner, too shaken to care if they were clean enough to wear. A pair of thick-soled sandals waited for him in front of the room's exit. Out of habit, he picked up his communicator from the random pile on the desk and put it in his ear.

He placed his hand on the plexiglass palm reader embedded in the hull and the door slid open with a loud hiss. From the outside, he slapped the matching panel to close the door and trudged out into the hallway.

His footsteps gave a soft metal echo as he wandered in no particular direction through the dimly lit tunnel. This was no luxury liner; a subtle vibration could be felt at all times from the tech and mechanicals hidden behind the scuffed and weathered walls. The *Santa Claus* was sturdy, but not designed for creature comforts. Captain Danverse had purchased the decommissioned cargo ship nearly a decade ago and offered Liam a job when the pair had left the military following the Centauri Prime civil war.

Intelligently, Danverse had populated the *Santa Claus* with a crew of men who could stand the long distance between stops and appreciate the company of their fellow men. Ports were few and far between, and it was a small world to live in for an extended span.

The planetary cluster of Alpha Centauri's binary star hosted an unparalleled fifteen or more planets that were capable of sustaining life, but travel between them could take weeks or months, depending on the quality of the ship engines. Faster-than-light capability was restricted to military-class vehicles. Subspace Link kept the information systems of every planet connected, and a space station-sized hub kept the entire cluster in range and part of a vast system of cultures and technologies. The current run to Luxoria had taken weeks, and they would only be docked for one twenty-four-hour cycle to load and refuel before making a return trip to Centauri Prime.

Danverse had chosen this way of life because, after the civil war, he had lost interest in planetary life, with its conflicting politics and the reminders of all the wasted lives. Liam had similar incentives to live off planet, bearing the invisible scars of a wartime job well done. He lived on the transport ship in an attempt to bury the memories, but the dreams always returned to reignite the guilt in his breast.

And he was remembering it oh so acutely at this late hour.

Liam knew the blueprint of the *Santa Claus* like it was imprinted in his brain, but that night, he wandered without recognizing what deck he was on or what passageway he was in. A strange sadness filled him, weighing him down as the confusion thickened. He knew he had ridden a lift and walked down several corridors, but he was damned if he was aware of where he was as he rounded a corner.

"Boss? You look like shit." Mac knelt in front of an open access panel, various tools around his feet and hanging from his utility belt.

"Mac? What are you doing up?" Liam straightened to hide his fragile frame of mind. Even now, his military training was too ingrained to stop maintaining the illusion of rank.

Mac was a rugged, dark-haired man with a sturdy body under the dirty coveralls he wore as the ship's head tech mechanic. Short and thick, with rounded muscles, Mac was smaller and less defined than Liam, but no less powerful. Dark hair covered his forearms and could be seen on his chest through where his zipper lay open. His youthful complexion was stained with machine oil and other occupational hazards—and too many hours on the job. Mac was the youngest man on the crew but made up for it in his diligence to his profession.

"Look who's talking. I'm giving the systems a few checkups and prepping the environments on Beta deck. We're going to have a couple guests taking the cruise."

"Why don't you let Mrs. Claus run the diagnostics and environmental presets and get some sleep?"

"First, I didn't get this good by letting the tech take care of itself. Second, I don't live on this boat because I trust anything to do my job, boss. That's kind of the same thing, but that's beside the point. Synthetic or not, if she strokes out on us, I'll be the one who gets blamed when we all start screaming 'Oh God, oh God, we're all going to die.'"

Usually Mac's crass sense of humor was infectious, but Liam was having difficulty holding himself together. A tremor was building, making it hard to stand still. Mac's brow flattened, and his scrutiny only made Liam's nerves worse. He could imagine the calculations going on in the tech's mind; he couldn't hide how disturbed he was. Mac couldn't know the cause, but he had to see the damage as Liam's facade started to erode.

"You okay, boss?" Mac's genuine concern was clear. Still, Liam was not about to share his past.

"I'm fine." He shifted his feet as he searched for a polite excuse to step away. The rising awkwardness only amplified his tension and made him pause when the ideas wouldn't form.

"The gym's always open. I bet no one else is up." Mac picked up a small tool and began making adjustments to the open logic boards.

"Thanks, Mac. That's not a bad idea." Liam was relieved Mac let the matter drop. "Don't take too long with that. We need you during the docking."

"Don't worry. I'm almost done. Besides, I only sleep about four hours a cycle anyway. My brain rarely shuts down enough. Too much nervous energy, I guess."

"Sounds like you could use a workout, too."

"How do you think I get the four hours in the first place?" Mac nodded down the hall. "Go on, boss. I have to get this finished, and you're distracting me."

Liam called out over his shoulder as he turned away. "All right. I'll see you before we get to port. You do good work, Mac."

"Go away, boss."

It took a few moments for Liam to process his location and head toward the gym, a large section of Beta deck housing a sizable exercise room, connected with lockers, lavatories, and an open shower room for the entire crew and possible passengers. Since the *Santa Claus* was a former military vessel, most quarters did not contain private baths. The communal bathroom for thirty men was maintained in a near-pristine condition. Mac was obsessed with the sanitary and recycling systems working at optimal efficiency.

Liam stepped off the lift and rounded the corner, stopping in front of Captain Danverse's quarters. Still haunted and fidgeting, he stared at the plaque engraved on the door. He knew he should go to the gym.

Fists tight, he resisted the urge to ring the door com. He should not be there. Not like this. It wasn't fair to everyone concerned. He spun away, took one step, and stopped.

"Mrs. Claus, is Captain Danverse in his quarters?" He rubbed his weary brow with an unsteady hand.

"Yes, Sergeant. The captain's status is marked as *In* and *Do Not Disturb*. Would you like me to contact him?"

"No, Mrs. Claus."

He stood unmoving for countless minutes, admonishing himself over and over. The dream had left him so anxious he could feel his skin crawling. Muscles twitched in uncomfortable patterns as he barely held himself still. In the end, desperation and need won out.

Hands shaking, he turned and pressed the door chime. With his gaze to the floor, he waited the endless seconds for the door to be answered, his guilty conscience overwhelming his senses.

CAPTAIN DANVERSE AWOKE with a start. The last three cycles had been long, with little sleep, so he had marked himself out to get some rest before they landed on Luxoria. A chime rang in the room, making him growl. Someone was at his door. *Can no one here read?* He took a quick look at the clock. *Son of a bitch!*

Throwing back the light covering, he stepped out of the bed, wearing a pair of lightweight sleeping shorts. He only wore them when he was alone in bed, and lately that happened more often than he'd care to admit. Just another thing to be annoyed at tonight. After commanding the lights on low, he stalked to the door and struck the control panel with a closed fist.

"Who the fuck doesn't know what *Do Not Disturb* means? This place better fucking be on fire." Whatever fool was idiot enough to wake him was in serious trouble. The heavy door shifted open. Even clad in his shorts, he knew he exuded authority. Upon recognizing his security chief, Danverse threw out his chest and stretched up tall. The dominance display was so practiced he barely realized he'd done it.

"Liam? What's going on? Do you know what time it is?"

Liam began to stammer. "I...I'm sorry. I shouldn't be here."

Hearing the fracture in Liam's voice and seeing the tremor in his stance, Danverse tamped down his intensity, his tone becoming one of quiet concern. "Are you all right, Liam?"

"I shouldn't be here. It's not fair. I just don't know how to handle it, sir." Liam's hazel eyes were shining, rimmed in red, and he refused to look at Danverse. The sergeant's breathing hitched, the ragged swell of his chest giving away the emotion about to crest over his defenses. Danverse knew what Liam was asking for.

*Don't do it.* It wasn't the first time Liam had come to his door. No matter how bad the idea was, his inner animal screamed to be let loose even as he tried to tell himself to send Liam away. But the hedonistic need wouldn't stop its relentless pleading. So he gave in to it.

Standing up tall, he summoned an air of command.

"Get inside, boy." Danverse placed a strong hand on the back of Liam's neck. "I know what you need."

A subtle pressure led Liam inside as Danverse reached out with his other hand and tapped the panel to slide the door closed. Liam made no effort to resist as Danverse held him in place, his authority well established.

"Mrs. Claus, captain's privilege. Privacy mode on."

"Yes, Captain. Door lock established. Soundproofing field on. Subspace Link firewall on. Surveillance scrambling field on." Mrs. Claus listed the security protocols as they were established. No one could see or hear anything that took place within the room's confines now.

The captain's quarters were the largest on the ship and included a private bathroom and living space. The general architecture was identical throughout the ship, but Danverse made a point to make a home out of his room. A vidscreen lined the wall under a small seating area with a fabric-upholstered chair and matching settee. Artwork from his private collection decorated the space, immaculate and ordered the way he liked it. The light panels were already on low as Danverse looked at his charge and uttered a simple command.

"Strip."

With his head down, Liam removed his few effects, folding each, and leaving them with his communicator in a careful pile near the door. Once his immense form stood naked and vulnerable before the captain, his breathing began to center itself. Danverse looked over the powerful man, admiring the swells of furred muscle and gruff good looks that made him popular with the crew. The sergeant's sleeping cock lay nestled in a thatch of hair between a pair of chiseled thighs. Everything about the man was impressive. With Liam perfectly posed with downcast eyes and hands behind him, Danverse welcomed the surge filling his cock.

"Stay."

Danverse walked over to one of the storage panels on the wall by the sleeping area and tapped a combination code on its keypad to open it. Reaching inside, he pulled out a series of leather straps and lengths of heavy metal chain. Liam didn't even raise his head as Danverse buckled the thick collar around his neck. The collar bit into his skin; Liam's eyes fluttered closed and a soft gasp escaped his lips.

Danverse spoke softly. "There are so many tech devices that can do the same thing, but I think the more archaic designs have a certain atmosphere." He fastened additional straps with sturdy, built-in rings around both of Liam's wrists. "The concept's ancient, but the leather's new. I had them made on our last run to Datham. They really outdid themselves."

Danverse clipped the chains from each wrist to rings mounted into either side of the collar before adding additional lengths extending from the manacles like dual leashes. Carefully, he stepped up onto the chair from the seating area and removed a painting from the wall above it, revealing a large metal hook welded into the hull.

"Come."

Pulling on the length of chain, he led the supplicant Liam to the wall. He stroked Liam's high-and-tight auburn hair and around the back of his neck before raising the chain over his head and fastening it to the hook. Liam's muscles stretched taut as he dangled, supporting his weight on the balls of his feet, arms raised like some obscene piece of art for Danverse's amusement. Once Danverse was satisfied that Liam was secure, he moved the chair well out of the way.

"You have no idea what the sight of you like this does to me." His words came out in a growl. "If the crew wouldn't miss you so much, I'd consider leaving you like this for several cycles." He roamed his hands over Liam's chiseled flanks and buttocks, causing Danverse's arousal to grow, his cock starting to leak. Without warning, he grasped a handful of auburn hair and pulled Liam's head into an awkward angle as he hissed in his ear.

"But we're not here for pleasure, are we, boy?" Danverse put as much menace into his voice as possible; Liam shivered in spite of the room's warmth.

In one practiced movement, Danverse's sleeping shorts landed on the other side of the room. Leading with his erection, he walked to the open storage, reached inside, and produced a coiled length of tightly braided leather.

"You're here over the blood you've spilled. Nothing will ever make that right." Danverse snarled as he allowed the braid to unwrap down to the floor, keeping only the thick black handle for himself. He stood surveying his prey, muscles going taut as he prepared to strike, his controlled breaths deepening in heat.

Liam yelped as the sudden hiss and crack left a deep red welt across his back. Two more searing strikes of the whip brought suppressed screams from his tight lips as he hung from the chains around his wrists and neck.

"The dead can't speak for themselves, but I know what you've done."

Another hard strike tore a forced cry from Liam. Sweat had already broken out in a thick sheen over his flesh, highlighting his glorious muscles. His strained shoulders pulsed with the series of quick, tight breaths he used to control himself between strikes. Danverse paused.

"If you need to cry out, go ahead. No one can hear you."

The next stroke was hard, and Danverse gave thanks for the privacy field to contain Liam's scream. Liam began to shake as lines of blood mixed with his sweat. Two more strikes punished his legs and buttocks. Danverse could hear Liam trying to restrain the emotions that were clawing their way out. This was nothing new. He'd seen it all before.

"I know what you need, boy."

*Hiss. Crack. Scream.*

"You need to let it out."

*Hiss. Crack. Scream.*

"You need to let it go."

*Hiss. Crack. Scream.*

Liam struggled to stay balanced. Unable to place his feet firmly on the floor, he swayed limply from the chains. A shudder ran through his tortured anatomy as the dominant touch of Danverse's hand stroked his head and neck and found its way into the sweat-soaked hair of his chest. Danverse cupped Liam's hardened nipple in his palm, rubbing in slow, tight circles.

Danverse spoke firmly to be heard over Liam's heaving breaths. "You can't change the past. We all did things we regret during the war. You need to release it." He moved his hand down the solid stomach and found Liam's swollen sex. "In more ways than one." Danverse gave a brutal grip to the steel-hard column, causing Liam to gasp and try to hide his face behind his suspended arm.

"I know you need this, boy." He released Liam and took several steps back. "You're here to be punished. I'm going to hurt you. I'm going to hurt you so you can't think of what you've done. There is no safeword. I'm sorry it has to be this way, but an exorcism is never painless."

Those were the last words spoken before the leather weapon truly came alive.

Danverse lost track of how many times the bullwhip blistered lines in Liam's flesh. It made Liam wail, bleeding and sobbing into the soundproofed room. Danverse struck the giant marionette like a sadistic artist possessed, his own hard member leaking glistening streams down its full length and heavy sac. He watched his charge closely as Liam teetered on the brink, his cries shifting into tortured moans. It was all about waiting for the right moment. It needed to happen soon; his own control was beginning to fray. Liam was almost there. With one last strike, Danverse saw the shift in Liam's countenance; the way his buttocks and hips flexed forward, the final precipice.

He dropped the whip and strode up to Liam, spitting into his palm and wetting his own flesh. Wrapping his brawny arms around Liam's head and chest, he thrust his slickened cock inside Liam, burying himself to the base in a single stroke.

A new kind of gasp escaped Liam as Danverse claimed him; Liam's passage spasmed at the intrusion and the quaking pressure on his rigid organ nearly brought the captain over the edge, but he held back. As satisfying as the sensation was, his own pleasure came second. Liam was here for a reason. Danverse understood that under the sobs and shame, Liam had a need to be broken. Pulling most of the way out before thrusting forward, he aimed his cock for maximum effect. No stranger to Liam's body, he knew Liam was near the end.

Still crying and grunting like an animal, Liam found the strength to push back into each thrust. Every time, his volume and movements grew more and more out of control. So Danverse pounded him even harder.

Liam shattered. His orgasm tore free to the sound of exhausted, harried cries. Pearlescent streaks painted the wall high enough that Danverse could see the dripping lines even with Liam's bulk obstructing his view. He continued his merciless rhythm for almost a minute until Liam's plateau began to fall and Danverse allowed himself to roar, filling Liam's channel with his own release, his arms tightening on Liam in surges with his own spasms.

As soon as he regained control of his body, Danverse carefully extracted himself. Holding Liam firmly with one arm, he unbuckled the straps around his wrists and neck. Long, thick rivulets of semen dripped down Liam's thighs, his muscles incapable of stemming the flow. Liam's head fell back on Danverse's shoulder and his arms sagged to his sides; he was barely holding up his own weight. His heaving sobs had faded into exhausted whimpers.

"That's a good boy." Danverse placed soft kisses along Liam's temple and stroked his chest. With a practiced hand, he turned Liam, who proceeded to curl forward and bury his ragged face into his superior's neck and shoulder. The captain's warm arms provided firm support as he sought to soothe Liam's heaving breaths.

Shifting his weight, Danverse led Liam into his private lavatory, keeping his arms around his broken charge. Over the sink, he slid the mirrored panel open, and pulled his personal medkit out onto the counter. He opened the case with one hand and drew out a small, worn metal oblong with a few protruding buttons that fit into the palm of his hand.

With careful steps, Danverse maneuvered the two of them into the shower stall. He pulled Liam close, ignoring the blood and sweat still seeping down his back, as he kissed the side of his head once again.

"Shower on. Soft. Thirty-seven degrees Celsius." A cascade of water washed over the pair. Danverse turned Liam around so he had access to his wounded back. He pressed a button on the device he carried, and an amber glow warmed the end.

He ran the device over the welts and lesions one by one, watching the marks fade and the flesh knit together. Under close observation, faint lines showed the remnants of earlier sessions to a knowing eye. The gentle shower washed away the blood as each wound was repaired. When the water ran clear, he turned off the device and traded it for the soap, carefully lathering Liam. With silent tenderness, Danverse washed the salt from every square centimeter of his friend's skin. Liam made no more than soft whimpers as he floated in blissful half awareness, the only time he found true peace.

Once the shower was complete, Danverse dried them both with a blue square of hyperabsorbent fabric and led them back into the main room.

"Water. Cool." The drink dispensed, and then he placed the glass to Liam's lips. "Drink. You need this. Slowly." Once Liam had his fill, Danverse finished the glass and dropped it into the washer/recycler. Then he led Liam to the bed, the covers still pulled back from earlier.

"Get in. I'll wake you when we're close to docking."

Liam climbed into the large bed, facing the wall, with Danverse following him. He wrapped his strong arms around Liam, caressing the furred abdomen while pressing his chest into Liam's back to comfort him. Danverse commanded the lights off and plunged the room into darkness as he relaxed.

He waited long minutes, taking in the sergeant's scent as his breathing leveled and Liam fell into a deep sleep. Once he was convinced Liam wouldn't awaken, he softly kissed the back of his head.

Whispering into the quiet of the still-soundproofed room, Danverse ran a hand through his hair as he settled into his pillow. "Damn it, Liam. Why do we keep doing this to each other?"

RUSHED FOOTSTEPS THUNDERED in the still night air. Stopping for a moment on the walkway, he looked back at the sumptuous house he was leaving, excited and anxious. As he hesitated, he took in the texture of his hooded cloak with his fingers like a security blanket.

The hooded man's gaze circled as if this was his first real chance to view his surroundings. A palatial mansion of metal and stone loomed in one direction and a massive, elaborate gate ended the walkway in the other. Rows of decorative trees manicured into perfect shapes lined the grounds as far as he could see.

Nervous, he turned first one way and then the other. With a resolute breath, he clutched the bag over his shoulder and strode for the exit. There wasn't much time. With a tentative hand, he touched the gate and it sprang open. The electronic locks had been disengaged.

Stepping out, he surveyed the quiet street. The black vehicle he had been escorted in was no longer here. Only a dirty yellow transport sat along the curb with its lights on and engine running. Sturdy but unkempt, the vehicle looked out of place amongst the affluence of this neighborhood. He understood the feeling. It was perfect.

The window slid open, and the driver stuck his head out. He was older, common and working class, but that was unimportant to the hooded man right then.

"Are you my fare to the spaceport?" The driver's voice had all the grace of road gravel.

The hooded man couldn't stop looking around warily. "Yes."

"Well, get in, already." The passenger door levered open. "I've been waiting for twenty minutes. If this wasn't paid for up front, I'd be gone by now."

The hooded man quickly climbed in. The seats were made from cheap fabric and well weathered. Odd smells came to his nose, and he was thankful this was a one-way trip. With a soft shudder, the transport lifted from the ground and glided down the road.

"You going anywhere special?" the driver asked.

"Please, just drive."

As a passenger without an escort for the first time in years, he couldn't help rubbing his hands together with a nervous twitch, unable to calm himself. Scenery flashing by the speeding vehicle sought to entrance him but only succeeded in making him more agitated. Everything around him was alien; he had no concept of where he was. That was nothing new, though. How many times had he ridden in darkened vehicles, unaware of the path he was taking?

He caught sight of the driver in the mirror and noticed the man trying to get a look at his hidden face. He pulled on the edge of the hood to conceal himself better.

"I would appreciate it if you watch where you are driving." He hadn't raised his voice, but it was full of warning. It surprised him how easy it was—he was unaccustomed to asserting himself in public. Reluctantly, the driver focused forward, grumbling under his breath.

He hoped the driver couldn't see his hands. In his discomfort, he couldn't hold them still. Splaying them out wide and then closing them into fists over and over, he couldn't stop looking at them. Were they stained? Were they covered in blood? In the night, it was impossible to tell. All he knew was that he needed distance from the mansion.

"How long will it take to get to the spaceport?"

"Spaceport Alpha is about an hour away."

The hooded man nodded in the dark. "Thank you."

He settled back into the dubious seat and tried to get comfortable. The plan was in motion, and he couldn't arrive at the spaceport soon enough.

# Chapter Two

THE HOODED MAN tugged at his worn leather cloak as he stepped out of the restroom. He had run his hands through the sanitizer at least four times. Although they looked fine when he turned them over to inspect, he still felt unclean.

Luxoria Spaceport Alpha was a sprawling center of commerce, and he felt dwarfed by it. Travelers marched through the concourse in all directions, performing some chaotic ballet that he didn't feel a part of. How could you be alone surrounded by so many people?

In spite of his size and strength, he felt very small and uneducated. The whole facility confused him, and it was unwise to ask for help. He needed to keep himself secret. How would he find his way in all of this?

A tall stranger walking over to an unusual kiosk a few meters from where he was sitting caught his attention. The man asked the object for directions, and a map appeared on its surface. He waited for the man to leave and cautiously stepped forward to the kiosk, taking a look around before facing the device.

Leaning forward, he asked his tentative question. "Where would I find the *Santa Claus*?"

Even though he'd just seen how the device worked, he still gave a start as the surface came to life.

A pretty, yet artificial voice spilled out of the kiosk. "The cargo-class vessel *Santa Claus* is scheduled to land at bay Alpha Gamma One Four. Boarding of passengers will commence in thirty-two hours and twenty-three minutes."

Holographic text and a map marked the location. From what he could tell, he was at the starting dot and the pulsating arrow told the direction. A quick scan of the area indicated the graphics matched the basic area he was standing in. This was good. He could follow this.

A few hours went by as he explored the station and found the landing bay for future reference. He attempted to stay quiet and unassuming, a relatively easy thing among the multitudes coming and going. Mere moments before two men in uniforms appeared from around the corner, he ducked into a small shop entrance. They never even noticed him. Even so, he kept looking over his shoulder, expecting to find his security escort, but there was no one there. Before long, he had retraced his steps back to the information kiosk.

"I need supplies. Men's grooming. Clothing." He paused for a moment. "And paper. Where can I find real paper?"

"All of these items can be found at Star's Department Store in the market district." A map image followed the kiosk's response, and he committed it to memory.

The shop was easy to find, the storefront larger by far than most he walked past. It took some work and more time than he wanted, but he located the things he was looking for. It was tempting to continue, but he felt leaving the shop and searching out a secluded place to wait would be a better option.

Following another customer, he found an available cashier, a middle-aged woman with a pleasant manner. As he watched, she ran his items over the scanner in the counter and read the total that appeared on her monitor.

"Will you be paying with an ID scan today?" she asked.

A chill ran down his spine at the thought. "No. No ID scan." He hoped he hadn't reacted too quickly.

A rush of panic began eating into his chest. He wasn't sure what he should do next; he had so little experience in this. It would be disastrous if she became suspicious and he attracted attention.

"Wait. I have this." His hands began to shake as he dug into his bag and pulled out a small card. It was translucent, with filament circuitry running along the surface in elegant patterns.

"A currency card? Of course, we can use that." Her voice was very helpful and warm, something else he was unaccustomed to. "Do you know how to use it?"

Realizing he was just standing still, he looked around and shook his head no.

"Touch it to here." She smiled and pulled out a data pad, extending it across the counter for him. Carefully, he touched the card to the pad, and it responded with an electronic chime. She gathered his purchases and handed him the package. His hands wouldn't stop shaking.

"Are you okay, sweetheart?" He could feel her genuine concern. A vague remembrance of his mother came forward. She might have been like this if she had the chance. "You look a little unraveled."

He admonished himself for losing his composure. Years of training seemed wasted if his practiced resolve could be fractured by this. He had endured far worse treatment with no visible effects over the years. *Find your center.* With a deep breath, a stoic calm came over him. It was a facade, but that was necessary. This was not the time to be unnerved.

"I am fine. But thank you for all your help." He bowed and left the store with a calm step.

Once he was back into the milling crowd, he could feel the edgy discomfort beginning to creep in. Everything around him was so foreign it strained his ability to find his center. He needed a quiet place to wait out the next step in the plan—preferably, someplace with a cup of tea and something to eat. Across the way, he spotted another information kiosk. Feeling more confident, this time he walked right up to the device.

"I need a restaurant that serves Jahrling tea."

"Checking menus with Jahrling tea... Café Aroma on deck four." Directions appeared, making the location easy for him to find. The restaurant seemed remote in regard to the rest of the market district. It would be easy to stay in that area until it was time.

Perfect. A nice, secluded place to wait for passenger boarding to begin. Twenty-eight hours and counting.

ONCE THE AUTOPILOT engaged, the station's homing beacon guided the incoming cargo vessel. The sturdy craft shuddered as it slowed to the designated landing pad at bay Alpha Gamma One Four and came to a halt. Vents opened along the bulkhead, releasing dense plumes of steam as the massive weight settled into itself. Liam stood sentinel at the exit hatch's viewport. The ship's engines powered down and the port's deckhands came out to greet the *Santa Claus*'s crew.

A voice piped through the ship's communication system. "Welcome to Luxoria Spaceport Alpha. You are cleared for thirty-six hours to refuel and reload. Please register with the dockmaster upon disembarking. Enjoy your stay."

With a loud hiss, the hatch pulled open and lowered itself to the hardened surface, forming a staircase. Captain Danverse and Sergeant Jacks were the first to disembark as the rest of the crew shut down the final systems.

A short, wide man in an olive jumpsuit, carrying a flat holographic pad terminal, walked up to the ship. He stopped short of the ship's hatch and waited as information about the *Santa Claus* was displayed over the device in his palm. With quick fingers, he filed and sorted through the floating information until he stopped, smiling with a raised brow on the image of Danverse. After an extended pause, he took a cursory glance through the rest of the ship's command staff.

"Greetings, Captain Danverse, Sergeant Jacks." His attention focused almost solely on the captain. "I'm Daniel Wallings, the Alpha Gamma dockmaster. I'll need a DNA ID scan, please." With a swipe of his finger, the data pad's graphics changed. Both men took turns placing their hands into the holographic display to confirm their identities. The pad's lettering turned green and Wallings smiled.

"Thank you, gentlemen. You are cleared for a thirty-six-hour stay. Fueling crews will begin their procedure in one hour. For safety and liability purposes, once fueling has begun, no one may enter or leave the ship for the following six hours. Customs scans and cargo loading and unloading will be done afterward. Passengers may board no sooner than within the last six hours of your leave. Do you have any questions?"

"Just where I can find a decent bite to eat." Danverse flashed a charming grin and a subtle growl. He puffed out his chest and subtly towered over the smaller man.

"The market district has the best range of cantinas, sir." Wallings began stuttering and a blush colored his cheeks. "It's where most visitors go to, um...eat. There are transports to every district." Wallings shivered slightly as he lowered his head, looking up at the captain through his lashes.

Danverse leered at the dockmaster. "Thank you, Daniel. I will be sure to get in touch with you if I *need* anything else."

Gaze locked onto Danverse, Wallings missed Liam rolling his eyes. With a polite nod, Liam and Danverse strode out of the landing reception area and headed for a transport to the market district.

Liam shook his head and sighed. "Was that really necessary?"

"It never hurts to get the man in charge on your side during business. If I have to fuck the little guy to get us out of here on time, I will." Danverse chuckled. "It's nice to hear you talking again, by the way. You've barely spoken since you woke up."

A sadness crept into Liam's features as he shifted, turning his face away from Danverse. He was feeling sane again, but an incredible shame came along with the method.

"I'm fine." Liam was a strong man, but being in the presence of the man who had seen him at his weakest, at his most unguarded, unsettled him. It wasn't the first session with his best friend, but this time had been more severe than any in the past. The force of his climax was devastating and mind-numbing; he had never come so hard before. The need for the pain and submission to release the rending guilt made Liam feel soiled. Not because he liked it so much, but because he couldn't be more than a good friend to the man who could bring that out in him.

Danverse had, on more than one occasion, been witness to the demons Liam harbored; his ability to help was one thing that drew Liam to him. Their sessions beat down the guilt and terrors, but it wasn't right. It wasn't romance bringing them together. They used each other to find something they couldn't find anywhere else, and they both knew it. Liam needed more even if he sometimes felt he didn't deserve it. They would always be connected in some fashion, but life mates? No. In the end, that wasn't possible.

The captain's firm hand wrapped around Liam's biceps, pivoting him and forcing his attention.

"Did I take you too far?" Danverse's focused blue eyes bore into Liam.

"No."

"Liam. Talk to me. I know I pushed you hard last night, but it's how I read it." The words were hushed, meant only for Liam.

"I know, Marc. You didn't do anything wrong. But it's still too fresh." Liam turned his head away and raised his outstretched hand. "Give me a little space. I'll be all right. I just need to clear my head a bit. Don't worry. I'll be back in plenty of time for cargo changeover."

With a gentle pull, Liam released himself from Danverse's hand. It didn't take much. The captain didn't resist as Liam put some distance between them and flagged a transport. He chanced a glance over his shoulder as Danverse stood unmoving, his demeanor deflating. Liam turned away when he couldn't look anymore at the pleading stare in his best friend's eyes.

AN ARTIFICIAL BREEZE wafted through the port. Every station had a similar texture. The miniature cities were the transition between the real world and his life among the stars. Danverse had little need for the real world and rarely visited it beyond the spaceports. His little piece of reality where he was king suited him better. Only right now he couldn't enjoy it. The transport carrying his best friend glided away and he wondered if he had harmed Liam more than helped.

Danverse had always been in the scene. He could barely remember his own indoctrination, but it began shortly after the death of his mother. The how and why never seemed to be important; it simply was. Danverse never apologized for his tastes and never hid them. He dominated his partners and they responded in kind...when he could find them.

Liam was never intended to be a part of it. They had become friends in the Marines well before Alpha Centauri plunged itself into civil war. Being five years older, he found himself taking Liam under his wing. He mentored Liam through his training and the two bonded. Finding two non-heteros without a sexual agenda was uncommon in the ranks. Danverse being the superior officer was never a factor in their jobs or their friendship. They found a common interest in vids, alcohol, and locker-room talk about their sexual conquests. Before long, they were inseparable.

Liam had never flinched over Danverse's tastes. He even seemed to enjoy the stories. Their relationship was a perfect camaraderie.

Then Belathius Pointe had happened.

Danverse closed his eyes tight as he paused and took a deep breath. It would be better if some memories never resurfaced.

Following Belathius Pointe, Liam had been swallowed by guilt and horror. His moods were uncontrollable and sudden; he'd vacillated between sullen and enraged without notice. He had been drowning. The captain had his own regrets but more self-control and managed far better than his best friend. Two weeks after the incident, Danverse had been having a drink with Liam, trying to help him find a way to cope.

He wasn't even sure how it happened. It hadn't been planned; he had no intention of ever bedding Liam. The whiskey, emotion, and closeness allowed them to cross a line. Liam begged to be fucked harder and rougher, and in the heat of the moment, Danverse complied. Afterward, once they were sticky and sated, Liam seemed to find a sense of peace.

There was some awkwardness the next morning, but they managed to survive it. The civil war had ended, and with the surplus of personnel, they were both offered buyouts on their military contracts. Danverse purchased the *Santa Claus* and began his life away from the chaos of the real world. Liam wasted no time in accepting his offer to be his first mate.

Before long, Liam began periodically appearing at his door, distraught, and the rough sex that followed would give him some form of absolution. It started simply enough, but over time, it escalated to a level more extreme than Danverse had expected Liam capable of. The sessions had become more and more brutal.

Last night had been especially scary. As exciting as Liam's complete submission was, Danverse was all too aware how tenuous his own control had been. Accepting Liam's trust came with an immense obligation, and Danverse had nearly abused him beyond his need. There had to be a better way to help Liam, but he wasn't ready to let him go. He felt too responsible for him and too connected to him.

With a heavy sigh, he drew a small com-pad from his pocket and pulled up his station itinerary. His time was limited, and he had errands to run. He tapped out a quick message to Gamin, the ship's cook, and then went back to his list. With a quick analysis, he put things in order to make the chores as efficient as possible.

Dropping the pad back into his pocket, he flagged a transport of his own. Liam had said he was coming back and would find his way home; Danverse had to believe that. He wasn't prepared for any other possibility.

LIAM EXITED THE transport and stepped into the herd of travelers and merchants in the market district. Distance made the earlier events seem smaller, and he began to immerse himself in the foreign place.

Luxoria had a reputation for opulence and quality, having been settled centuries ago by the wealthiest families and corporations during the Great Migration. The spaceport was no exception. The marketplace's architecture was immaculate and beautifully designed; the flawless construction was the obvious mark of the highest quality. Maintenance droids kept the rows of businesses free of dirt and clutter. The many shops occupying the district were stacked over each other in multiple levels connected by gravity lifts.

Not wanting to risk becoming lost, Liam walked over to a holographic information kiosk in the center of the walkway.

"Restaurant list, please. Moderately priced. Cooked, not synthesized. Quiet."

A list of options floated before him. Choosing one at random, Liam reached forward and touched its name. The blue text flashed yellow and, with a quick-sync transmission, a golden arrow graphic projected itself from the communication device around his ear. Liam followed the pointer as he looked around at the various stores along the way.

One store showed a menagerie of exotic pets from various worlds in the cluster. What an awful thing to deal with in space. Mac would have a stroke cleaning up Argarian bird shit. Liam was glad they didn't allow pets on the *Santa Claus.*

He walked past several women's boutiques and stopped in a men's shop where he ordered a few tunics and breeches to replace ones he'd torn over the last few months. He also picked out a few new jockstraps. *Never have enough of them.* Payment was made by DNA ID scan and Subspace Link to his private account. Once he'd ordered the purchases sent to the docking bay, Liam was back on his way.

Rising up one level via the lift, and following one more row to the end of a long string of establishments, Liam found himself at the entrance of Café Aroma. He stepped inside the darkened, intimate space and was greeted by the fragrance of exquisite spices that left him with an instant hunger.

The host led him to a tall bistro table barely large enough for two, leaving the menu pad in front of him. He felt ridiculous climbing onto the tiny stool and considered asking to be moved to a larger space, but he didn't have the energy to complain. Paging through the choices, he settled on a glass of whiskey and a large bowl of Bandish stew. Another DNA scan placed the order, and a server brought over the drink in a squat tumbler.

It was between main meal hours so the café population was sparse. Liam sipped the full-bodied drink as he surveyed the room's few occupants. A young couple talked quietly as they ate, their heated stares only for one another. An older gentleman chewed his meal while engrossed in his Subspace Link browser.

Liam was fascinated by the last customer. The man was covered in a knee-length hooded cloak made of worn leather, and heavy black leggings. He sat sipping his drink and eating his meal, doing nothing out of the ordinary. In the darkness and with the hood drawn, Liam was unable to see what the man looked like, and the bulkiness of the robe disguised his shape. Having the hood up indoors struck Liam as unusual, but having seen enough culture variations over the years, he let it pass. Other than looking in Liam's direction when he'd entered, the hooded man had done nothing to draw attention to himself.

Liam couldn't understand why he found the hooded man so alluring. He couldn't even see his face. Perhaps it was the way the man tried to be nondescript. It was subtle. Most wouldn't see it, but a good security chief would have a talent for noticing things that were out of place.

The man was sitting in a restaurant on a planet Liam was unfamiliar with. Maybe he just wanted to be left alone.

He finished his drink and signaled for a second. Minutes later, the server appeared with a steaming bowl of Bandish stew and a fresh drink. The savory aroma made Liam's mouth water. It had been long weeks since he'd had the opportunity to enjoy his favorite dish. For him, it was the ultimate comfort food, and he eagerly tucked in.

The server walked away in the direction of the hooded man. The man reached out, without looking, a split second before the server tripped on the rug and dropped the empty glass into the man's outstretched hand. He handed the glass back to her, and she stood there looking startled. She stammered a quick "Thank you" before rushing into the back.

How odd. That almost seemed rehearsed. His hand was out before she tripped.

Liam shook his head. It had nothing to do with him. He levered another heaping spoon of heaven into his mouth. The stew was far more important, and he still had at least five hours to burn before it was time to go back to the ship.

"PASSENGER BOARDING FOR the *Santa Claus* to Alpha Centauri Prime has now begun. Please stay within the yellow safety markers and have your itineraries available for review."

Liam always hated this part. He waited at the hatch with Captain Danverse to greet passengers. Well, Danverse greeted them while Liam verified their IDs and assigned quarters. It was a tedious project. As a cargo vessel, the *Santa Claus* was hardly a luxury excursion. Amenities were minimal and the ship was old. Passengers typically chose them because the cost was affordable. The trick was to make sure you didn't have someone on board who was homicidal or on the run from the authorities. Danverse had created a nice little world for himself with few issues. He wouldn't tolerate anything that might put himself and his crew at risk.

Station protocols required them to allow passengers a three-hour window to board, and there were only four reservations on this run. He knew Danverse didn't mind. The cargo was where he made the most money, but the occasional traveler kept things interesting. In near silence for almost an hour, the two men sat patiently in a pair of comfortable collapsible chairs from the ship, awaiting the first voyager.

Danverse finally broke the quiet. "Find a good batch of Bandish stew?"

Liam's brow arched as he turned to the captain. "How did you know?"

"It's what you always crave when everything implodes."

"Am I that predictable?" Liam grunted.

Danverse shrugged. "I wouldn't say predictable. I just know you."

"Bandish stew reminds me of my mother. She'd make it for me whenever I had a bad day. She never made it any other time."

"That's a nice way to remember her. My family life was a lot less maternal. No wonder I joined the military as soon as I was old enough."

Danverse turned to him, and Liam could see the question before it was asked.

"Liam, are we going to be all right?" Danverse hadn't stopped fidgeting since he returned to the dock. The air of unease was so out of character for the captain. Liam didn't like it. Danverse not being in charge would upset the sense of order to his universe.

Liam sighed. "Yeah. We'll be fine. I'm just a little embarrassed by it all. I wish I could find a better way to bury the past."

"You will. And you let me know if you need help with anything."

Liam snorted. "Pervert."

"Not just that." Danverse laughed. "I mean with anything you need."

"I know." It felt like the first time he'd smiled in days.

Soon after that, the first passenger came aboard. Dr. Davis Cellus was a professor in his fifties who had been on sabbatical and would be heading back to his regular life. He was heavyset, with a thin goatee and shaved head, dressed in comfortable clothing that spoke of a meager wage, but his manner indicated a modest lifestyle. Liam was convinced his accounts were heavier than he let on.

They turned the second passenger away. Clearly she had ignored the "No Hetero, No Female" rule. She had to be escorted off by station security when she started arguing. Danverse maintained that Mrs. Claus insisted she would be the only female on the ship. Liam knew better.

Danverse hadn't always placed such restrictions on passengers, but the ship wasn't designed with separate facilities. Privacy wasn't a focus on a military vessel, and he didn't want to spend the currency on making the changes. Voyages lasting easily six or more weeks at a time became tedious with complaints from hetero passengers unhappy about walking in on crew members having sex in the shower room or other areas. Danverse had no interest in changing the men's habits. Non-hetero passengers complained less or joined in. According to Danverse, since they didn't have passengers on every trip, removing orientation and gender issues made the whole process a lot easier. The captain liked it that way. Liam never saw the need for the policy and discussed the sense of it to Danverse on several occasions, but in the end, Danverse had final say. It was his ship after all.

Marley Keyes was next. He was a rough-looking man with a medium build heading for a new job opportunity on Alpha Centauri. He seemed uncomfortable and maintained an iron grip on the satchel strapped around his shoulder. Marley claimed to have never been off planet before. Liam was suspicious of the twitchy man, but the background check came up clean, so Marley joined the ship.

The boarding period was almost over before the last person on the manifest appeared. Liam had to remind himself not to stare. It was the hooded man from the café.

"I am Hadrian Jamison. I should have a reservation for passage to Alpha Centauri. I hope I am in the right place." The man's rich voice bore a delicate accent. Liam checked his list and scanned the man's hand. He seemed hesitant to be registered. Wanting him to feel welcome, Liam gave the data a cursory glance and then turned the pad off. Danverse threw a questioning look in his direction.

"I'm Captain Marc Danverse." He shook Hadrian's hand. "And this is my security chief, Sergeant Liam Jacks." As Hadrian turned and traded greetings, Liam got his first proper look at the hooded man. Hadrian was above average in size, just a little shorter than Danverse. His hand was veined and strong. He sported wild, long, dark hair and facial stubble over an olive complexion and had the most entrancing eyes Liam had ever looked into. Thick dark eyelashes outlined the white in stark contrast to ice-blue irises ringed in sapphire. It was otherworldly, and he was gorgeous. Liam found a heat rising in his chest as those beautiful eyes looked up at him through the haphazard locks of hair falling around his face.

"Do you have any other belongings to load?" Danverse asked, glancing at where Liam's and Hadrian's hands were still touching.

"No, thank you. The bag I am carrying is all I need." Hadrian nodded to the pack slung over his shoulder. He hesitantly removed his hand from Liam's.

"Then I can show you to your quarters." With one outstretched hand and the other lightly at Hadrian's back, Liam directed this last passenger up the steps. He noticed Danverse watching them with a crooked eyebrow as they passed. His mouth was slightly open, but he didn't say a word as they stepped on board. *What the hell was that odd look about?*

"THESE ARE YOUR quarters." Liam keyed open the door as Hadrian watched the simple procedure with an unusual intensity. The room was virtually identical to every other living space on board, save the captain's. Basic amenities were provided: bed, storage, lights, and privacy.

Hadrian's reply was gentle and polite. "Thank you, Sergeant. But I did not require a personal escort."

"I don't mind." He pointed at the panel mounted to the wall. "This screen has all the info, maps, meal times, et cetera you should need while on board. Subspace Link works through this panel as well. Mrs. Claus, the ship's AI, only responds to ship personnel." Liam was trying, with little success, not to stare like a lecher at his guest. He couldn't even see Hadrian's physique through the bulky robe, but he was drawn to him. Somehow he resisted the urge to reach out and touch.

"Is this a business trip?" Liam asked.

"I have someone to meet on Alpha Centauri."

"Oh. Is it a permanent move?"

"If I am fortunate, I will never set eyes on this planet again."

Liam could hear the sadness and exhaustion underlining the words. Recognized them because he knew their soul-deadening weight so well. Hadrian was bearing it admirably, but the weariness was beginning to seep through. An urge to help welled up in Liam. He wanted to wrap his arms around the smaller man and let him know it would be all right, but had no idea where the sensation was coming from.

Hadrian softened for a moment and looked up into Liam's eyes, exploring their depth. Liam had the distinct impression he was being examined. While Hadrian didn't smile, Liam could have sworn his expression shifted to some kind of innocent gratitude. It had been a long time since anyone fascinated Liam so quickly.

"Thank you so much for your kindness, Sergeant." Hadrian turned away. "I should get some rest, and I am sure you have many responsibilities more important than me before we lift off. It has been a very long day."

Liam couldn't help noticing Hadrian's fatigue. "You don't look like you've had much sleep."

"I could say the same to you, but I think that would be a story for another time."

"Okay." Reluctantly, Liam backed out of the room. "If you need anything, I'm in number 204, on the other end of Beta deck with the rest of the crew. If I'm not there, the status panel can let you know where I am. And please, call me Liam."

Hadrian nodded. "I will. Thank you."

"You're welcome. Seriously, if you need anything..."

"Thank you, Liam. It was a pleasure to meet you." Hadrian gave a small but genuine smile as he pressed the panel, sliding the door back into place.

Liam stared for several minutes at the closed hatch, feeling giddy and stupid. He made a silent oath that he would get to know Hadrian Jamison better. He had plenty of time; the trip would take several weeks. But first, he needed to adjust himself. He was aroused and uncomfortable in a way that hadn't happened since he was a teenager.

THE *SANTA CLAUS*'S rough vibrations stopped once it cleared Luxoria's atmosphere. A few calculations and the bridge crew directed the large vessel into the vector of Alpha Centauri. Once free of the planet's gravity well, Danverse gave the order to open up the throttle and get the ship up to cruising speed. The engine's fuel cells were full and more than ready to burn for the next seven weeks to their next port.

Once the pilot and navigator were settled, Danverse headed back to his private quarters. The takeoff had gone smoothly enough, but he was on edge. The crew had learned long ago to ride these moments out. They followed orders and did what they were told but stayed out of his way.

As the door closed behind him, Danverse stripped off his shirt and threw it on the desk. He opened a storage panel and pulled out an amber bottle of Centauri-distilled bourbon. Pouring two fingers into a glass, he took a deep drink, wincing as the vapors assaulted his throat and nostrils. Reaching back with a firm hand, he tried to release the tension at the base of his skull. He didn't know where this temper was coming from.

That wasn't true. He knew full well why he was so pissed off. *Fucking Hadrian Jamison.*

Liam couldn't take his eyes off of him.

Of course, he couldn't. The man was stunning.

Usually, Danverse was rational enough to know Liam would never be completely happy with him. The natural dominance that made him a good captain extended to every aspect of his life, including—someday, he hoped—his mate. Being in charge wasn't enough; he required an extreme level of control as well.

But Liam only responded to that level of direction and discipline as a method of self-punishment. When Liam finally freed himself of his inner demons, and Danverse hoped someday he would, Liam wouldn't need that side of his best friend. A rational man would accept it and let his best friend go to find a way to make himself happy.

Danverse wasn't feeling 100 percent rational at the moment.

How could he? Every time he relived the previous night's session with Liam, even for a moment, he would start to harden, which wasn't easy to hide in these trousers. So far, Liam was the only one who had indulged his darker side to this level. Others had tried, but no one else needed him the way Liam had.

It wasn't as if he hadn't tried. He populated his crew exclusively with non-hetero men to increase his chances, but it could be very lonely in space. He had once thought about Mac filling that role. The brawny tech was the physical type that caught his attention and was always eager to please. Amid all the raucous jokes, there was a glimmer of innocence in Mac's eyes Danverse found appealing. But he knew he would ruin that if they became close. He always did. Perhaps that was the real reason he couldn't give Liam up.

Danverse wasn't quite ready to face that reality.

"Mrs. Claus." He polished off his drink with a hard swallow. "Subspace Link. I want all available information on passenger Hadrian Jamison. Send everything to my monitor."

"Of course, Captain."

Pouring another bourbon, he walked with drink in hand to the monitor mounted on the wall above his desk. Mrs. Claus had fed the statistics to the screen. An image of Hadrian was displayed on the left, with his biodata and information in a scrolling pattern down the right. He eyed the information carefully, looking for any discrepancies. Over and over, he read the data. Everything seemed in place. It all looked legitimate.

But there wasn't enough of it.

Danverse glared at the screen as he gripped his drink, threatening to shatter the glass. The history and data were minimal. A citizen of a planet like Luxoria would have endless pages to view. Even the lowest-born men and women were cataloged ad nauseam. Sorting through the other passengers' histories before their arrival had taken a ridiculous amount of time. What was in this data sheet could have been written in ten minutes.

This was a fake. He was sure of it.

# Chapter Three

LIAM DIDN'T UNDERSTAND what was wrong with Danverse. The captain had been short with him since they left Luxoria the previous day and would offer no explanation. The man who wanted to delve into his psyche after an explosive whip-and-come night was suddenly not being very forthcoming. Whatever was at the core of his mood would fade, and everything would soon be back to normal. It was just so fucking annoying when Danverse was surly. Maybe the rest of the crew had the right idea: steer clear of their grumbling commander until the storm passed. However long that would take.

Thankfully, Liam had duties that would keep him busy through the majority of the voyage.

He sighed and rubbed the base of his skull as his pad continued scanning yet another cargo container. The jet-black pad fit in the palm of his hand, sporting a few scuffs and scratches along the edges. The outside might not have been pristine, but like everything else on the ship, the tech was top rate, something Mac prided himself on.

The cargo bays were nearly full, which would bring a healthy wage. One of the few things to pull a grin from the captain's face—even if it was short-lived given his current mood. Large chests were stacked high in the endless rooms. The *Santa Claus* had four main cargo holds at the rear of the vessel. They were designed to transport military vehicles, so the space was vast. Liam made a slow pace down the narrow alleys between the crates. Severe shadows loomed in every corner with the lighting blocked in so many directions. If he didn't know he was the only person in the area, he might have been nervous.

In spite of customs prescanning, Liam insisted on screening each box himself after leaving port. If something dangerous appeared, it was going out the airlock. After finding a micro-nuke in a container three years ago, he was taking no chances. It was a long process, but it was a duty he took seriously.

Liam continued to catalog the contents. A number of crates were filled with clothing being shipped to various shops. One crate was filled with all the personal items Dr. Cellus had acquired on his sabbatical. Another contained Luxorian jade and Irithium jewelry, a collection of exceptional value. This list went on and on.

"Boss?" Mac's voice came through the com. Usually every decibel would echo there, but in the packed room, it sounded normal for a change.

"Yeah, Mac. What's up?" Liam continued reading the scan of the next crate in line.

"Uh...lunch. You coming?"

"No, thanks. I'm only in the second cargo bay." Liam fingered the hologram of the crate's interior, spinning the three-dimensional image, and inspected the contents. "This place is full."

"No kidding, boss. But you already missed breakfast. That shit can wait. You have weeks to catalog it all."

"Really, Mac. I need to make some more progress on this. I'll see you at supper." Liam tapped the screen, dissolving the image, and then aimed the pad to begin the next scan.

Mac's voice continued to chirp through the com. "Mrs. Claus, I'm going to run personal diagnostics on Sergeant Jacks's equipment. Please power down and disconnect all tools and scanners connected to his work protocols for one hour. Tech command alpha-papa-one-zero-seven-alpha."

Every device in Liam's possession went dark and lifeless. With an exasperated growl, he pressed the pad over and over to resume his work, even though he knew it was hopeless. He dropped his arms to his sides and rolled his eyes, releasing a defeated breath.

Liam chuckled as he spoke. "Oh, you little bitch."

"See you in the mess hall, boss." The com shut itself off.

Liam slipped the dead data pad into his pocket and stowed the rest of the scanning tools in the various pouches lining the legs of his work pants. The well-worn, sturdy fabric was meant to fit loosely, but around Liam's thick haunches, it showed off every curve and bulge. Liam couldn't really say he minded.

As soon as he began thinking of the mess hall, his stomach growled, and he laughed. There was so much work to do, but he shouldn't have skipped breakfast. Mac was right, as usual. Liam couldn't remember the last time the man had been wrong about something. The hyperactive little guy was constantly analyzing everything around him. It wasn't surprising he had every option calculated before he proceeded with anything.

Once Liam exited the hold, the large blast door hissed shut and he punched his personal security code into the keypad. With the potential value of the contents and their paychecks at stake, Liam insisted on something more than a DNA scan to access the hold during flight time. The last thing he wanted was a group of raiders boarding the ship and chopping off his hand to run rampant through the payload. The captain called him paranoid but acquiesced in the end.

The *Santa Claus* had been fortunate. Raiders seemed to leave the ex-military vessel alone. They had one of the highest safety records in the cluster for transport. An attack was still a real possibility, but this ship came with weapons, and most raiders didn't carry the firepower to overwhelm it. So far, it seemed it wasn't worth the effort.

After checking the locks on all four holds, he proceeded to the lift. When he stepped off into the hallway, his stomach groaned even louder. The mess hall was to the right, and it smelled wonderful. Apparently Gamin, the cook, was trying to impress the guests.

The hall was clean and, like the rest of the ship, full of gray metal. The benches and tables were set up in rows with a cafeteria-style buffet separating the dining zone from the visible kitchen. The majority of the crew were seated and enjoying the meal. Gamin, a prematurely gray man in his early fifties, was behind the counter serving. The personable polar bear was a master at working with real and synthesized rations but admitted a penchant for sampling his own work as he patted his rounded belly. Liam picked up a tray and Gamin immediately placed a full bowl on it.

"Only one choice today?" Liam asked.

Gamin winked at him. "For you, yes. Captain's orders." Liam was about to protest when the scent hit his nose. Bandish stew. He looked down at the savory concoction, his mouth open, and then back up to Gamin. It smelled just like his mother's recipe.

"How did you get the ingredients for this?"

"I have my ways. Now go sit down before it goes cold, son."

Liam grabbed a cup of water from the dispenser and looked across the mess hall. The majority of the crew were eating and socializing, except those who were on a night shift or unable to leave their station. Even the passengers were there. Dr. Davis Cellus was talking with a few of the men and clearly availing himself of the *Santa Claus*'s hospitality. No doubt some of the men were looking at him as a new playmate. He seemed quite happy to be on board. Marley Keyes sat alone, looking as agitated as he did when he arrived. He continued to keep his satchel close to his side as he glared suspiciously at every man around him. Liam wondered if Keyes thought he was going to be robbed, riding with this group of roughnecks. It might be worth keeping an eye on the man.

Liam turned to find Danverse waving him over to a table, dressed in a black thermal and gray breeches. Sitting next to him was a certain head tech mechanic with a giant toothy grin. He wore one of his usual sets of overalls, with a grease mark gracing his nose. Some things would never change. Liam put his tray on the table and sat across from the pair.

"I told you I could get him to come to lunch, Cap'n." Mac puffed his chest out with pride.

"I was beginning to think you were going to catalog all the cargo nonstop." Danverse said as Liam stuffed a huge spoonful of the stew into his mouth. His eyes nearly rolled back in his head. It was just like he remembered his mother's. "I almost did." Speaking while still chewing, he pointed his spoon at Mac. "Until this little fucker did an override shutdown on all my equipment."

The captain began laughing out loud. "I do love your ability to get things done, Mac."

"I may be a little crazy, Cap'n, but I know how to take orders."

The grin Danverse gave Mac was almost heated. "That's a good thing. I'd hate to have Gamin's efforts go to waste." He gave a satisfied smile as Liam continued to devour the bowl in front of him. "How's the stew?"

"Fantastic." Another loaded scoop filled his mouth. "Thank you."

Danverse nodded as Liam inhaled the obvious peace offering. He must have had Gamin collect the ingredients for the stew at the Luxorian port. Liam's embarrassment over the scene after his nightmare seemed unimportant and petty, as his best friend was proving his ability to take care of him in a different way altogether. He found he could set aside his problems for a short while and enjoy a good meal in the home of his choice.

Mac smiled at Danverse. "Would you like another drink, Cap'n?"

"Thank you, Mac. I would, yes." He smiled back, his gaze trailing after Mac as the tech eagerly hopped up from his seat. Danverse turned back to Liam.

"How's the inventory going?"

"Barely half done. We need to adjust a few clients' invoices. Some of the contents were more valuable than declared on their orders…" Liam trailed off as he saw Hadrian enter the mess hall.

He was still wearing the bulky robe and leggings, but his hood was drawn back, revealing his unruly head of dark hair. Even through the thick locks attempting to cover his face, his eyes could be seen across the room. His full lips shone inside the dark stubble painting his jawline. He walked to the buffet where Gamin served him with a jovial, yet mesmerized, smile. Carrying his tray, he headed toward a table in the far corner of the room. Throughout the hall, curious crew members turned in Hadrian's direction, the lust on their faces a tangible thing. Hadrian winced and hastened to his seat, avoiding the stares.

Liam shifted his chair back. "Excuse me." Danverse's smile dissolved, just as Mac returned with a cold glass of fruit juice. Liam rose and began to walk over to the solitary guest.

Liam approached Hadrian, who was eating a bowl of the stew. His lips caressed the spoon as he took a bite. Hadrian even ate in a beautiful fashion. Despite his wild appearance, there was a natural elegance to his manners. Liam stopped a respectful distance away before speaking.

"Can I join you?"

Hadrian gave him a gentle smile and nod, and Liam took the seat opposite him.

Awkward moments passed in silence before Liam got up the nerve to speak again. "How are your accommodations?"

"They are much appreciated, Sergeant." There was an artistry in the way Hadrian brought a spoon of the stew's broth to his lips.

"Are they comfortable? And please, call me Liam."

"Better than I had expected on a transport vessel, Liam."

Hearing his name in the exotic man's soft accent made Liam's chest throb.

"Was the Link information unclear?"

Another bite of stew entered Hadrian's open mouth.

"I did not make the reservation. It was made for me in haste, and I never had the opportunity to preview it. I assumed incorrectly."

Liam tilted his head. "Why the rush?"

"That is a story for another time." Hadrian smiled sadly as he took another taste of his meal.

"Do you like the stew?"

"It is magnificent."

Liam beamed and his thoughts drifted. A memory of his mother came to mind. Her arm was wrapped around him as he ate his beloved stew at the kitchen table. She was wiping the tears from his face and kissing his head after he'd broken his arm playing with the other children. She told him over and over that it would all be all right in the end.

As Liam came back to the present, he found Hadrian studying him. The warm glow on his features somehow matched the contentment in Liam's memories.

Liam sat upright in a rush. Realizing how closely Hadrian was scrutinizing him made him feel exposed. A voice inside urged him to tell Hadrian all about his mother and bare his soul. He wanted to tell Hadrian stories about her he hadn't even shared with Danverse. But he hushed the voice. You don't do that with people you've known for less than a day. The warmth began to fade from Hadrian's expression.

"How are you planning on spending your time on this trip? You'll have a lot of free hours on the way to Alpha Centauri."

Hadrian straightened in his seat. "Do not take this the wrong way, Liam. Your attentions are strangely honorable and respectful."

"Strangely? That's a surprise?"

"Call it a newfound experience. You are one of the few on board whose first thought has not been some variation of throwing me down over the table and fucking me senseless."

Liam felt himself blush at the image racing through his brain.

Hadrian appeared amused by his reaction. "I said not your *first* thought."

Liam had to clear his throat to reply. "Some of the guys can get pretty rowdy, I admit. But not all of us. Not all the time."

"My life is very complicated, Liam, and I would hate to drag you into the drama."

"Is there anything I can do to help?"

"It is very unlikely."

"Tell me what's going on."

Hadrian smiled bitterly at Liam and let out a tired breath. "You are a good man, Liam. Perhaps in another lifetime. Thank you for your company." Hadrian smoothly rose from the table, leaving a crestfallen Liam behind. As Hadrian exited, he cast a glance back over his shoulder. "I can see why your mother took such special care of you."

Hadrian's remark stifled Liam's urge to follow. He couldn't actually have known what Liam was thinking? No. It must have been a coincidence.


LIAM'S MUSCLES FLEXED under the grueling exercise he forced upon himself. One repetition after another made his arms swell and heave. Sweat ran down his back, soaking his shirt as he pushed through yet another set. One last curl caused veins to bulge as his endurance failed and his arms descended under the weight. He dropped the bar to the floor, and it automatically reverted the magnetic resistance to zero. Panting from the stress, he wiped at the salt running into his eyes.

He'd lost track of how long he'd been in the gym at this late hour. The workout had only marginally alleviated his frustrations.

It had been three days since they left the station, and Danverse's disposition had soured again. He wasn't angry and raging, but there was a constant undertone of unhappiness to his day. Liam had tried to get him to say what was on his mind, but he was impossible to squeeze information from, as usual.

Then there was Hadrian Jamison. Liam had only fleeting glimpses of the man since finding him in the mess hall. Cataloging the cargo had taken longer than planned. He didn't understand why Hadrian was being evasive. He didn't understand why he'd left the mess hall so suddenly. He didn't understand why Hadrian continued to invade his thoughts. Yes, Hadrian was beautiful, but there was a quality to him that made Liam crave his presence. In the past, Liam couldn't recall ever feeling more than an immediate and short-lived need for anyone.

Liam looked down at the weight bar and debated continuing his punishing routine, but his arms were beginning to feel like lead, and his clothing was so soaked in perspiration it was beginning to stick to him in uncomfortable places. Besides, it was late and he had duties that would no doubt come sooner than he would be happy with.

He lumbered out of the exercise room, viewing himself in the mirrors lining the walls as he walked past the weightlifting equipment and treadmills. Swollen with exertion, his body looked powerful and strong, even if he was a sweaty mess. The white sleeveless shirt and thin shorts he wore clung to him in obscene ways. The hair on his head and body was drenched and matted. Entering the locker area between the gym, lavatories, and showers, he sat on the changing bench. A shower was running in the next room as he peeled the garments from his sticky skin. Black leggings and a white shirt lay on the other end of the bench.

Liam entered the shower room and chose a nozzle a reasonable distance away from the stark room's other occupant. He touched the pad under the showerhead, ordered the temperature and water pressure, and began washing away the day's exertions. As he rolled his head under the steamy spray, he noticed his neighbor but, at first glance, didn't recognize him.

The man was built. His body was covered with corded muscle that reminded Liam of a coiled spring. The water flowed over a powerful back bearing an elaborate sheet of tattoos spilling from the stranger's left shoulder diagonally down to his right thigh, working around the firm, perfect buttocks. Another coordinating tattoo spun down the length of his left arm.

In his hand was a small shaving device. He glided it over his skin, its ultraviolet glow burning away the hairs. He stroked the razor over his chest, covering every square centimeter, and Liam nearly gasped as it moved lower and denuded the most perfect set of genitals he'd ever seen. Realizing he was staring, Liam raised his eyes to the man's face. His head was clean-shaven and he sported a neatly trimmed goatee that looked...

It was Hadrian.

Liam was unable to look away. Hadrian went about his business, continuing to remove the hair on his buttocks and legs. A warm, pleasant swell started between Liam's legs. Unable to stop it, he turned, hoping to hide the growing evidence of his arousal. Without so much as a glance, Hadrian seemed so engrossed in his project, Liam wondered if Hadrian knew he was there.

"Of course, I know you are there." Hadrian's voice echoed in the metal room, shocking Liam out of his trance.

Frozen in the awkward moment, Liam had no idea what to do. It was obvious he had been caught staring at the breathtaking man, who was now even more exotic than he'd thought before. Hadrian continued shaving without even looking in Liam's direction.

"This is quite a drastic change of appearance. What brought that on?" Liam made a desperate attempt to feel less like a voyeur as he continued to point his hard cock at the wall.

"I felt a need to change. I never liked the other look."

"Why did you have it, then?"

Hadrian continued to face away. "My...ex liked it that way."

Liam held back his discomfort. The flash of jealousy surprised and shamed him. "Are you trying to escape from him? Is that why you're on board?"

Hadrian paused. "That is also a story for another lifetime."

"I'm sorry. I don't mean to pry. It's none of my business." Liam started rambling; he couldn't backpedal faster if he tried. An anxious heat grew in his face as his confidence degenerated into something like awkward adolescence. "Anyway, I like the new look on you."

Hadrian gave him a sly smile. "Yes, the erection made that obvious."

Liam blanched. His penis was fully hard, standing straight and swollen upward to his navel. Hiding it had failed, and now he looked like a sex-starved creep. He had never been so mortified.

"I'm so sorry, Hadrian. It has a mind of its own these days." The hot water beating on his engorged member did nothing to quell its condition. Liam closed his eyes, trying to will his errant dick to go down. No such luck. If anything, the skin tightened further.

"There is nothing to be ashamed of, Liam. It is as impressive as you are." From the corner of Liam's eye, he watched as Hadrian turned off his shower, palmed the razor, and began to leave.

"If this life were different, Liam, I think I would like to know you better. But it is not. I am truly sorry about that." Hadrian sounded sad. Liam lowered his head, feeling juvenile and stupid.

"Do not worry. Someone will be along shortly to take care of you." Hadrian hesitated for a moment and then exited the room.

"Shit." Liam buried his head even farther under the spray. An overwhelming urge to pound his head against the hull came over him.

What was it about this man that made him so crazy? He hadn't thrown a rigid cock without being touched first since he was a teen. Ever. Now he'd done it twice in as many days over the same man, who hadn't done anything more than talk to him politely. Okay, he'd been ogling Hadrian like a horny schoolboy, but it had been a long time since he couldn't trust his dick to behave.

And Hadrian pointed it out. How embarrassing was that? And it still refused to go down!

Liam wondered if the day could get any odder.

"Nice rod, boss!" Mac had his usual toothy grin as he chose the nozzle next to Liam. Liam closed his eyes again in a sad attempt to hide. "Was that Hadrian Jamison?" Mac turned on the water and began soaping his compact body.

"Yes, it was."

"Damn. No wonder you're all boned up."

Liam couldn't stop from deadpanning out of embarrassment. "Thanks for noticing, Mac. You can just fucking shoot me now."

Liam returned to his shower and lathered himself head to toe. Having spent his time gawking at Hadrian, he had neglected his task. On a mission, he lathered every muscle and crevice diligently, rinsing away the grime, but his erection refused to flag.

"Um, boss?" Mac's voice was unusually timid.

"Yeah?"

"Um...if you want, uh...I could take care of that for you." Mac's cheeks flushed as he continued scrubbing soap through his fuzzy chest and stomach, keeping his gaze down and forward. Liam noticed how Mac's cock was also swelling.

"I thought you were seeing the supply officer."

Mac snorted. "You're listening to too much gossip. First, you know James's husband is on the ship with us."

"True. Not that I think he minds."

"Second, I'm not into a threesome with him and Barrus, and two bottoms bumping pussies doesn't a relationship make. We had a stupid hookup once, over a year ago, and some of the guys are still talking about it like it was yesterday. I haven't been with anyone since."

"Oh."

"I don't know about you, but I could use some human contact right about now." Mac's soft, pleading tone was not lost on Liam.

"I'm not sure, Mac." Liam's protest lacked conviction as he stared at the swollen length pointing out from Mac's hairy thighs.

"I don't want to marry you, boss. I just want to help out a friend. I can tell you're ready to burst. I'm not like a lot of the guys here. I don't do stuff like this very often, or ever these days. But, you know what they say, if you can't have the one you want..."

"I don't know..."

"It's not like this place hasn't seen this before."

Liam knew it was true. With a crew of thirty men in space for weeks at a time, the ship sometimes resembled a floating bathhouse. More than once, he had heard stories of the shower room becoming a mass of wet, interlocked bodies. The captain knew about it but didn't try to stop it. At times, he seemed to encourage it. Liam had joined the men on one occasion, but he didn't make a habit of it. He wasn't a prude, but ultimately, he was interested in something more private and bond-forming.

Liam gasped as Mac's rough hand encircled his flesh. He reached for the wall to steady himself. One stroke and the glans was already soaked and slippery, and it wasn't from the water.

"Damn, boss. You're not gonna last long." Mac dropped to his knees, never releasing his grip on Liam. He aimed the purple organ to his lips, ran a heavy, flattened tongue around the head to swipe away the juice, and slid the pole down his heated throat.

Every thought told him Mac was not the man to be playing with. As attractive as he found the short, hairy bulldog kneeling before him, this was not who he wanted sucking off his overheated organ. Frustration made his mind drift, and he pictured Hadrian's soft lips pursed around his shaft. Liam imagined Hadrian's startling ice-blue eyes looking into his own, making that connection, while the power and restrained strength of his chiseled physique danced under Liam's hands. Liam caressed his willing servant's head with his free hand as he gave rein to his inner beast.

Liam's mouth dropped open, uncontrolled noises escaping him while he watched Mac work his cock. Mac grunted in a happy cadence as he swallowed the fat piece of flesh over and over while stroking his own turgid member. There was nothing subtle about his craft. One hand slid up and down the shaft as it disappeared into his greedy mouth, while his hungry tongue ran firm, wet pressure along the entire length with each movement. He was obviously trying to finish Liam hard and fast.

Mac was about to get his wish. Liam's arousal was already skating along his breaking point, and the tech's enthusiastic feasting pushed him over the edge. A groan echoed with each burst into Mac's mouth as he pulled back, keeping the swollen head firmly against his tongue. After the initial surge, Mac swallowed down to the base, holding Liam's cock down his throat. Seconds later, his own self-choked moan matched the explosion firing streaks over Liam's leg all the way up to his hip. A long time passed before either man's breathing returned to something resembling normal.

With careful slowness, the men extracted themselves as Mac wiped his mouth with the back of his hand. "Thanks, boss. I needed that."

"We probably shouldn't have done that." Liam turned and faced the wall as pangs of guilt crept in along the edges, staining the moment.

"This hasn't changed anything, boss. We just helped each other out. That's all."

"All right." Liam wasn't sure.

"It won't hurt my feelings if you were thinking of someone else." Mac's voice became small and vulnerable. "I was."

Liam looked over and saw the hint of heartache on Mac's face as he ran his head under the shower. Heavy streams of water flowed down his shoulders and back, and Mac took a silent, deep breath, his composure seeming to fray. Liam knew the signs all too well. The welling in Mac's eyes as he chewed his bottom lip. He was pretty sure he knew who had Mac's heart. Hopefully, he would be worthy of it.

"Shit, this was stupid." Mac squeezed his eyes closed. "Of all people, you're the last one I should be blowing in the shower."

"Don't punish yourself over it, Mac. I think we both needed the distraction."

"This ship's too small. I don't want to start any gossip. No one needs to know." He opened his eyes wide to face Liam. "Don't even tell the cap'n, okay? It's not a big deal, but I'd rather he not know."

"No problem." Liam placed a comforting hand on Mac's shoulder. He could feel the underlying tremor and knew how close Mac's emotions were to the surface.

"Thank you." Mac raised his face into the deluge as if to wash away the evidence of his near outburst. Liam wanted to wrap his arms around him. He understood the humiliation, but knew Mac would break if he did. Instead, Liam ran a paternal hand over Mac's neck and head in the same soothing manner Danverse did when Liam was overcome.

Mac's eyes closed at the contact, and his tremors began to abate.

"Looks like I'm going to need to re-shower. For fuck's sake, you painted my leg!" Liam chuckled as he looked down at the wild, spattered streaks coating his muscled limb. Dropping his hand, Liam moved back to the actual shower he had neglected.

Mac's laugh was sheepish. "I was a little pent up."

"Welcome to the club."

# Chapter Four

HADRIAN JAMISON WAS running from someone. Liam was sure of it.

One—a hastily crafted stellar voyage with minimal possessions. Two—a radical change in appearance. Three—evasive behavior. Four—counterfeit personal data. An elementary school student could add those numbers together.

Alone in his quarters, Liam was clad in only a rust-colored T-shirt with a retro spaceship imprinted across the chest and his favorite black jock, his preferred lounging outfit in his private hours. The T-shirt stretched tightly around his torso, its fabric buttery soft with wear, the once-vibrant color washed out over time. With a drink in hand, he padded barefoot over to the vidscreen mounted on the wall.

Liam studied the data illuminating the screen. Danverse had sent an urgent private message with his suspicions on the report's legitimacy, and Liam had to agree. He kicked himself for glossing over the details earlier because he couldn't look away from the entrancing blue eyes in the photo. He never should have been so sloppy.

He was thankful he was now on a trail to gain some insight into Hadrian, but he didn't understand why Danverse cared enough to mark the message "urgent." The captain had good reason for background checks on all passengers, wanting no trouble from the authorities. He had a right to pick and choose his charges, but he was demanding a deeper investigation. Liam couldn't understand Danverse's personal animosity toward Hadrian. When had Danverse ever turned away from an attractive man? There was an answer to this puzzle somewhere, but he couldn't put his finger on it. The captain's moods had been a bit of a carnival ride since their last session before they landed in Luxoria.

A shudder ran down Liam's spine as he recalled his last night's dream. It had been far less vicious than the previous nightmare but still left him awake in a cold sweat. And he knew it would continue to return—it always did—ultimately with devastating force if he allowed himself to ignore it for too long. This was not the time to ponder his mental health.

Cyber-green text scrolled across the monitor for the third or fourth time as Liam scanned the all-too-brief history. There was still nothing there, and reviewing it again wasn't making a damn bit of difference. He took a swig of his favorite Centurian-brewed ale, glad he'd been able to replenish his private stock while they were in port.

He looked at Hadrian's portrait and ran a finger over the digital cheek, disappointed in the cool, hard feel of the glass. The sterile image only captured a hint of Hadrian's beauty. The face on the screen was barely recognizable when compared with the version Liam couldn't help picturing from the shower: ragged locks of hair gone and all clean shaven. If not for the unmistakable eyes and lips, he might not believe it to be the same man at all. Lost in fantasy, his jock shifted as his flesh started to swell.

Liam grumbled at his dick. "Down, boy." There was work to be done. He was glad Danverse had sent his suspicions. The captain had started looking into things, but Liam was far better at unburying pasts.

He sat at his desk, ignoring the initial chill as the faux-leather cushion touched his bare buttocks.

"Mrs. Claus, I need an encrypted Subspace Link to Luxoria. I don't want any sniffer hacks following me home."

"Of course, Sergeant Jacks. The link is ready when you are." He settled into his chair and began his work in earnest.

Two more hours and three more ales and Liam was no further along than when he started. He'd lost count of how many different searches he had run over the Luxorian Link and had come up with nothing more than the fake ID he began with. He'd read it so many times he'd nearly memorized it.

He pushed away from the desk and fired his empty bottle into the recycler. Rubbing the base of his neck, he growled as he paced the small cabin, looking for inspiration. How could his efforts come up with nothing? He was no novice, but the lack of even the beginning of some kind of lead was making him feel like an amateur. It wasn't so much that he couldn't find what he was looking for, he realized. The details weren't there. All evidence of Hadrian's existence on Luxoria was wiped clean. No trace. Who could wipe a person from an entire planet and do it so completely? Whatever Hadrian was hiding had to be significant.

That reaffirmed his belief that Hadrian needed his help.

There was a mutual attraction between them. During the random moments when they crossed paths over the last week, even after the shower, he could see the way Hadrian stole glances when he thought Liam wasn't looking. How he turned those ice-blue eyes away at the last second when Liam caught him. He knew there was something there, if he could only get a chance to explore it. Liam assured himself he wasn't suffering from some insane stalker syndrome. He was convinced if he could help Hadrian, he might have a chance. But he had to discover Hadrian's secrets first, and he hoped he could stomach them. When someone holds on to secrets with a tenacious grip, they're either too scandalous to bear or too dangerous to share. Liam suspected it was the latter, because he had the distinct impression Hadrian was trying to protect him from something. Of course, that could just be the wishful thinking of one man crushing on another.

Liam turned back to the screen and viewed the results of the last search. Nothing. Useless lines of code mocked him from the screen. It was as if Hadrian hadn't been born on Luxoria at all.

"Son of a bitch."

That was it. Hadrian wasn't a native of Luxoria. He couldn't believe it had taken him so long to see it. He needed to continue his search elsewhere. Fifteen other possible planetary colonies to choose from...where to start? Hadrian was heading to Alpha Centauri. That was as good an option as any other.

"Mrs. Claus, redirect the secure Link to Alpha Centauri. Redo all search parameters."

"One moment, Sergeant. Search results will be complete in approximately fifteen minutes and forty seconds. I am condensing all previous searches over the last two hours into relevant Alpha Centauri substitutions."

Liam slumped backward on his unmade bed while he waited, his bare legs straddling the corner of the mattress. He was sure he could help Hadrian. He needed to. He would do anything for a chance to kiss those supple lips and feel that kiss returned.

Without conscious thought, he reached into his jock and cupped the swelling mass inside as he thumbed a hardened nipple through his shirt with his right hand. Visions of Hadrian in the shower danced through his head as a firm squeeze to his balls brought him to full size.

The thought of the smooth skin that barely contained the rippling sinews beneath it raised a rapid fire in Liam. If only he could examine those tattoos up close. He longed to follow the designs with his gaze and trace them with his tongue. Did they taste as good as they looked? Did Hadrian? The salt of his flesh was no doubt the finest natural flavor.

A rough pinch to his already-sensitized nipple made Liam arch his back off the bed. He gasped as his left hand worked its way down beneath the straining pouch. When he stroked the opening between his cheeks, the gasp blurred into a moan. He began to press a finger inside, and his brain became a smear of lust. Reaching out, he popped the drawer on the wall next to his bed and pulled out his favorite toy.

Rolling the synthetic phallus in his palm, Liam raised his feet to the mattress. The toy, made of realistic synth-flesh, was self-lubricating, self-cleaning, and could change length and girth to the user's preference. Even Danverse didn't know about it. This was Liam's special secret. With a few quick adjustments, the device was the size and shape of what he imagined Hadrian's erect cock to be.

Liam's need was so intense, he hardly had to prepare himself before the slick dildo was buried to the hilt. His eyes rolled back in relief. Once he recovered from the initial shock, he hefted his dick from the pouch and started stroking with both hands: one on his real cock and one on the artificial. The internal and external friction was sending him into orbit. His head thrashed as he pounded himself harder, imagining himself with Hadrian. This could be Hadrian's hand on his cock. This could be Hadrian's cock in his ass. What would it be like to have Hadrian come inside him?

That was the thought that finished him. His moan turned into a roar and semen sprayed like a burst artery, jetting across his shirt and bedcovers in time with the spasms clamping the phallus inside him. Slowly the crescendo faded, and Liam found himself sprawled on the bed, the bleachy scent of bodily fluids and sweat filling the room.

Once his breathing began to level, Liam looked down at the expressionist painting coating him as he wiped a stray streak from his jaw.

"Shit. This is my favorite shirt. I hope it comes clean."

Liam stared at the ceiling. He couldn't believe how strongly Hadrian affected him. Picturing Hadrian fucking him through the mattress brought him to the end a lot faster than he expected—faster, and explosively. Would he survive the real thing if given the chance?

What was he going to do?

"Your search results are complete, Sergeant."

Liam jumped at the sound of Mrs. Claus's voice. He had started to drift away, lying there feeling the cooling wetness on his shirt and skin. Even though she was the ship's AI, he still felt like he'd been caught playing with himself. In a way, he had been.

The screen showed three possible Hadrian Jamisons on Alpha Centauri. One was a seventy-three-year-old botanist. The second was his fifty-year-old son. The last entry grabbed Liam's complete attention.

Hadrian Jamison. Deceased ten-year-old orphan. Dead for over eighteen years.

Liam called up the archived picture and felt more confused than ever. A familiar pair of ice-blue eyes stared back from the monitor. There was no mistaking the eyes and mouth. It was a ten-year-old version of Hadrian. Facial recognition and age extrapolation confirmed it.

Why did Alpha Centauri think Hadrian was dead, and what was he doing on Luxoria?

THE NIGHTMARE WAS fresh in Liam's memory, as it always was when he woke in a cold sweat. The chaos, the screams, and the gunshot's deafening report echoed in his ears. The blood glistened wet on his hands, its stains refusing to wash clean. The sheets fluttered to the floor as he tore himself from the bed. Sleep was over for the night.

Grabbing a cup of water from the dispenser, he drank in desperate swallows. He stared into the darkness as he wiped his mouth across his forearm, his hands still shaking. How many years had it been? How long would the horrors of war plague his tortured soul? Was it possible to make amends? Could he truly bury the past?

Concentrating on the soft hum of the ship's engines, he tried to focus past the craziness threatening to crawl out of him. The sweat cooling on his body chilled him, heightening the haunted sensation. This was a bad one. He was moments away from bolting to Danverse's quarters and having him lash the demon down.

With a scream born of sadness and rage, Liam hurled the cup at his desk. It smashed across the surface, caroming off the wall and apparently taking half the desk's contents with it. In the near darkness, Liam listened to the items raining on the hard floor like shattered puzzles. He would not go to Danverse. He couldn't, no matter how enticing the lure that could drown the pain and bring silence. It wasn't fair to Danverse when Liam harbored no romantic feelings for him. A voice kept telling him his liaisons with the captain would only ruin their friendship. The voice was right. Liam needed something else to pour his attentions into.

"Mrs. Claus. Give me the location of Hadrian Jamison."

For a week, since discovering the forged death notice, Liam had kept a constant watch on Hadrian. Whether he spied him in the mess hall or had Mrs. Claus give him access to the security-vid feed that ran throughout the ship, he knew Hadrian's whereabouts at all times. Liam was becoming obsessed. He had continued his search for more information, but beyond the death certificate, there was nothing. Hadrian's parents had died in a transport accident when he was eight. Without surviving relatives, he had been remanded to the local orphanage. Cause of death was marked as cardiac infarction, which was ridiculous. A medical condition that severe in a child could never be hidden. It would have been found and corrected at the time he entered the facility.

He needed to know more.

Hadrian's activities over the past week had provided little information to alleviate the mystery. Eating, showering, and reading stories from the Link in his quarters, Hadrian spent most of his time alone. When Liam saw him in person, the sadness in Hadrian's eyes mirrored his own.

Mrs. Claus was polite as usual. "Hadrian Jamison is in Cargo Bay Two."

Liam snapped. "How the hell is that possible? That bay is locked. All of them are. Who let him in?"

"The access codes used to unlock the bay were yours, Sergeant." Liam's confusion turned to anger as a wave of betrayal washed over the lingering pall from his dream. He'd found a new focus.

"When?"

"Forty-seven minutes ago."

"I was in bed. Show me the security feed." The wall screen came to life. There sat Hadrian on top of a stack of cargo containers, wearing the same outfit and robe he'd entered the ship in. Liam studied the scene. Other than accessing the space, Hadrian didn't appear to have disturbed anything. He was just sitting there...meditating?

Liam quickly clothed himself and stalked down to the cargo bay. The door opened with a loud hiss. In the middle of the piles of crates, Hadrian sat unfazed by the intrusion. Liam felt an uncomfortable mix of anger and arousal at the sight of him but spoke with authority.

"What are you doing in here?"

"I am sorry. I was looking for a quiet corner. Sometimes, it is difficult to block out the voices." Hadrian turned to Liam and began a graceful climb down from his perch. Liam marveled at how effortlessly he landed on his feet.

Refusing to be distracted, Liam growled. "How did you get in?"

"I did not mean to overhear. Some people's voices are harder to quiet than others. Yours in particular. You have a habit of repeating the code after you perform your rounds."

"I do not." Liam stared into those ice-blue eyes, crossing his arms over his chest in defiance.

Hadrian sighed and averted his gaze. "Not out loud, no."

"That makes no sense."

"Please, Liam. I am only interested in making a quiet journey back to Alpha Centauri. I should not have used your access code. I just needed some distance. It has been harder and harder to keep you out. Your nightmare tonight was..." Hadrian's eyes became unfocused and mercurial, his expression fading.

"Liam, we have to go. Now."

"What?"

Hadrian's voice was becoming hurried, almost panicked. "We have to get out of here."

"We're not leaving until I have some answers."

"We cannot stay here!"

"You're not making sense."

Hadrian gasped. "It is too late."

He grasped Liam's wrist and dragged him into an aisle between two tall stacks of crates, nearly causing him to stumble. He was about to protest when Hadrian covered his mouth with his hand.

Hadrian's voice dropped to a whisper. "Quiet." He peered around the corner of the stack they were hidden behind. Liam stiffened when he heard the sound of the outer airlock hiss open. They were in space. Someone was docked with the ship. Where was the intruder alert? He could hear voices. Multiple voices.

Liam crawled between the rows to get a better look. Seven men in dirty militaristic clothing were talking amongst themselves. They seemed to be coordinating their efforts as they scanned crates the way he had done at the beginning of the trip. There were a lot of valuable items in the bay. No doubt that was what they were after.

*Fucking raiders.*

Each raider was armed with combat knives and projectile weapons, and everything became a lot more serious. Projectile weapons were exceptionally dangerous on a spacecraft. One misplaced bullet and an explosive decompression would kill everyone on board unless the emergency bulkheads could close fast enough.

He admonished himself for rushing out so fast he'd left his quarters without his communicator. The only way to contact the ship was a verbal connection to Mrs. Claus, which was too risky right then. Why she hadn't raised an alarm, Liam couldn't guess. He was unarmed and unable to summon help as the raiders worked their way through the bay.

He snuck back to the spot where he had left Hadrian.

"We have to get out of here. When I tell you, run for the main door."

Hadrian's grip on his wrist held him fast.

"You cannot. Every path that way ends in death. It is too far. They see us every time we go."

"What are you talking about?"

Hadrian wasn't making sense, but his manner was so matter-of-fact that Liam found himself trusting him. He just didn't understand why.

Hadrian caressed Liam's cheek. "There is only one path that guarantees survival. Your threat has to be removed. They know you are the security chief. I am sorry, Liam." Liam shuddered at the contact even if he didn't comprehend what Hadrian was telling him. It distracted him enough that he never predicted the gunshot and bullet that blew a hole through his upper chest, slamming him into the storage stack. He slid down the wall, leaving a wet smear in his wake, and slumped down into the aisle.

One of the raiders called out, "I hit the security chief!" Footsteps drew closer, the rest converging on his position.

Liam lay unmoving as the blinding pain held him still. A hot wetness spread over his shirt in contrast to the cold metal floor against his back. His body shook with trauma, refusing to move to save itself, but his eyes somehow stayed open. With a wet gasp, he tasted blood in his mouth.

He tried to call out to Mrs. Claus and send out an alarm, but he couldn't find the necessary breath to produce more than a pained whisper. Of all the ways Liam had envisioned his death, this was not one of them. Hadrian's warm, comforting hand touched his leg.

"Do not worry, Liam. Stay awake. It will be all right." Hadrian stood up and shed his bulky outer robe. The form-fitting black vest underneath blended with the snug leggings he had always sported. The winding tattoo down his arm was visible, and every exposed muscle flexed, ready to unleash itself. His expression was calm, cold fury. His eyes regained that unfocused stare as he turned and stepped out into the aisle and into the raiders' sight.

The first raider raised his weapon and fired, Hadrian sidestepping a moment before he pulled the trigger. Several bullet holes riddled the space where Liam and Hadrian had been standing. The other raiders came running, and Hadrian closed the distance with frightening speed. Gripping the first raider's gun hand, he turned it over, snapping the wrist as he struck the man in the throat. As he rode the man with dead eyes to the floor, he stole the combat knife strapped to his chest and launched himself at the second and third.

A single solid kick crushed the second raider's skull against the wall as Hadrian sank the blade to the hilt in the third's chest. Using the knife as a handle, Hadrian spun the body to shield himself from three more gunshots. Dumping the dead man, he headed farther into the fray.

Liam was mesmerized by Hadrian's capacity for calculated violence. Every move was natural. There was no hesitation in the punishment he inflicted. There was no rage in his face. In fact, his eyes continued to be unfocused as his body wrought efficient havoc on the raiders.

Time after time, Hadrian stepped aside at the last moment to avoid being shot, always one moment ahead of all their actions, like perfect choreography. The fourth raider died as Hadrian wove inside his defenses and snapped his neck in one ferocious twist.

The fifth pulled his knife and attempted to fight hand to hand. From his trained stance, it was obvious the man was a deadly combatant. It didn't matter. In two seconds, Hadrian broke the man's left wrist, crushed his right knee, and jammed the raider's combat knife into his upper chest. The gurgling, blood-spitting man hadn't even hit the floor before Hadrian was stalking the last two.

Panicked gunshots echoes bounced through the crowded space as Hadrian stepped effortlessly between them, as if he knew where they would be beforehand. Each missed shot made the remaining raiders more agitated. Liam witnessed Hadrian's vacant stare as he pounced on the sixth man, twisting his gun hand away from him, while the seventh circled around behind them for a better vantage point. Liam was helpless to warn him. Hadrian couldn't possibly see the last man.

Without looking, Hadrian pulled the man's dagger from its sheath and buried it under his chin. The sixth raider gasped and spasmed, pulling his trigger in sympathetic reflex. The bullet ricocheted off a metal crate, blowing a chasm in the approaching raider's forehead. With a shrug, Hadrian dumped his charge to the floor with the rest of the bodies.

It was all over so quickly. Liam was still staring in shock and disbelief. Hadrian was untouched, the blood on his hands and body clearly not his own. His stance softened, and he gave only a cursory glance at the carnage. There was no need to check the men on the floor. They weren't moving.

Hadrian blinked, a gradual awareness and concern solidifying as his gaze zeroed in on Liam's. Were the lights dimming? Liam's vision darkened as the taste of copper filled his mouth. The floor seemed colder than he remembered. Hadrian stepped forward, but the sound of a door hissing open stopped him in his tracks.

There was shouting. Liam recognized multiple voices, but the words had become garbled nonsense with a strange echo. A blur was forming around the edges of his sight. Short, shallow breaths accompanied the cold numbness seeping into his body. The frenzied outcries became a cacophony of rage and fear.

It was all playing in slow motion. Hadrian's body jerked as the flash of multiple particle weapons struck him. The peculiar smell of burning flesh assaulted Liam's nose. Hadrian slumped to the floor, unmoving and twisted, sharing space amongst the dead. Liam soundlessly screamed out his name, but his broken body remained motionless. More voices shouted his own name as the darkness came over him, and there was only numb silence.

# Chapter Five

*"WHY DID YOU call for me, Leo?"*

*"I enjoy your company."*

*"But in all the time I have known you, you have never laid a hand on me. You have never asked for a single service that I am trained for."*

*"I don't need physical intimacy from you, sweet. I would never treat you like a common prostitute."*

*"It seems like a great deal of currency for quiet companionship."*

*"It's my money. I have more than I know what to do with."*

*"You are the only one who ever requested conversation from me."*

*"Then your other clients do you a disservice. You are an intelligent, breathtaking man, Hadrian. I don't seek to possess you like the others."*

*"Why do you insist on calling me Hadrian?"*

*"Because it's your name, pet. No matter what that troll keeps telling you."*

*"Father has his reasons, I am sure."*

*"You know very well he's not your father. His relationship to you has nothing to do with parentage."*

*"Father takes care of me."*

*"As long as you behave like a good little slave. Oh yes, Hadrian. I know how easy it is for him to mete out punishment. I have watched him and his consort-whore abuse you at his whim. His need to have you call him Father is rather telling, and sickening at the same time."*

*"He is one of your closest friends."*

*"Friends. Rivals. Whatever. There are a number of words to describe it, all of them contradictory. But it has allowed me to keep a close watch on you."*

*"You have been very generous on my behalf."*

*"Because in spite of all your skills, you are highly vulnerable."*

*"My life could be worse."*

*"I worry that if you outlive your usefulness, it will be."*

*"I do not believe that."*

*"Don't placate me. You're not a fool, Hadrian. You know as well as I do what will one day await you."*

*"I am Adonirati. I am not my own man. I do not have a say in my destiny, Leo. There is no alternative."*

*"What if I told you I had a solution? That I could engineer your freedom. Tonight."*

*"Then I would call you a cruel man. There is no real freedom for me."*

*"But there is, pet. Everything is already set in motion."*

*"That is impossible."*

*"No, Hadrian. I assure you. You're leaving tonight."*

*"You cannot be serious. How am I supposed to leave? There is no way."*

*"Relax, Hadrian. There isn't much time left. Before you say anything, let me be very clear. Your freedom comes at a price."*

The darkness began to lighten as Hadrian's consciousness rose through the mire. He opened his eyes slowly, their weight resisting the effort. Light poured in, making him wince and moan.

"Captain, he's waking up." The voice was new and unfamiliar. A wave of distrust and suppressed anger with a light dose of fear washed over him. None of the emotions were his own. Beneath him, the bed was firm with harsh, clean sheets. Unspoken layers of voices whispered secrets to him. There were others nearby. He tried to rise, but a flat pressure across his chest and limbs held him down.

Another voice growled. "The stasis field is on until we're sure no one else will end up like those dumbass raiders."

As the haze lifted, Hadrian recognized Captain Danverse standing next to his bed. A quick scan made it clear he was in a hospital of some kind, or more likely the *Santa Claus's* sick bay. The walls matched the ship's cold metal structure, with flat monitors lining them. Familiar artificial light panels lit the room. There had to be more beds, but the stasis field limited his ability to move his head. Another man of slight build kept glancing between Hadrian and the monitor to the side of his bed, no doubt checking his vitals. Soft digital tones relaying the rhythm of his heartbeat came from the display above him.

"Raiders?" Hadrian asked with a hazy awareness. He was weak, and it affected his ability to create silence. The additional voices were only adding to his confusion.

"Do you remember what happened?" The captain's question was insistent. "In the cargo hold?"

"Cargo hold? Raiders?" The reply was slow and muddled until his memory rushed forward. "Liam!" He tried to rise again, but the pressure held him down.

"Where is Liam? I cannot hear him! Where is he?" Hadrian's eyes went wide as his own frantic terror flooded him.

DANVERSE WANTED TO hate the man who had slaughtered seven men. Panic blossomed behind Hadrian's eyes as he struggled to leave the sickbay bed. Hadrian was stealing his best friend away, and he knew, deep down, there was nothing he could do about it. At first, it had seemed Hadrian was rebuffing Liam's attentions, and Danverse had been content. He knew if Hadrian ever returned those attentions, all was lost. And here Hadrian was, asking for Liam without giving even a thought to his own welfare. *Damn.*

"Liam is fine. He's in stasis to keep from waking up and injuring himself worse." Dr. Bosch's voice had a soothing bedside manner. "The gunshot did a lot of damage. It took me several hours to stabilize him."

Danverse took a closer look at the doctor. In spite of his pleasant demeanor, subtle shadows under his eyes threatened to expose his weariness. It was clear Liam's condition was more tenuous than he was letting on.

"Is he going to survive?" Despair rolled off Hadrian. It made Danverse reflect the emotion in sympathy; it was so genuine.

"He's a strong man. I have every reason to believe he'll pull through." Dr. Bosch was never a man who offered false promises. "Right now, I have more reason to wonder how you're awake so soon. The dermal regenerator made quick work of your phaser burns, but you seem to be recovering much faster than expected."

"How long have I been in bed?"

"Twenty-seven hours."

Hadrian's voice was weak and disbelieving. "I cannot believe I was unconscious from a phaser stun for so long."

"Um...make that six phaser stuns. At point-blank range." Danverse didn't like having to admit it and tried very hard not to sound embarrassed.

The doctor shot a dark, accusing glance at him before turning back to Hadrian. "You're lucky to be alive."

"It will not be worth it if Liam does not recover." Hadrian's voice was thick with shame.

"I'm sorry we shot you. It was all happening so fast. You were the only man standing. I don't even know who fired first. But I've reviewed the security vids and know you weren't responsible." Danverse cleared his throat. "Thank you for saving Liam. If you hadn't put those men down, I hate to think how many others might have been hurt...or worse." He looked away from Hadrian. "I also want to apologize for shooting you twice."

"Why am I confined to this bed?"

Danverse stared into Hadrian's eyes. "Because you scare the fuck out of me. I saw what happened. I watched you kill seven armed men in seconds with your bare hands because they pissed you off. You have to understand I have a crew I'm responsible for. If there's any chance they aren't safe—"

"I understand, Captain. I have never taken a life that did not try to take mine first." The somber confession broke Danverse's train of thought. He wanted to ask more, but for some reason, it seemed inappropriate. His own history in the military had exposed him to many horrors. He'd seen and shed his share of blood during the war. But the vid of Hadrian dispatching the group of raiders gave him pause. Deep down, he knew Hadrian was safe to set free, but the alpha male in him didn't feel ready to let the most dangerous man he'd ever witnessed loose on his ship.

"You are still the dominant male on the ship. That has not changed."

Even the doctor paused and looked at Hadrian with a tilted head and curious stare. Danverse looked deep into the stunning man's eyes with an unnerving sense of realization.

Dr. Bosch spoke first. "Apart from the captain's concerns, I want to keep the immobilizing field on until I'm sure you can't injure yourself. You were seriously wounded."

"I feel fine."

"Trust me. You're well medicated."

"When Dr. Bosch clears you as fit, I don't have any right to hold you," Danverse said. "But I will monitor your movements on the ship until we've landed on Alpha Centauri."

"That is perfectly understandable. With your and the doctor's permission, I would like to stay and watch over Liam, if possible." Hadrian was sounding weaker; Danverse was going to have to work fast to get the information he wanted.

"We'll see. I have some more questions for you—"

Dr. Bosch interrupted. "That's enough of this conversation. Mr. Jamison needs to rest." He rested a brief hand on Hadrian's shoulder. "You're recovering quickly, but you're far from healed. Your body is still showing signs of system shock from the multiple particle beams. I'm going to sedate you until it's safe to turn off the immobilizing field. At this point, you need sleep more than anything else."

Hadrian nodded in assent. The doctor tapped a few keys on the screen and the dermal regenerators on his wrist and shoulders hissed quietly. Hadrian's eyes grew heavy and closed. After checking a few more items on the monitor, the doctor left his slumbering patient and beckoned Danverse to follow him to his adjacent office. Bulky doors with large windows for patient observation closed behind them and the doctor sat down at his desk.

"Doc, that man should be dead."

"I know." Bosch picked up a digital pad and scanned the medical readout on the two men in sick bay. "I've extrapolated the range and angle of all the phaser burns. The shot to his face that I healed happened while he was unconscious on the ground." The doctor made no effort to conceal the disdain in his voice.

That moment of rage and despair flashed through Danverse's mind. "I thought he killed my best friend." Hadrian was down on the ground among the raiders. Liam was bleeding out on the floor, not responding to anyone or anything. The doctor had been summoned, but Danverse was convinced he wouldn't arrive in time. A swell of anguish rose inside him, its deafening silence burying all rational thought. He'd stalked over and aimed his gun at the beautiful man's head and pulled the trigger one last time.

"That's why I haven't reported you."

"It wasn't my proudest moment."

"That's an understatement." The doctor closed his eyes and took a slow breath. "But that's not why I brought you in here. I've been so focused on Liam I haven't had the chance to do a full medscan on Hadrian. I'm just starting the full workup on him, and I'm already finding anomalies."

Danverse's brow began to rise. He didn't like oddities. "Does he have any contagions we should be concerned with?"

"Quite the opposite. The man is perfect. A little too perfect. I suspect some genetic tampering."

"That would explain his strength, speed, and recovery time, if he's been modified."

"It also looks like his body is filled with subdermal circuitry."

"What for?"

Bosch shook his head. "I don't know. I don't have a medical history to compare against, so it's going to take some time to analyze the data. I've only just begun my profile."

"I don't like surprises on my ship, Doc. When you get your findings sorted, I want you to send me a copy. Even if it's nothing."


HADRIAN SAT WITHOUT saying a word as Liam's chest slowly rose and fell. He was out of the greatest danger but still lay in stasis to protect the fragile tissues that had been so meticulously regenerated. Soft digital tones chimed in sympathy with Liam's vital rhythms while the devices strapped to his wrist and shoulder made his body breathe and live.

Liam was paler than normal but looked healthy. A soft sigh escaped Hadrian as he started to believe this man who'd invaded his peace of mind might recover.

After spending long hours meditating to block out the voices, Hadrian wished he could hear Liam once again. The stasis field limited Liam's brain activity to autonomic functions, so he had no real responsiveness. The silence Hadrian had sought had become something he loathed.

How did this happen? Hadrian had known many men over the years, and not one had ever made him crave their presence. He had never been allowed the experience of a real relationship, and clients' motives could not be trusted. Hadrian had only explored romantic matters through entertainment vids and others' stories. But the moment he'd laid eyes on the rugged sergeant, Hadrian had heard the genuine desire inside him. For the first time, he began to understand what poets wrote endless sonnets about.

Hadrian resisted the urge to reach out and touch Liam's skin as he slept. The thought of making real contact terrified him. He wondered if he would have the courage even if the doctor hadn't warned him not to interfere with the stasis field. Instead, he squeezed his hands into fists and pressed them against his forehead.

THE SIGHT OF Hadrian standing watch over Liam had yet to make Danverse comfortable.

"Thank you for allowing me to be here, Captain." Hadrian spoke softly, his attention never wavering from Liam.

Danverse leaned against the hull, surveying the scene. "That's very unnerving, Mr. Jamison."

"I do not understand your meaning, Captain."

"Fine. Keep your secrets. But you'll keep them better if you stop telegraphing that you hear things without your ears."

Danverse stepped closer, keeping a respectful distance. Hadrian had yet to look away from Liam, but Danverse knew he wasn't being ignored. After everything he'd seen, he was well aware Hadrian didn't need to look at him to know his surroundings.

"How is he doing?" Danverse focused on his unconscious best friend. The last few days had been exceptionally stressful. Keeping the morale of the crew up without his security chief was harder than he expected. He was beginning to realize how accustomed to Liam's counsel he had become. How many years had they been in each other's lives?

"He is being kept in stasis for another day or two to prevent any accidental internal bleeding. Repairing the gunshot was apparently very problematic. But the doctor says he will recover."

"That's good to hear." Danverse felt a wave of relief. He hadn't received an update from Dr. Bosch on Liam's condition. In truth, he'd been so busy trying to maintain the ship and calm the crew after the incident, he hadn't had the chance to check his messages. "As much as I appreciate your saving Liam, I have to ask you a question. Why are you here in sick bay, Hadrian?"

"I do not know."

"Liam is my best friend. I don't want him hurt."

Hadrian shook his head, the movement tiny and nearly invisible. "I would never hurt him."

"But you're not staying on board. What happens when we get to Alpha Centauri?"

"I cannot answer that."

"You might want to think about it. He's been fawning over you since you arrived. It's going to crush him when you leave. If he thinks you might be interested, I'll be cleaning him off the floor for months." The statement was harsher than he'd intended, but Danverse wasn't sorry. The man before him threatened to undo everything. Liam was smitten. If Hadrian returned his affections, Liam might follow him to the gates of Hell.

Hadrian's shoulders sagged and he lowered his head to the side of the bed. He reached out to the bed frame and traced the line of the molding, his fingertips stopping short of the life-saving aura's edge.

"I have tried to stay away. I barely know Liam, but I cannot deny how drawn I am to him. I never realized how lonely I was until I met him."

Danverse couldn't help hearing the raw need in the dangerous man's voice. It was stronger than his own. The struggle to restrain himself was written in the tightness running across Hadrian's shoulders.

"I'm not going to tell you to stay away from him. I'm just asking that, before you start anything, you think about how it will end."

Danverse turned away and left the sick bay. He couldn't continue to watch Hadrian at Liam's bedside. He'd watched the scene of Hadrian dispatching the group of raiders more times than he cared to admit. The man was a trained killer. The sight of him unraveling at Liam's bedside was unnerving. Danverse had no interest in humanizing Hadrian at this point.

The door closed behind him with a loud hiss, and Danverse looked down the hall. He deflated with an excruciatingly slow breath. Pressures of being captain had never weighed so heavy on him before. He was beginning to understand the age-old concept of the captain going down with the ship. Being the captain meant forever standing alone.

Did it always have to be that way? He wasn't ready to concede that.

"Mrs. Claus. Where is Mac Smith?"

Mrs. Claus chimed in. "Mackenzie Smith is in his quarters, Captain Danverse."

Danverse turned down the hall and entered the lift to Beta deck. Once there, he stopped in front of Mac's door. He pressed the door chime, and the panel replied back in amber digital letters: *Do Not Disturb*.

Danverse frowned. It was time for the mess hall to start serving dinner, and he wasn't ready to eat without company. Mac hadn't surfaced since the scene at the cargo bay, and Danverse needed his proximity to take the edge off. He pressed the panel's com again.

"Mac. Open the door. That's an order."

An extended pause followed before the heavy door slid open. Mac stood in the doorway, but he wasn't the man Danverse was accustomed to.

The customary jovial energy was gone. Dark circles painted his eyes. His disheveled hair was way beyond the usual, and he still wore the same filthy T-shirt and breeches from two days before. A dirty sheen glossed his skin. Mac was often unshaven, but right then, he was a wreck. He looked up at the captain and turned away, disappearing back into the darkness of his room. Danverse followed him in and was surprised by the sight.

The lights were low, the room primarily lit by the active data screens on multiple monitors. The uneven, harsh light threw unnatural shadows across the normally uncluttered room. Mac was known for making a mess of himself during his duties, but his living space had always been immaculate. That was not the case now. Tools and com-pads were thrown about the room. Every storage panel was open, their contents spilled out. Empty bottles littered the floor. It looked like his quarters had been ransacked.

"What the fuck happened here, Mac?"

Mac ignored Danverse, picked up a random com-pad, and deposited himself in front of a monitor. He tapped the screen impatiently as he compared details between the devices. Apparently unhappy with the results, he threw the com-pad to the floor and picked up another, his eyes wild and unsettled. Danverse didn't like what he was seeing.

"Mac." With a whisper, he placed a firm hand on Mac's shoulder. Danverse could feel the tension in Mac's muscles. Mac paused and turned to look at him. The agitation and emotion floating under the surface couldn't be denied. It reminded Danverse of when Liam came to his door after his nightmares had gotten out of control.

Mac's words were as rough as his appearance. "I have to find how they got in."

"What? The raiders?"

"They bypassed my systems and nearly killed the boss. They would have killed more of us, too, if they'd had the chance."

"But they didn't, and Liam is going to be fine."

Mac twitched as he shook his head. "I should have been able to keep them out."

"It's not your fault, Mac."

"*Of course it's my fault!*" Pain flooded his voice, making his words coarse and agonizing to hear. "*If I'd done my job right, they wouldn't have found a way in!*"

Danverse stared into Mac's watering eyes. It took everything he had to maintain a comforting tone.

"If someone wants something badly enough, they usually find a way. Motivation is a powerful tool. All you can do sometimes is plug the holes so it can't happen again."

"That's what I've been trying to do since it happened. I can't figure out how they got in! I'm smarter than those assholes! I don't understand why I can't find it!" Mac pulled away and snatched up another com-pad.

When Mac came to work on the *Santa Claus,* he had been twenty-two years old. He'd applied while in port on Alpha Centauri two years ago. The boy's good looks and personable nature got him noticed. He was eager and talented but far too young. Danverse would have turned him away if he hadn't read his background check. Mac had grown up in an orphanage, surrounded by people, and wasn't handling life on his own well. The world was too big for his overactive intellect. Living on the ship with its contained community was exactly what he needed.

But Mac was so young. The men aboard the ship would've eaten him alive if they'd had the chance. Danverse had felt an immediate need to watch over the boy. He'd mentored him and loved watching how good he was at overhauling the ship's systems. Mac's intellect and skills were amazing. There was nothing tech-oriented he couldn't modify or fix. He was naïve, but with just enough street smarts to keep him from being gullible. The captain had even quietly scared off the supply officer, James, when it looked like he had designs on his tech. James was a good crew member, but a notorious rogue. Danverse didn't want to risk Mac falling for him and being wounded in the process. He'd seen it happen enough with young ones.

Mac's natural spirit was infectious, and this level of darkness was unlike him. It was destructive and painful to witness. He wanted to be able to make Mac back into the amiable young man he'd hired. Mac was the positive energy in his life, not this distraught stranger.

A vid playing on the monitor over Mac's desk caught his attention: it was the security vid of the incident in the cargo bay. He watched Liam being shot and the subsequent bloody fight. Then Hadrian Jamison was gunned down, with the execution-style shot afterward. Then the vid repeated itself from the beginning.

"Mac. Why are you watching this?" He was shocked enough to whisper. "You shouldn't be watching this."

Mac began fidgeting, eyes locked on his monitor. He seemed to be having trouble keeping his hands still as his shoulders slumped and his breathing became uneven.

"I've never seen anyone die before." Mac's fragile reply tore at Danverse. "Not for real. You see it in entertainment vids, but it's not the same."

"No. No, it's not." He came up and rested his hand on Mac's shoulder again in an attempt to quiet the rising tremors.

"You were in the Centauri civil war. How do you kill someone or see it happen over and over and come out of it the same person?"

"Some of us didn't." Danverse thought back to his unconscious best friend. The horror of the last mission they shared had forever changed the man he knew. Liam had been left in hell and had yet to be purged of his sins. At the moment, Mac's innocence was eroding before his eyes, and he wasn't about to sit back and let it happen.

"You need to take a break, Mac."

"I have too much work to do. Leave me alone." He shrugged Danverse's hand from his shoulder.

"You need to get some distance from this. You need a fresh perspective. It's not working right now. Step away."

"*No.*"

That did it. If there was one thing Danverse couldn't tolerate, it was insubordination. The alpha dog came out and snarled its displeasure. He slapped a firm hand on the back of Mac's neck and gripped him tight.

"I said step away. That. Is. An. Order. Boy."

Mac stiffened and exhaled in a sharp rush before his shoulders relaxed into submission under the captain's touch.

"Yes, sir." Mac's voice was soft and compliant. Danverse led him away from his work and to the center of his room.

"I don't like seeing you like this, Mac. I don't find self-destructiveness an attractive quality in my men." Danverse rumbled in Mac's ear, his dominance established. "I'm going to take care of you now. Grab a set of clean clothes. I'm taking you to the showers."

Mac nodded. Probably for the first time in days, he came into focus. All at once, Mac's only order of business appeared to be the captain's. The crazed light in his eyes seemed far, far away as a calm came over him.

"I will wait in the lockers while you shower, and then you will accompany me to the mess hall for dinner. Are we clear?"

"Yes, sir."

# Chapter Six

"I WON'T LIE. You had us scared for a while."

Danverse laid a hand on Liam's arm, taking care not to disturb the medical devices still attached to him. Monitors continued to chime to the pulse of his vitals, but he was awake. Danverse couldn't have masked his relief if he'd tried. He sat on the edge of the bed while Liam rested. The stasis field was off and he was able to move freely, if carefully. The sheets were rolled down to his waist and the previously gaping bullet wound was now a lightly raised mark on the swell of his pec.

"Dr. Bosch says I can go back to my duties tomorrow. I'm a little stiff from being in this bed so long, but it looks like I'm going to be around for a while. I can't wait to get out of here." Liam's eyes were alert, if a bit tired. "You mind filling me in now?"

The smile began to fade from Danverse's lips. "How much do you remember?"

"Pretty much all of it." Liam's visage darkened as he turned his eyes away. He reached across his chest, the tips of his fingers grazing the remaining scar. "How did you guys know I was in trouble?"

"The gunshots set off Mrs. Claus's sensors and she issued the intruder alert. They managed to block their bioscans and some other sensor feeds, but didn't get everything. We came running. Dumb luck, really."

"How did they get in?"

"Not sure yet. Somehow they bypassed all the security protocols. Mrs. Claus didn't even register their ship's presence when they docked. Mac's working on it."

"Still? He's got to be going crazy if he hasn't solved it by now."

"You have no idea." Danverse's volume dropped to a murmur.

"Marc? What happened?"

Danverse rolled his head back to face the ceiling as a soft sigh escaped him. "It was bad, Liam. Mac's feeling guilty that all this happened because they got past his security systems. He was taking it personally, and for some reason, he started watching the cargo bay's security vid of the assault...on endless repeat."

"Shit. For how long?"

"I don't know. By the time I found him, he was in complete meltdown." Danverse rubbed his hand down his forehead and face as he struggled to contain himself. The memory of Mac coming undone was still upsetting. "Mac doesn't have experience with this kind of shit. We've been to war, but Mac... It was scary, Liam. It was like someone had taken my...tech and replaced him with a complete stranger."

"Is he going to be okay?"

"I think so. I got him under control."

"Under control?" Liam's eyebrow arched.

Danverse paused as he read the meaning behind Liam's words. "Not like that."

"Why not?"

He shook his head. "I couldn't take advantage of him in the state he was in."

"Seriously?" Liam's sarcasm was too loud.

Danverse flinched. He never hesitated when Liam came knocking on his door at three in the morning, but Mac was different.

"He's too young."

"Mac is hardly a child."

"He's just a boy."

"*Boy* being the operative word."

The only sounds in the room for long moments were the synthetic chimes of Liam's heartbeat. They seemed to echo. Danverse shifted uncomfortably as he thought.

"I see the way he looks at you, Marc. He would do anything for you."

"It's not possible."

"That's ridiculous. He's here. On your ship, and he's not going anywhere. You love this life, but it can be lonely."

"That's enough," Danverse snarled, using his most commanding tone, hoping Liam would take the hint. This conversation was not something he wanted to delve into. Even with his best friend.

Liam didn't take the hint, but his response was more pleading than he'd expected. "Talk to him. From what Mac told me, he has his sights on someone, but he thinks they aren't interested. You might want to do something before that guy pulls his head out of his ass."

Danverse snapped around, his face heating. The thought of Mac with another crew member made his teeth grind. He knew he wasn't a proper match for Mac, but he didn't want to hear about anyone else laying claim to him either.

"How's things with Hadrian?" he spat back.

Liam's brow creased with a frown.

A sad, angry fire rose in Danverse's chest. That was a dirty evasion, and he didn't typically resort to such tactics. But he knew Liam well enough to know that if he didn't, the subject of Mac would never come to a close, and he couldn't handle that right then.

He didn't understand why, though. It wasn't the first time Liam had said he thought an eager-to-please cub matched up with a controlling dom seemed like a perfect pairing. Was he afraid Mac would reject him?

How could Mac not, once he discovered what Danverse was capable of behind closed doors?

"There's nothing to say. Hadrian's made it very clear that he's not interested."

"Really? The man who killed seven armed men to save your life isn't interested? The man whose first concern when he woke up was whether you were okay, before his own welfare? The man who's been sitting by your bedside since Dr. Bosch released him? Is that the guy you're talking about?"

The words rolled off his tongue without a filter. He didn't know why he was telling Liam this at all. He didn't want the two of them together. Confirming Hadrian's interest was sure to end in disaster, but he had to get Liam to stop questioning him about Mac. That topic was off-limits.

With his tirade ended, Danverse formed a thin line with his lips. He was suddenly agitated, and being near Liam was making matters worse. The confused look on Liam's face spoke volumes. He was processing every word Danverse said. It would only be moments before Liam started believing in Hadrian's attraction, and what would Danverse do then?

*Stupid, stupid, stupid.*

Mac couldn't be an option. No matter how good it would be, Mac was far too innocent to be exposed to Danverse's more sadistic needs. Liam was the only one who allowed him to indulge at that level, and the guilt accompanying the pleasure was becoming a burden.

He didn't know what to do.

MARLEY KEYES WAS not happy.

He sat in his assigned quarters and paced like a trapped rat. While the metal apartment was nicer than he was used to, it still felt unnatural. Having barely set foot outside his room, he was getting claustrophobic. How the hell was he going to get through the next several weeks?

He caught a whiff of his unwashed body and cringed. He needed a shower but was so worried about the others on board seeing him naked that he'd resigned himself to bathing only when absolutely necessary. If only he could get to Alpha Centauri without getting ass-raped in the process.

Yes, he'd lied on the application for passage. He'd expected the members of the *Santa Claus* to be a bunch of girls in men's clothing. They were far from it. Most of the guys were bigger than he was and a few were so muscular they were outright scary. He didn't want to admit if something went horribly wrong, the homos could probably kick his ass before he could stop them. The crew was nothing like what he'd been told all his life.

The mining colony he had grown up in was a small community that had limited contact with the merchants and cities outside and whose people were extra careful to avoid the stain of the degenerate upper classes. The cities of Luxoria had a reputation for decadence and affluence. Marley was the tech of his particular division, which gave him an opportunity not to be stuck in hazardous labor. From an early age, he had been taught all people outside the commune were dangerous to the virtuous. The rich had always earned a living off the backs of the laborers.

But the crew on board were laborers, right? The idea they were all a bunch of depraved swine was beginning to lose fuel. The men hadn't groped him in the corridors or mess hall, although he was sure it was only a matter of time. He had always been warned about the crazed sexual appetites of the non-heteros.

Whatever he had been expecting, though, this wasn't it. The captain and the crew were no batch of sissies. Captain Danverse seemed like military, and Marley's first instinct was obedience. The rest of the crew were pretty regular guys. Then there was the whole thing in the cargo bay.

He'd heard the whispers in the mess hall. One man had singlehandedly dispatched seven armed men. Unthinkable. The whole incident left him shaken and wishing for an end to this voyage. This wasn't how it was supposed to be.

Marley started when the door chime rang. He wasn't sure what it was at first, having never heard it before. Fear ripped through his chest at the thought of who could be outside.

The com flared to life. "Mr. Keyes. This is Captain Danverse. I would like a word with you, please."

Marley froze. The trembling in his hands became stronger as he crept away from the door until the bed stopped his progress. Where did he think he was going? All he knew for sure was that he was not letting one of *them* into his room.

"Mrs. Claus, unlock the door to Beta deck, room two-two-seven. Captain's override alpha-eight-zero-six-beta-five."

The door hissed open as Captain Danverse, Mac Smith, and two armed men stormed into the room. In spite of having nowhere to go, Marley bolted for the door, trying to plow through the men at the entrance. A stiff arm battered his chest and slammed him to the floor. A guard's foot on his neck held his head still as Marley looked up at the gun in the guard's outstretched hand. Preservation got the better of him and he stopped resisting.

The unfamiliar guard hissed. "Please, give me a reason."

DANVERSE LOOKED AT Marley Keyes with disdain. Convinced Keyes was now harmless, he allowed Mac to move from behind him. With a small scanner in hand, Mac began combing through the small room.

In spite of being restrained, Keyes believed he had rights. "You can't do this!"

"Shut up, you piece of shit." Mac turned to the guard holding Keyes to the floor. "If he yells like that again, you have my permission to shoot him in the head."

Keyes yipped in submission.

The guard training his weapon on him turned to Danverse, his brow hiked up in question.

Danverse couldn't help but roll his eyes before shaking his head no.

Mac quickly ran his scanner over the deck, bed, and storage panels in Keyes's quarters. Finally, he came to the worn satchel Keyes never seemed to be without. Keyes's eyes grew wide as moons when Mac reached inside and drew an object out of the bag.

"Here we are." Mac stepped back over to the group with a piece of homemade tech. Parts had been soldered together along with the small viewscreen. The buttons on the front were mismatched, looking to have been scrounged from multiple sources. The device powered up, and Mac fixated on the lines of code scrolling over the screen.

Danverse nodded at the device. "That's what you were looking for?"

"Yep. This little baby overrides Mrs. Claus's privacy systems. Looks like it's set up to block out the long-range sensors and bypass bioscans, among other things. Basically it puts the selected area into tech blackout." Mac continued to press buttons and manipulate the device.

Danverse stared at the man subdued on the ground before him. Keyes had broken out in an uncontrollable sweat that only became worse as Danverse stooped down and stared him in the eye.

"You're saying that this is the device he used to allow those seven raiders to slip onto my ship and shoot my security chief?"

Keyes lay unmoving.

"Was your cut of the Luxorian jewelry on board really going to be worth it? Was it worth the lives of your buddies who are lying in the morgue?"

Controlling his rage at the man under him was a supreme test of will. His fury was shared by Mac and the two guards, which was why he made a point to keep it in check. With the tension so high, it would take little effort to add another corpse to the body count.

"Why?" Danverse asked a question, but the tone was more of a command.

Keyes was on the verge of stammering. "It wasn't supposed to be like that. It was supposed to be quick and easy."

"Who were they?"

"I didn't know them. They contacted me when word got out I was heading to Alpha Centauri. They had me build the scrambler and were going to pay me so I'd have some credits to work with planetside. The ride was cheaper than anywhere else, but it still broke me. It was all supposed to be easy. No one was supposed to get hurt. They said you'd all back down because you were a bunch of..." Keyes looked away. His guilt was too easy to read.

Mac finished Keyes's sentence with a snarl. "Fags."

With all the menace he could muster, Danverse glowered at Keyes. "I ought to order this guard to shoot you between the eyes and end you for all the trouble you've caused." He was sorely tempted. This man was responsible for the near murder of his best friend, and possibly others, if the reckless band had left the confines of the cargo bay.

Marley barked out in desperation, "You can't!" The dirty man was one second away from wetting himself.

Danverse knelt down, their faces a finger's width apart. "Tell me why not."

"Those jewels were made with the labor of my people to enrich the lives of the decadent wealthy." Keyes was sad to listen to. Filled with violent shakes, he contained all the conviction of a parrot.

"I don't give a shit about your politics. You helped a group of raiders board my vessel, raiders who had no qualms about killing any witnesses. All over a bunch of fucking rocks. But you still haven't answered my question. Tell me why I don't execute you right here and blow your stupid ass out the airlock."

"Because I surrender!" Keyes's eyes were wide with a sudden revelation. "That makes me your prisoner, and by Interstellar Convention you can't abuse me. The security feeds are watching, and if you're found out, you'll lose your license and your ship. If I don't show up on Alpha Centauri, there'll be an inquest."

How fucking annoying. Keyes was right. No matter how tempting, he had worked too hard to get to this point and he'd be damned if he was going to lose it all over a moment of revenge. Even if he had crossed the line when he thought Hadrian had killed Liam. He stood, never taking his focus off Marley Keyes, while letting loose an angered sigh. The urge to punish this man was nearly overwhelming.

"Pick him up. He'll spend the rest of the trip in the brig."

Reluctantly, the guard lifted his foot and dragged the prisoner to his feet. Keyes continued to tremble as the second guard took his other side and patted him down for weapons and similar tech.

"Hold on to this for a minute." Mac handed Danverse the homemade scrambler. The screen glowed. The item was still on. Mac turned on Keyes. "You boarded our ship and nearly got us killed. Then you have the nerve to threaten the captain over Interstellar Convention guidelines? Did you honestly think I wouldn't figure out that elementary-school piece of crap in about five seconds?

"You know what really pisses me off? You blackout the cargo hold but leave the security vid on so you can watch, you worthless piece of shit." Mac turned to face the captain. "By the way, I turned that on when I found it, but unlike this asshole, I didn't leave the security vid feed on. There's no record of his surrender. You can pretty much do whatever you want with him. We've been in full privacy mode since this started."

Mac spun and threw a brutal knee into Keyes's groin. His anguished scream was cut short by three quick punches to the face and stomach. The guards stood in shock as the unconscious prisoner slumped like a broken doll in their arms.

"How's that for a bunch of fags." Mac was breathing heavily as he took Keyes's tech back. "I told you I was smarter than these assholes."

Before he did something stupid, Danverse spat an order to the guards. "Get him the fuck out of here."

With little effort, the two men walked out the door, Keyes's feet dragging behind him.

Shifting beside Mac, Danverse placed a commanding hand on the back of Mac's neck, his thumb stroking the base of his skull. A satisfied grin spread across Danverse's face.

"Good boy."


LIAM HOVERED HIS hand above the keypad outside Cargo Bay Two. He was having difficulty willing his fingers to travel the last few centimeters to type in his security code. It was his first set of evening rounds since the attack, and he hadn't expected to need to convince himself everything was fine. Danverse had offered to cover the cargo hold on his rounds, but Liam had refused. No one was going to treat him like a frightened child. He was fine.

It had been two days since he was released from sick bay, and he had grown tired of the crew fawning over him. The first day, he'd walked like an old man while his body worked out the kinks from being confined in a stasis field for almost a week. That didn't last long, but everyone was still trying to do things for him. Mac carried his meal tray. Danverse wanted to take over his responsibilities as security chief. James, the supply officer, was even "helpful" enough to offer to give him a hand in the shower. Liam wasn't amused. Two days had passed and he was already pacing. He just wanted it all back to normal.

Closing his eyes, he drew a slow, deep inhale and exhaled over an even longer span. Steeling himself, he pressed his finger to the touch pad and typed in the proper sequence. The door opened like a dragon's maw and Liam braced, waiting for the scalding heat to burn his skin. However, all he felt was the soft rush of air-conditioned atmosphere escaping the room. He stepped forward when the light came on, banishing the darkness. His eyes were wide as he scanned the bay filled with high stacks of cargo, expecting something to leap out of the shadows. He stopped for a moment to calm his nerves.

In an effort to distract himself, he reached into the pocket along his thigh and pulled forth his trusty scanner. With a few quick touches, the item came to life.

Walking slowly through the quiet aisles, he moved his hand back and forth, all but ignoring the images on the small screen. Rounding a corner, he came to a halt at the path running along the hull less than a hundred meters from the airlock.

This was where it had happened.

There was no blood. The walls and floor had been scrubbed clean. It was so spotless Mac had to have been involved. Liam couldn't even tell anything had occurred there.

Until he turned around and found the bullet holes.

A tight series of hollows riddled the crate where Liam had been standing before he'd been shot. He could still feel his body slamming against the unyielding metal as the round punched through his torso. His breathing quickened as his gaze drifted down, replaying the moment he slid to the floor with a gaping wound in his chest. No. Not in his chest. Through his chest. Liam's pulse began to drown out his thoughts. The scanner slipped out of his hand and bounced on the floor. When he leaned over to pick it up, his hands shook. Gripping the device was awkward, so he returned it to his pocket.

A light, cold sweat had broken out over his body, and Liam realized he should have taken Danverse up on his offer. *Fuck this. This job can wait.* Liam turned and strode back to the entrance and out into the hallway. Seconds later, the door was locked, and he pressed his forehead to it as he gulped air to center himself.

"Liam. Are you all right?"

He started at the soft, accented voice.

Liam turned to find Hadrian watching him with concern.

"I'm fine, Hadrian. I can walk on my own two feet and everything." The words came out harshly. Liam hadn't seen Hadrian since he was released, and his ego bristled.

"I do not think you are weak, Liam."

"I'm fine. Thanks for caring."

"I can feel how agitated you are. I cannot ignore it."

"Really? You sat by my bedside for days, but when it's time for me to wake up, you're nowhere to be found."

Hadrian frowned and averted his eyes.

"I've been out for two days now, and I haven't seen a hint of you on board. I'd say you've been ignoring me just fine."

Liam wasn't shaking anymore. Frustration had turned into rancor over the last few days. When Danverse told him of Hadrian watching over him, he'd allowed himself to hope that the mysterious man might be moving past whatever bullshit he was holding onto, and Liam might actually get to know him. But as everyone else on board looked in on him, one person was absent.

And now here he was trying to convince Liam he gave a shit.

A furrowed brow and twitching grimace spoiled Hadrian's expression. The regal poise Liam had associated with him was melting as he shifted his weight from one foot to the other. Hadrian seemed unaccustomed to this level of clumsiness, the words somehow frozen on his tongue. His mouth opened and closed as the explanation Liam was waiting for never emerged.

"Have a good night, Mr. Jamison." Liam shouldered past, using his larger size to voice his resentment.

It probably wasn't the smartest move to bully the man who'd killed seven men with his bare hands. No matter how much bigger Liam was, there was no doubt as to who would win in a fight. Hadrian snapped out a tattooed arm to grip Liam's wrist. The hallway spun as Liam was shoved into a shallow maintenance service alcove. Hadrian pinned Liam's arms with shocking strength.

"I am trying to apologize, damn it!" The tension and remorse were written in Hadrian's eyes. If Liam weren't so annoyed, he might have taken it better. Hadrian had his hands in the perfect spot to negate any leverage Liam could use to free himself, but it didn't stop him from struggling.

"Why the fuck are you here?"

"Because I cannot stay away from you no matter how bad an idea it is. I could feel your desire the moment we met. Like nearly everyone else's on board. I was content to travel to Alpha Centauri in peace, but no. You had to be a decent human being. You had to show me that you genuinely wanted to help me. I do not know what to do with that." Hadrian's usual composure was eroding as his voice rose, an audible blend of anger and predatory heat.

"I should keep to myself and move along. I should be minding my own business and not involving you in the disaster that my life may yet become. But the longer I stay on this ship, the more I find myself wanting to know you." Hadrian took a deep breath as his eyes began to smolder. "Personally and biblically."

A long pause followed. Hadrian continued to hold Liam against the wall, but Liam was no longer resisting. Hypnotized by ice-blue eyes, he swallowed involuntarily.

"You could have just said so." Liam's anger began to soften and become something altogether needier.

"I wanted to. I was so frightened when you were shot. I had my doubts you would survive, even though I had seen it." Hadrian's voice began to shrink. "I know I said we would have to know each other in another lifetime, but watching you struggle to survive was agony. I want to know you in this one. I have been denied so much. I need you."

Liam whispered back. "I've tried so hard to give you space, Hadrian, even though it's exactly the opposite of what I want. Do you mean it? It's not only me falling for you, is it?"

Hadrian shook his head, his gaze never leaving Liam's. "It was never only you."

"See? You can say it. Was that so hard?" Liam couldn't help but tease.

Hadrian's reply was uncharacteristically shy. "You have no idea. I have never done this before."

"You can't expect me to believe you're a virgin."

"Hardly, Liam." His voice rose back up with confidence. "I know how to seduce a man. I have never *courted* one before."

Hadrian's grip softened, but neither man moved, except to lean closer. Liam could pick up Hadrian's heated scent at this distance, and it was making his lingering indignation wane. Hadrian was wearing a white, sleeveless shirt with three buttons undone at the chest. The valley between the planes of his chest was easily visible from this vantage point. Liam's gaze traced the intricately inked dragon winding its way around Hadrian's rippling arm.

"You can court me later." Liam shifted his hazy sight to Hadrian's lips and then pressed forward to taste them.

The kiss rose to a feverish heat as their arms snaked around each other's bodies in a desperate effort to get closer. Liam melted as Hadrian's tongue caressed and dominated his own. Breaths slid into soft moans as both men lost themselves.

Hadrian separated them, pressing Liam against the wall. Panting hard, Liam couldn't tear himself away from the glassy, needy stare of the man holding his arms. His lips felt swollen and puffy as Hadrian held him down with one hand and explored his body with the other. The possessive strokes massaging Liam's head and neck made him nuzzle into Hadrian's firm touch. Rushes of lust surged deeply through Liam as Hadrian's kneading fingertips worked down over his shoulder and chest, examining the mass of muscle under the shirt. Hadrian found a hardened nipple and rubbed a firm circle over and around it, making Liam shudder.

Liam's eyes rolled back in pleasure as Hadrian's hand worked its way down, massaging his abdomen and hip. When Hadrian palmed his rigid cock through his pants, he thought he would die right there. His eyes snapped open when Hadrian unbuttoned his fly and brought his erection into the air.

"Hadrian...what are you doing?" Liam's question was a throaty pant. He wasn't sure he wanted to be this exposed in a public corridor, no matter what time of night it was. However, Hadrian's talented grip was making such thoughts start to bleed into ineffectual whispers.

Hadrian bit the muscle at Liam's neck and spoke into the skin. "What I should have done the other night, instead of leaving you to the mechanic's skills."

When Hadrian went to his knees and slid his wet tongue along Liam's aching length, Liam almost came. He gripped Hadrian's shoulders to keep from falling.

Hadrian nuzzled into the heated flesh, taking in long breaths, as thin, sticky lines of arousal were drawn along his face. The warmth of Hadrian's skin against Liam's cock raised an unbearable fire as he tasted his way down to Liam's balls and beneath.

Liam made needy whimpers as Hadrian continued his assault. Having never believed this would happen, Liam knew he wouldn't last long, and given his noise level, Hadrian had to be aware of this. Clear lines of fluid flowed down his shaft, the head already glossy and swollen. In one strong lick, Hadrian spread the slick juices, coating every centimeter of Liam's exposed genitals. Apparently, it made swallowing the entire length easier.

Liam cried out when the sweltering wet enveloped him and pulled back with mind-bending suction. Mac was good, but Hadrian was an artist. Every bit of his bare flesh was being sucked, held, or stroked simultaneously. Happy noises issued from Hadrian as he practiced his craft. Not only was he skilled, but it seemed he was enjoying every moment on his knees.

Hadrian's movements increased and Liam's body rocked in sympathy. He was getting close. He wasn't even making intelligent noise anymore. His hands fluttered about Hadrian's head and neck, unable to decide where to place them. Hadrian reached along Liam's perineum with his finger and found his sweat-slicked opening. It breached him with ease, and one brush to his prostate was the start of the end.

Liam tried to stifle his cry as he came undone. His hands gripped and released Hadrian in rhythmic spasms. Hadrian continued stroking, gorging himself on every salty gush that fired into his mouth. Liam tried to pull him off, but Hadrian refused to release him until every tremor had calmed.

With Liam slumped against the wall and barely standing, Hadrian gracefully stood and kissed the life back into him. Slow, nourishing caresses soothed Liam as he held Hadrian to show him how precious he was to him. It took a great deal of time for Liam's breathing to settle.

Hadrian pulled back, smiling, his eyes hypnotizing. Liam couldn't remember the last time he'd been so content. Gently, Hadrian returned him to a decent state and whispered in his ear.

"When you finish your rounds, come find me. What I want to do to you next requires privacy and a comfortable bed."

DANVERSE SAT AT his desk in his sleeping shorts, staring back at his empty bed. Sleep eluded him as he imagined what a certain young mechanic would look like wrapped in his blankets. He traced mindless circles on the desktop with his hand as his thoughts wandered. He had never hesitated when it came to a man before. What stayed his hand with this one? Perhaps because he had never wanted anyone so strongly.

Mac was exactly what he wanted in a mate: attractive, compliant, and intelligent. Every time Danverse saw him, it made his day brighter. The urge to touch Mac was powerful. It tested his self-control not to throw him down and fuck him through the floor whenever they were alone. He had made himself content with the occasional possessive contact on the back of his neck. That would have to do for the time being. He was afraid of what would happen if Mac came face-to-face with his darker side. If they were together, he would need to restrain his boy and punish him. At some point, he would hurt Mac and then take care of him, like he did with Liam. It was who he was. He knew better than to deny that need, but he couldn't bear to see Mac run from him if he didn't understand. He didn't believe Mac *could* understand. So he'd restrained himself and hadn't claimed his boy...no matter how fiercely he wanted to.

Damn. Now he was referring to Mac as *his boy*. Liam was probably right about all of it. Not that Danverse wanted to admit it.

The chime of a new personal message coming into his mailbox broke his contemplation. It was late. He wondered who would be sending mail at this hour.

A quick touch brought the monitor to life and opened his message board. A new post from Dr. Bosch sat in the in-box. Rather than reading it, he tapped the screen and waited for a vid link to connect. Moments later, the doctor appeared on the monitor.

"Captain. I didn't expect you to be awake. I would have called."

Danverse shook his head. "I couldn't sleep. You're not usually up at this hour either."

"I had an emergency call."

"Anything serious?" He began to rise in his chair, stiffening at the thought of a problem. The raiders' boarding continued to leave him on guard.

"No. I've already treated James."

"What happened?"

"He didn't take no for an answer in the shower room earlier and got thumped."

"Fantastic. How bad was it?"

"Not that bad. James admitted he pushed too far. Mr. Jamison declined a personal scrub down not once, but three times. When James touched him, Jamison grabbed his wrist, flipped him, and slammed him onto the floor. Just once." The doctor had a mild grin on his face.

Danverse's eyes went wide in surprise. "Hadrian Jamison? He's lucky to be alive."

"He has some pretty bruises and a dislocated shoulder. He's staying in sick bay overnight with a regenerator strapped on. He'll be fine in the morning."

"Is Jamison pressing charges?"

"James already apologized, and Jamison is the one who brought him to sick bay." Dr. Bosch rolled his eyes. "He actually seemed sorry he had been so rough."

"So what made you send the message?"

"It was Jamison's medical profile. When he came in, I realized I hadn't sent it to you."

"What's it say?"

"You didn't read it?" The doctor shook his head. "Not that you had the time, but of course you didn't read it. Why would you start doing that now?" The doctor's bedside manner had faded.

"Because you write novels. I want to hear the abridged version."

Dr. Bosch straightened in his chair. "Fine. Hadrian Jamison is one of the most perfect human specimens I have ever examined, down to a cellular level. He has most certainly been genetically modified. His strength, agility, and speed are all at the borderline of para-human."

"We guessed that. Is he a clone?" Danverse sat back in his chair and settled his chin in his hand.

"No. The DNA is too perfect. There would be distinct genetic degradation markers that can't be corrected. You can't copy something that complex without flaws."

"What about the subdermal tech?"

"His nervous system is flooded with it. Brain stem, spine, nerve endings, all of it. Completely interwoven."

"Any idea why?"

"This stuff is way beyond my pay grade. It's not medical tech, but it's amazingly intricate. The manufacturing codes I was able to find didn't explain the circuitry's purpose, but when I cross-referenced it, I came up with the word Adonirati in the Luxorian database. Have you ever heard of it before?"

"No. Should I?"

"Adonirati seem to be a small group of cloned men who serve as highly prized gladiators. They're owned by only the wealthiest members of Luxorian society. There were also some veiled references that describe them as high-class prostitutes. The details on all of it are very sketchy."

"They sound like slaves."

"Slavery is illegal in the cluster. That's why they use clones. No legal rights."

Danverse paused for a moment. "Why is Hadrian Jamison loaded with Adonirati subdermal tech, then? You said he's not a clone."

"I don't have an answer for that." Dr. Bosch looked defeated, his shoulders sagging.

"Thanks, Doc." Danverse began to stretch in his chair. "I'll read over the detailed report tomorrow. Have a good night." With a polite wave, Danverse tapped the screen and ended the connection. Pushing against the floor with his right foot, he rotated his chair while he pondered the new information. There were even more questions to be asked now. Too many conflicting stories. Too many details that refused to make sense. All of it pointed to Hadrian Jamison.

What had they gotten themselves into when they brought this man aboard? If there was one thing he hated, it was unknown quantities on his ship. He needed information, and his last attempt had been next to useless. Danverse knew he'd have to be less subtle this time.

"Mrs. Claus. I need a Subspace Link to the Luxorian government."

# Chapter Seven

LIAM'S DOOR OPENED with its familiar hiss, and he entered his quarters. Every step was like slogging through mud. His legs had been weak and rubbery ever since he'd run into Hadrian earlier. Pleasant memories of the encounter in the hallway should have sparked a new arousal, but he was far too fatigued. His body had been healed, but his stamina was in the toilet. Perhaps he wasn't fully recovered after all.

Painfully slow, he shut the door behind him and peeled off his pants. When the cloth became tangled at his ankles, he grumbled as he realized he was still wearing his boots. Ankles bound, he shuffled to the desk chair and settled into it to unstrap his boots and relieve himself of the offending material.

Clad only in his T-shirt and jock, he gazed longingly at his bed. It looked so comfortable. Getting to its comfy sweetness was going to be a challenge, though. With a mighty effort, he rose and took a step toward sleepy heaven.

The door chime rang.

Liam's half-open eyes, paired with a muddled brain, stared at the door. Who could be at his door right then, when he was so close to happy sleep time? Confused and frustrated, he shuffled to the door and opened it.

"You were supposed to come find me after your rounds." Brow arched, Hadrian stood in the doorway in a simple pair of lounging pants that flowed down and hugged every curve of his lower half. Even the faint outline of his cock could be seen under the lightweight garment. Liam tried not to stare but took another peek.

"I ran a lot later than I expected. I thought you'd be asleep."

Hadrian stepped inside and invaded Liam's personal space, bringing the scent of a recent shower into the room.

"You should have come for me." Hadrian placed a hand on Liam's chest and looked down at his remaining clothing. The soft shirt fit tightly over his thick torso, and he hoped Hadrian found the jock a good choice. The approving grin that met his gaze as he looked up said yes.

As happy as he was to see Hadrian, Liam was exhausted. His eyelids were struggling to stay open under their own weight.

"You didn't wait up for me this whole time, did you?"

"Well, I did take a long shower." Hadrian brushed his gentle hand over Liam's chest and shoulder. "And I had to help your supply clerk to sick bay. But otherwise, yes."

"James? Is he okay?"

"He fell down in the shower. The doctor has treated him. He will be fine." Hadrian's hand slid up to the back of Liam's neck. Liam's eyes closed and his mouth opened with the warm sensation. Hadrian gave the base of his skull a firm stroke and Liam's head began to sag on its perch.

Hadrian's whisper was so comforting. "Liam, I can see and feel how exhausted you are. It is time to put you to bed."

Liam didn't even speak. Eyes still closed, he nodded and let Hadrian lead him to the bed like a half-conscious child.

Liam flopped onto the bed and burrowed into the covers. A deep, satisfied groan escaped him as he settled into his haven. The soft rustle of Hadrian shedding his pants was the only sound before Hadrian slid in next to him. Liam reached out to wrap an arm around Hadrian's waist and pull him closer.

Liam murmured under his breath. "Mine." Hadrian nestled into him as he lost the battle to stay awake.

A WAVE OF terror and guilt tore Hadrian out of a restful sleep. His eyes snapped open in the dark as he heard the pitiful cry so close to him. The anguish tore at his heart.

"Lights. Lowest setting."

He spun around to find Liam curled up at the corner of the bed, his face hidden in his shaking hands as he tried to press himself farther into the wall. Ripples of disquiet slammed into Hadrian as Liam wailed into his hands. Liam's whole body was quaking. His feet dug into the bedcovers as he twisted himself, lost in the horror of his dream.

"Liam?" Hadrian murmured, laying a hand on Liam's shoulder, and then immediately pulling back to avoid being struck in the face by Liam's elbow. Liam's nightmare and reactions were intensifying. He grabbed Liam's wrist and spun him face-first to the bed, subduing him through a few key pressure points.

He didn't want to shock him awake, but he had no choice. *"Liam! Wake up!"*

When he felt the shift of awareness telling him Liam was awake, he relaxed his hold. Liam shook and sputtered as he pulled out of his sleep-induced terror. Eventually, he turned over. His eyes were wide and skittish as he found Hadrian on top of him.

"Hadrian? Oh God. I'm so sorry." The shame on his face was unmistakable. Hadrian could hear the urge to run and hide as Liam looked around for an escape route.

"This is your room. There is nowhere to go. You need to calm down."

He kept his volume at a soothing level. Liam was on the verge of hyperventilating. Closing his eyes, Liam shook his head as he worked to slow his breathing down to a sane pace. Hadrian stroked his chest while he found his center.

"I have felt your nightmares before. This one seemed especially bad."

"Yeah." Liam's voice was shaky and harsh. "I'll be okay. It happens."

Once he was sure Liam was calm, Hadrian walked over to the cold storage and brought back a tumbler of water.

"Drink."

Liam emptied half the glass in one series of swallows.

"Thank you." He wiped his mouth with the back of his hand. "You seem awfully calm about this."

"In my life, meeting people with night terrors is not uncommon. I wanted to be sure you would not hurt yourself or me." Sitting close to Liam, he stroked his sweaty hairline.

"It doesn't happen every night. It seems to happen if I get too happy." Liam's gaze shifted away into a dark corner.

"I want to understand." Hadrian pulled Liam's attention back with a gentle hand on his chin. "I know I do not have a right to ask you this, and I know I have hardly been forthcoming, but I want to help, Liam. I want to know what you have done that makes you need to punish yourself over and over."

As Liam looked deep into Hadrian's eyes, Hadrian could hear his search for a hint of deception. Felt him strain to find any and come up empty. Even so, Hadrian could feel Liam's internal debate over sharing with him. He clearly wanted to. He wanted to bare his soul and see if Hadrian could stomach his past.

He tried to keep his tone safe and comforting. "I doubt there is anything you could reveal that could truly shock me."

Liam closed his eyes and upended the water, finishing it before he began to speak.

"I was a sniper in the Alpha Centauri Marines. We had our hands full for several years as we dealt with the civil war between the main government and the migrant workers' uprisings. My unit was regularly deployed for special missions. Captain Danverse was my commanding officer. He kept me together when the job got all fucked up.

"It's hard to look through a scope and watch someone's head blow off when you pull the trigger. The only thing that would get me through was that I knew I was removing someone whose whole plan was to kill others to achieve their goals. Killing select targets to help bring an end to the war was something I could get behind. It had gone on for so long.

"Our last mission was a security detail at Belathius Pointe. A summit had been established between the faction leaders that we hoped would bring an end to all the fighting. It was very public. They wanted everyone to see they were committed to peace. We were in place to scan the crowds. You know, keep a lookout for something suspicious. Everything was running smoothly. Then we got the urgent com.

"Intelligence had discovered a radical group that opposed the summit was planning an attack. A bomb had been planted on a civilian in the crowd and would be set off by a com call. Our job was changed to find the device and remove the target if necessary.

"I turned on my tech scanner and I got lucky and found it. I picked up a micro nuke powerful enough to incinerate five city blocks." Liam took a deep breath and a tear rolled down his cheek. "It was in the shoulder bag of a little boy. He couldn't have been more than ten years old."

"I called it in to Danverse and he confirmed it with his scanner. The kid wasn't involved. He went to school with the son of the guy who set the bomb up. They picked him because his class was on a field trip to the capitol building.

"Then the scanner picked up an incoming call to the kid's com.

"We couldn't stop the call, there wasn't time. The kid started to reach for his wrist com. Danverse ordered me to shoot. I hesitated and he screamed at me, 'Shoot or we all die!'...so I fired.

"It was so different from all the other kills. The way he jerked and exploded." Liam gasped as tears welled from his eyes. "Oh God. I watched that boy die in my scope in front of all his schoolmates... I still can't shake that image out of my head. He was innocent. And I killed him."

Heaving sobs tore free as he wrapped himself around Hadrian, the weight of his sins making him fall forward. Shamelessly, he cried into the shoulder that kept him from collapsing. For long minutes, he clung to Hadrian, his crushing grip threatening bruises. Hadrian let him, continuing to hold and stroke his head and neck, encouraging him to draw strength where he could.

"The bomb scare didn't keep the summit from happening. The war ended shortly afterward. But once it was over, I couldn't stay in the military." Liam scrubbed his eyes and nose with the back of his hand. "Danverse left with me. He felt responsible, I guess, but I think the war took a lot out of him too. So we ended up here." Liam raised his head, looking around at the room.

Hadrian refused to release Liam as he spoke. "It is never an easy thing to end another's life, even if they deserve it. You may never be at ease with it, but your actions brought the end of wartime suffering to many. That boy's sacrifice no doubt saved thousands of lives. I am sorry it had to be you. I will never attempt to diminish the gravity of your experience, but you cannot punish yourself for eternity for the death of one that saved so many."

"But he was an innocent."

"War always makes victims of the innocent. All you can do is try to bring an end to it."

Liam still held tight to Hadrian, but his anxiety was down to a manageable level. With both hands, Hadrian raised Liam's face. He looked into his swollen eyes and haggard expression, and pressed their lips together in a soft, nurturing kiss.

As he drew away, he pulled Liam back down to the bed.

"Lie with me, Liam. This has been a hard night for you. You need more rest." He guided Liam back into place on the large mattress as he canceled the lights and maneuvered the covers back over them without losing contact. Liam's breathing gradually calmed and evened out as Hadrian kissed his head and held him tighter still.

HADRIAN WAS STILL unaccustomed to how dark it became on board with the lights off. Never having been off planet before, he hadn't been prepared for how absolute the shadows could be. Thankfully, he didn't need light to feel what was in front of him at the moment.

He had woken spooned to Liam's back. His hand rested on Liam's firm stomach under the ridge of his shirt, while grazing his little finger along the border of his jock. Soft hair tickled his palm as he began to make small circles, quietly exploring Liam's body.

He had never known this kind of freedom. To have sanction to touch your partner without contract or obligation was virtually unimaginable to him. He nearly wept at the joy. Sight wasn't needed to be aware his manhood nestled between the bare mounds of Liam's backside. He pressed tighter, allowing the warmth to envelop him, causing a surge of blood into his organ as he pulled Liam closer. The resulting friction was making his breathing hard to disguise.

The heat threatening to swallow his cock was making him push in a short, gentle rhythm. He found himself unable to resist. Sweat and his arousal were, little by little, gaining him access.

Liam moaned and Hadrian froze. Liam began to move and Hadrian heard the sound of spitting.

"You need to be wetter." Liam twisted around and ran a slippery hand over Hadrian's length. A moment later, he backed himself onto Hadrian's cock with a happy sigh as he sank to the bottom. The tight, searing heat wrapped itself around Hadrian, and he couldn't help pushing forward and back, Liam matching each thrust.

Liam grunted like an animal every time Hadrian slid in to the hilt. He reached down to cup Liam's cloth-covered groin, but Liam stopped him, pulled his hand up to his chest, and rocked ever stronger with the ride.

Pulling out, Hadrian abruptly rolled Liam onto his back. Liam gave no resistance as his legs were lifted and Hadrian unerringly found his way back inside, making Liam groan.

Liam panted between each plunge. "You don't have to be gentle."

Hadrian knew Liam couldn't see his answering smile, so he just snapped his hips forward harder than before. He was determined to give Liam exactly what they both needed.

The heat built in the room faster than the atmosphere generators were prepared to compensate for as the two men accelerated into full rut. Only nonverbal communication was of use in the frenzy, and the sounds of flesh gained volume.

Leaning forward, Hadrian found Liam's mouth. The kiss was messy and primal. Liam wrapped his arms around him and held him tight as Hadrian moved into a brutal, erratic pump, making sure to press himself down against Liam's cock. Hadrian could feel the rising tide in Liam as his own made him howl into their kiss. With a few forceful pushes, he unloaded as deeply as possible, with Liam finishing right behind him.

Moans faded as they refused to break the kiss, absorbing every iota of intimacy they could. Both of them seemed determined to caress every spot of skin they could find. The embrace tightened as Liam wrapped his legs around Hadrian, refusing to let him out. The pouch of Liam's jock was damp against his stomach.

"Damn. That's another piece of clothing that'll be hard to wash." With his cheek pressed to Hadrian's, the pair laughed to themselves in the dark.

DANVERSE WAS RESTLESS. Liam had been out of the infirmary for over a week and they had barely seen each other. There were no late-night chats over whiskey or vids in the entertainment room. He had been forced into working out by himself as well. All because Liam was spending every spare moment with Hadrian Jamison.

He felt a sharp twinge of jealousy at the thought. He knew he should be happy for Liam, but he wondered what would happen next. Would Liam leave with Hadrian when they arrived on Alpha Centauri? Would Hadrian disembark, leaving a shattered Liam behind? He felt that no matter how this ended, his relationship with Liam was at a critical point.

He didn't want Liam to leave. Their sexual history aside, he relied on the companionship they shared. Life on board the *Santa Claus* without Liam would be very different indeed.

"Mrs. Claus, has the dinner meal service begun?"

"Yes, Captain. The evening meal service began thirteen minutes ago."

"Where can I find Mac Smith?"

"Mac Smith is in engineering, Captain Danverse."

Recently, every time he thought about Liam and Hadrian, he sought out Mac's company. Mac's amiable nature soothed him, and Danverse realized he needed Mac's presence more and more. It was a practice in self-control. Mac had no idea how close Danverse was to simply claiming him, but he resisted. He couldn't bring Mac that far into his world. He would be content with having him near and absorbing the positive nature that brought a smile to his face.

As he strode down the hall, he repeated to himself Mac's friendship would be enough. He wouldn't ruin the boy by sullying him with his carnal needs.

He took the lift down to Gamma deck, which housed most of the main engineering and mechanical access. The doors hissed open and he rounded the corner to engineering. A harsh, staccato beat of metal on metal was echoing through the hallway. Following the noise, he found Mac working inside a large open bulkhead. Mac was on his hands and knees, his upper torso hidden inside the crawl space as he banged away on something. Tools and multiple data pads surrounded his workspace, as usual.

Danverse didn't need to see Mac's face to know it was him. He recognized the thick legs inside the weathered overalls he was wearing. During work shifts, most of the maintenance crew wore traditional coveralls, but Mac never cared for them. Danverse wasn't complaining. He visually traced the seam that wrapped between the curves of Mac's ass, the meaty globes straining the fabric. Smudges of grime stained Mac's skin. He wasn't wearing a shirt. Danverse shook his head to clear the indecent thoughts brimming to the surface.

"Dinner, Mac."

The pounding stopped as Mac jumped at the sudden voice. "Cap'n? Is it that time already?"

"Yeah. I'm hungry. Let's get moving."

Mac growled. "Gimme a sec. This last piece won't drop into place." He reached behind him with an oil-stained hand. "Pass me the hammer."

"Hammer?" He stepped closer to Mac and slipped the tool into Mac's outstretched hand. "What have you been beating that thing with up until now?"

"Don't ask." The banging resumed, louder than before.

Mac's legs shifted apart, and Danverse could see the bulge dropping down between his thighs. The worn fabric was showing off every smooth detail. Perfectly smooth. There wasn't even a hint of elastic strap or barrier fabric beneath. The buttons at the side of the overalls had come undone, revealing bare skin all the way down Mac's flank.

Danverse's breathing hitched as arousal made his breeches bind. A growl escaped him, or maybe it was more of a moan.

"Mac, why aren't you wearing any underwear?"

There was the unmistakable sound of a hammer clattering to the ground as Mac stilled. Danverse watched as Mac's upper body rose and fell in quick, shallow breaths.

"I said, why aren't you wearing any underwear?"

Mac cautiously backed out of the enclosure. Eyes wide, he looked over his shoulder. There was something very enticing about the way Mac licked his lips as he hesitated.

"I didn't think you would care."

Danverse leaned forward so close Mac could no doubt feel his breath. Goose bumps rose to the surface over all that exposed skin. Mac's flesh was searing hot as Danverse snaked his hand into the open seam of Mac's overalls, gripping the vulnerable crease of his hip. Mac's gasp urged him on. Sliding his hand farther in, he cupped Mac's package, the erection growing in his fist.

"I don't like my things being put on display."

"Y-your things?" Mac's heart was beating so hard, the pulse pounding straight through the eager cock in Danverse's hand.

The beast inside him snarled as he gave the hard flesh a squeeze. "Yes. Mine." Releasing him, he tugged Mac's hip, pulling him up until they were standing, facing one another.

"Really?" Mac's lips trembled and his gaze dropped to the floor.

Danverse slid his hands up Mac's neck, weaving his fingers into the thick locks of his hair so they were again face to face, though he couldn't force Mac to meet his eyes.

"Was I unclear?"

He licked his lips at the heated trembling of Mac's body. Mac's mouth hung open, panting as he shook his head. Mac curled his hands and pulled them close to his chest. Danverse memorized the lust on his face as he stroked his scalp.

Danverse knew this was a bad idea. He'd resolved to leave Mac alone, but the sight of him, the scent of sweat and grease... Everything about Mac beckoned to him, making him ignore all the reasons this couldn't work. Need rose up and stamped out all the rationality he'd spent so long hiding behind. He might go to hell for it, but at least Mac would be with him.

Mac's whisper was faint. "Please…"

"Please what?"

"Please don't…"

Danverse stiffened as an icy rush ran over his spine. He swallowed harshly. "What?" Had he read this all wrong? A terror built with every worry he'd ever had over Mac refusing him behind it, threatening to crush him.

"Please don't start if you don't plan on keeping me." Mac looked at him, finally, tears forming in his eyes.

A burst of relief tore down the fear. Danverse gripped his thick hair and brought Mac so close his breath brushed over his lips. If he still harbored any doubts, they were smothered by the lust in his head at the moment.

"I'm sorry, Mac. I should have done this a long time ago."

Mac gasped as Danverse closed the gap between their mouths. A hot tear slipping free from Mac became trapped between their cheeks, and Mac found a place for his arms around Danverse's neck. Needy whimpers filled the air as their embrace tightened.

Danverse pulled back slowly. Mac continued to lick and nip at his mouth, his desires nearly out of control. A firm grip on his hair was necessary to snap him back to reality and remind him who was in charge.

A pleased growl slipped out of him. "Now, boy. You will wear a jock from now on unless I tell you otherwise. I want you contained. I don't want anyone getting more of a show than they should."

"What about in the shower?"

"You'll shower in my quarters from now on."

Mac's uncontrollable, beaming grin warmed Danverse's soul.

"Why a jock? There are other types I could wear."

He leaned forward, lips brushing Mac's ear. "Because if I strip off your pants to get to that ass, I don't want anything in the way."

Mac gasped. "Yes, sir."

Danverse chuckled as he stood up tall, bringing Mac with him. There was no way to hide the obvious tents in both their trousers. He eyed Mac's endowment and chewed his lip. Mac's blush could probably be seen across the cluster.

Danverse cleared his throat. "Let's get these dicks to go down and get something to eat. We're going to need the energy. Besides. A little denial builds character."

"Easy for you to say. You're wearing underwear."

He grinned with a leer. "Actually, I'm not."

Mac frowned. "You're not helping."

SEVERAL LONG MINUTES passed before the pair could walk the corridors toward the mess hall. Danverse kept a hand on the small of Mac's back, refusing to let him go now that he'd finally thrown out his reservations but making sure his hand never left the fabric of Mac's clothing. He wanted to touch his skin but knew they'd never make it to dinner if he did. There would be time for more exploration soon enough. He had a great deal to teach Mac about the art of discipline. It was going to be a slow process, but he was determined. Mac was his now, as he always should have been.

Leaning forward, he spoke so only Mac could hear. "I'm going to lock us in my quarters and breed you so many times tonight."

Mac's shudder was visible, his eyes half-closed at the thought.

Leading the way, Danverse kept Mac close as they entered the mess hall. They went to the food line and filled their trays, all the while brushing against one another. He was barely aware of his choice of food. Each soft touch sent fire through his skin. He inhaled, taking in Mac's natural musk, to prove to himself this was real. He never wanted to spend another lonely night staring at the empty side of the bed.

Mac wasn't his usual chatty self, but his glowing smile told the story. Danverse met his sparkling eyes, trying to show Mac how prized he was without saying a word. Intense and shimmering, Mac's gaze only darted away when a rosy blush colored his cheeks.

They sat together as usual, but their body language was more familiar tonight. A little closer than normal. Conversation more private than typical. Food on the plate being neglected. He could feel the happiness radiating off his boy and returned it in kind. Mac took a long drink from a glass of water. The way his lips caressed the rim as he swallowed made Danverse's mouth dry. He couldn't help leaning in closer to the heat of Mac's body. With his nose mere centimeters from Mac's ear, he began memorizing the scent he planned to wake up to every morning from now on.

"Are you two finally an item?" Danverse and Mac broke their fixation on each other to turn to James, standing in front of them with his own tray in hand.

"Hi, James." Mac tipped his head and turned away, smiling, as if he didn't know how to respond.

Danverse found the newfound shyness endearing. "We're getting to know each other better. How's your shoulder, James?"

The blond rolled his shoulder. "A lot better. I almost can't tell anything happened."

"You're lucky Hadrian didn't do worse."

"Oh, I know. But, enough about me"—James's grin was huge—"I'm glad to see you two get together."

"Thanks. I might just keep him." Mac reached over and squeezed Danverse's arm.

Danverse chuckled. "He hasn't learned who's in charge yet."

"Well, go easy on him, Captain. He's had to wait a long time for you to come around. I thought after you ran us all off, you'd have gone after him a lot sooner."

Mac stiffened, the grin fading from his face. "Ran you off?"

"Oh, hell yes." James laughed. "He made it very clear you were off-limits. It was an order."

Danverse ground his teeth. "James…"

"Oh, sorry, guys. I don't want to intrude. I'm glad to see the two of you together. Have a nice dinner." James walked away to join a small group at an adjoining table.

Mac's glow was gone and his posture was rigid as his eyes went unfocused the way they did when he calculated in his overactive head. All traces of happiness were gone. There was no way this could be good.

"Mac…" He grazed Mac's arm with gentle fingertips, but Mac flinched away.

"Don't."

That same icy touch he'd felt when he thought Mac was rejecting him was back.

"Do you have any idea what the last year has been like?" Mac's whisper was rough. "After James and I got together, everyone stopped talking to me. They weren't being mean or impolite, but I wasn't being included either. I wondered what I'd done. I wondered if I was such a lousy fuck that they'd all talked about me and no one was interested in getting near me. You and the boss have been the only ones I could talk to."

Mac shook his head as he spoke. His eyes were growing wider and his hands and face were starting to twitch. It reminded Danverse of the manic state he'd found Mac in after the raiders boarded the ship.

"You know, it was like being back in the orphanage. You have a few friends if you're lucky, but in the end, no one wants to adopt you, and then you're out on your own." Mac dropped his glass as if it were something vile. It bounced across the table, spilling its contents and sending his silverware clattering to the floor.

"Do you remember what it's like to be my age? How much you crave being touched? Do you have any idea how horrible it's been, feeling so unwanted on a ship filled with men who fuck each other all over the place?" Mac's eyes began to fill and he closed them tightly. "Do you know how bad it gets, knowing that all you have is your hand while everyone else gets to be intimate with another human being, even if just for a night to take the edge off?" Mac's stuttered gasp bordered on agony. "It's not that I wanted to run around and screw every member of the crew, but I wanted to feel like someone, anyone, wanted me."

The ice was strangling his heart. Mac was only moments away from meltdown, and this time, Danverse knew he couldn't dominate him into submission. Mac's reddened eyes zeroed in on his.

"I've had a crush on you from the day I applied to come on board." Mac's twitches had become full-on tremors. "I never thought for a second you might show an interest in me. If you wanted me all to yourself, why couldn't you tell me right from the start?"

Danverse sat there, mouth open, not knowing how to respond.

Mac shook his head, his volume increasing. "What were you waiting for? To make me so lonely that when you finally decided I'd suffered enough, I couldn't refuse you? Is that it?"

"It wasn't like that, Mac. I swear." Even to his own ears, he sounded small and unconvincing.

A tear escaped Mac's eyes. "A whole year of feeling unwanted. A whole year of feeling repulsive.

"It might not be so bad if I thought you'd done without too." A bitter sneer formed on Mac's lips. "But I know better. I've heard your locker-room talk with the boss. I've seen the security vids. You've taken turns with most of the crew. Just not with me. Because, supposedly, I'm special." Danverse grabbed Mac by the arm. The shudder he felt under his palm showed how unwelcome his touch had become. He pulled Mac close so he could look into his eyes.

"You are special to me. I shouldn't have waited."

Mac snatched his arm away. "Don't touch me. I have work to do." Slamming his hands on the table, he shifted his weight to press his chair back.

"Finish dinner with me, please. I want to talk about this."

Mac's voice went cold. "I don't."

The chair scraped the floor with an alarming noise as Mac stood. The movement felt very final.

"I don't have an appetite anymore." Mac spoke through gritted teeth as he struggled to contain himself. "Find someone else to eat with. That shouldn't be hard for you."

Shoulders trembling, Mac spun and strode out of the room. Danverse finally understood what other people meant about having your heart broken. The eyes of every present crew member were on him, layering the pain in his chest with humiliation. He knew he should race after Mac to convince him they were meant for each other, because he believed it, but he couldn't. What if Mac refused him?

# Chapter Eight

WHAT HAD IT been, a week since the scene in the mess hall without a word from the captain? Mac grumbled as he pulled his heavy coat tighter around himself. The raiders' ship was bitterly cold. The environmental systems were on minimum for the time being until Mac could give them the overhaul they desperately needed. He could see his own breath as he rummaged through the computer's mainframe. He shivered hard. He wasn't used to these conditions. It was much nicer on the *Santa Claus*.

"How did seven of them fit in this place? It took us weeks to get out this far." The security officer, Barrus, stepped through the airlock and surveyed the room in confusion, his footsteps clunking in the cabin. There were four seats on the small ship, with an open space behind for staging or other workspace. Efficient storage panels lined the wall, with a small aisle down the middle leading to facilities and mechanical rooms. A lot of the tech and materials looked to be added through crude repairs. Bulkheads were mismatched and forced to fit. It was spaceworthy, but it wasn't pretty.

Mac tapped at the pilot's keypad. "According to the logs, they were only in here for two days." He strummed the pad with his fingers as long lists of code ran across the screen. His gaze flickered back and forth as he absorbed everything.

"Bullshit. How is that possible?"

Pulling up his handheld data pad, Mac compared the readouts. "It looks like the engines have faster-than-light capability. Sneaky bastards."

"I thought only military vehicles were allowed to have warp engines."

"Subspace Link says it's a decommissioned Luxorian stealth craft. Model Alpha-65. Full cloaking capability. Sensor and visual camouflage." He continued reading the endless scrolling text between the two monitors, comparing every detail. "Someone spent a lot of time and money putting this baby back together."

"Explains how they managed to dock without us knowing."

"That and Marley Keyes's homemade scrambler. Once I pull the specs on all of this, I'll update Mrs. Claus. She won't be fooled a second time."

"Seven heteros jammed into this place couldn't have been too much fun. What would they do for two days?"

Mac managed to pull himself away from the tech readouts long enough to watch Barrus zip his coat up to his shivering neck. He was a large, imposing man with a shaved head that didn't help keep him warm. It wasn't long before Barrus was standing with his arms clenched to his sides, looking around aimlessly.

Mac pointed at the back wall. "Why don't you start cracking those storage panels. I've got the mainframe. Let's get this done. It's too damn cold in here."

Barrus nodded. "Ain't that the truth." Rubbing his arms for warmth, Barrus began opening the storage panels in the back wall. The first panel was refrigerated, filled with rations and water. The second was filled with repair tools and the ship's medkit. "Remind me what we're here for, again?"

Both men had received the order via Link message. Mac was still bristling that the captain hadn't bothered to speak to him directly.

"This far out, we have salvage rights. I'm here to assess the tech, and you're here to inventory the ship's contents so we can see if there's anything worth selling. It could mean a nice bonus for us. Speaking of supplies and inventories, why isn't James doing this? This should be his job, shouldn't it?"

Barrus paused a moment. "Because the captain won't let James be in a small, enclosed space with you." The response was barely audible, as if only for his own ears.

Mac ground his teeth and shook his head. "But he doesn't mind me being alone with James's husband?"

"You're not my type, and he knows it. Besides, if I touched you, I'd probably have to be the captain's bitch again, or I'd be without a job when we hit the spaceport. I'm not interested in either."

Mac cringed at Barrus's confession. Just one more person the captain had entertained while he sat up at night alone.

"Barrus, how do you handle James's reputation for sleeping around?"

"I don't care who he fucks. We both like to play around. In the end, I know who he comes home to." Barrus shrugged. "The only night he hasn't slept in my bed in twelve years was when he wound up in the infirmary for hitting on Hadrian Jamison."

"Really?"

"Yep. He deserved it. I told him one of these days... Whoa." Barrus stood still in front of the largest storage panel.

Mac moved over next to him. "Holy shit." The space was filled to capacity with weapons. Explosives, automatic rifles, and ammunition were just a few of the items he could see with a quick glance. He even saw a large-caliber, rotary-cannon machine gun, complete with carry harness, that would be capable of shredding an area in seconds. There was enough artillery inside to lay a small siege.

"I guess we don't have to wonder if they were going to come after the rest of us." Barrus whistled. "It makes me a lot sorrier I shot Jamison."

"Remind me to thank him again." Mac stepped closer, accidentally brushing against Barrus's arm. The large man flinched away.

"Oh, for fuck's sake, relax! I'm not with the captain!" Mac closed his eyes tightly and clenched his fists as he caught himself. "Sorry." He stomped back to the pilot's station, where he roughly keyed through several screens as he continued his scan of the ship's data. Glancing over his shoulder, he found Barrus looking at him, wearing a sympathetic frown.

"It's all right. James told me what happened in the mess hall."

"I'm surprised he had to, the way gossip runs on the ship." Mac grumbled as he read the data. "These security protocols are a joke." With a few additional touches, his device began downloading all the raiders' digital drives. He set the tech on the dashboard and leaned back in the chair, surprised at how cozy it was.

"We're a small town. You can't keep too many secrets." Barrus pulled a data pad and small scanner from his coat pocket and began inventorying the weaponry.

Mac crossed his arms over his chest, and it had nothing to do with warmth. "Unless it's from me. No one seems to have a problem with that."

"Mac, everyone stepped aside to keep from getting in the captain's way. He's a great guy and I don't want to serve under anyone else, but he's got a wicked dominant streak."

Mac scowled at him. "What's that supposed to mean?"

"You mean you and he never...?"

"No." The word came out in an endless syllable, soft with regret. Stopping his scan, Barrus shifted to face him. His shoulders dropped as he tilted his head the way people do when they feel sorry for a person. Mac hated that.

"You don't even see it, do you? The captain's tastes aren't average. You need to be ready to deal with that."

"Not average how?"

"Oh, no." Barrus's face went pale as his eyes widened. The clouds of breath appeared larger and more rapid. "You find that out from someone else. I might as well fuck you as give up those kinds of details if he hasn't told you already."

"It doesn't matter. He and I aren't together." Mac's hand went out as if to push away the notion.

"Then you have time to find out more about him before he comes after you."

Mac snorted and shook his head. "He's not going to do that."

Barrus looked him in the eye. "Are you sure about that?"

BOTH FRESHLY SHOWERED and smelling clean, Liam gave a happy hum as Hadrian pressed closer amid the sheets of the unmade bed. Liam reveled in the warmth of the touch. The metal walls of his quarters had never been this comfortable. The lights were dimmed, and the monitor on the wall was alight with an entertainment vid as they lounged, watching the story unfold.

Hadrian leaned his cheek on Liam's shoulder. "I have to admit this is not the story I would have expected you to choose."

"What's wrong with the vid? You don't like love stories?"

A grin reached the corners of Hadrian's cheeks. "Let us say I would have expected more explosions and far more violence."

Liam turned to face him.

"Do you want to watch something else?"

Hadrian crawled over Liam, placing him on his back. "I am not really watching the vid." A need began to rise in Liam as he watched Hadrian lick his lips, fixated on Liam's mouth. Achingly slow, he lowered his head until Liam whimpered at the resulting kiss. Liam wrapped his arms around Hadrian as they shared a lazy, loving moment. When Hadrian pulled away, Liam couldn't stop looking into his sparkling eyes.

"Hadrian, what happens when we get to Alpha Centauri?" Liam unconsciously tightened his grip as a wave of fear sparked in his chest.

"I am not sure. I have a man I need to meet with. Once my business is done, I am free."

"What kind of business?" Liam stiffened in jealousy. The way Hadrian tensed, he had to have noticed.

Hadrian reached up and stroked Liam's cheek. "It is not like that, Liam. I am meeting a doctor."

"Are you sick?"

"Not exactly." Hadrian's voice dropped as his brow furrowed.

"What do you mean?"

"I cannot tell you all of the details. I do not understand much of what is happening, myself."

"That makes no sense."

Hadrian sighed. "Liam, you have to understand. I have not been in control of my own life since I was a child. I have been nothing more than a slave for years, and I cannot go back to that life."

"You are running from someone—your ex—aren't you?"

Hadrian nodded. "Father will come after me if he finds out where I've gone."

"Your father is your ex?" Liam's eyes went wide in alarm.

"He is not actually my father. He simply likes the title."

"Why did you need to run?"

"Because I can no longer be his possession. I no longer wish to fight and pleasure others for his profit." Hadrian's frustration grew, bordering on anger.

Liam paused as he processed the words and the shock set in.

"You're not exaggerating. You really have been a slave, haven't you? How long has he been whoring you out?"

Hadrian rolled away and sat at the edge of the bed, staring at nothing, his shoulders sagging. Liam tried to tone down his reaction. If there was one thing he understood, it was shame.

"Since he collected me from the orphanage. I was still a child. I wasn't the only one." It was little more than a murmur.

The new outrage in Liam's chest burst forward before he could stop it. "How can he get away with this?"

"He is very powerful and connected, and the Adonirati have no legal rights on Luxoria. We are property." Hadrian's sorrow tempered Liam's offense. He had been suspicious that Hadrian suffered some form of abuse in the past, but hearing it out loud was more difficult than he'd expected. Swallowing down his discomfort, he lowered his voice to a more sympathetic volume.

"How did you get away?"

"A friend sacrificed a great deal for me. I owe him a debt I can't repay."

Liam crawled to Hadrian and turned him by his chin to look into his eyes. "How can I help?"

"Get me to Alpha Centauri. Once I am there, Father will have no ability to retrieve me. It will all come to an end."

"What about us?" Liam held his breath as he waited for the answer. Anguish welled inside of him as he feared the worst possible response.

Hadrian climbed up and held Liam's head between his warm hands.

"I need you, Liam."

Liam couldn't help but stare into Hadrian's eyes as they bore into his own.

"I do not even understand how compelled I am to be near you. No matter what happens, I will find a way back to you. I will not live without you." Pressing his mouth to Liam's, Hadrian worked to convince him.

THE TIME DISPLAY turned over from 24:00 to 00:01 hours in Danverse's quarters. He took a deep drink of his whiskey and placed the empty glass on the desk. With a flick of his fingers, it skidded across the surface until it hit the wall with a small thud.

"Well, that was a great fortieth birthday. I should do this more often."

He knew he shouldn't be resentful. It wasn't as if he'd announced his birthday, but it would have been nice if anyone had noticed. Liam was besotted with Hadrian Jamison, so it wasn't surprising he'd forgotten. Danverse just wished he hadn't.

With slow fingers, he stroked the metal necklace that lay against his skin. Small square links made up the chain, with a single blood-red crystal running horizontal with the length, completing the masculine design. He'd worn it constantly since the scene in the mess hall. It had been his gift from Mac the previous year. Due to the length and timing of their runs, Mac would have had to buy the necklace far in advance to have it ready for his birthday. He should have paid closer attention back then or at least stopped being so stupid. Now it was his only connection to Mac, and he wasn't willing to take it off.

He stared at his empty bed. He'd hoped Mac would bring the salvage report to him, to set the stage for them to talk. It was the reason he'd sent Mac the order to inventory the raiders' craft in the first place. It could have waited until they were in port. Unfortunately, it didn't work.

He wanted to apologize. Never in all his years had he wanted to fall on his knees and beg forgiveness. Never had he felt willing to appear weak for another man. For Mac, he would consider it.

Just the opportunity to lick his eager mouth would be worth debasing himself. To feel him writhe under his oral ministrations, begging to come, would be heaven. He imagined what it would feel like to peel Mac's clothing off and bite the flesh of his rounded ass before claiming him in a sweaty, dripping rut.

He growled at himself. He should have gone after Mac when he'd walked away in the mess hall. Now that he'd waited, he no doubt looked guilty or uninterested. He had been so close. Mac had been his until James showed up with his congratulations. And he couldn't even really be angry with James. There was no way James could have known how much damage he'd done. All the blame ultimately lay within himself.

He leaned back in his chair, looking up at the ceiling. The loneliness had become stronger these days as the reality of Liam drifting away settled in. He'd known it would happen eventually, just not so soon or so suddenly. Who knew it would only take one devastatingly attractive passenger? Liam's absence made his isolation so much more obvious.

He looked at the empty bed again. Mac should be there, exhausted and recovering, waiting for him to come and claim him again. Grinding his teeth in frustration, Danverse came to a decision. He needed his boy.

"Mrs. Claus, where can I find MacKenzie Smith?"

"MacKenzie Smith is in his quarters, Captain Danverse."

Danverse sat his elbow on the armrest and chewed on his knuckle. The mere thought of being near Mac was arousing him, but he had no idea if Mac would accept him. It would crush him if he was rejected again.

But he couldn't live without knowing the answer.

Raising the necklace to his lips, he brushed a hopeful kiss to it. He stood and stepped into a pair of shorts and pulled a T-shirt over his head. With a hurried shuffle, he was slipping a pair of sandals onto his feet on his way to the door when Mrs. Claus interrupted him.

"Captain Danverse. You're receiving a voice com from Corporal Childers."

"Put it through. Childers. What is it?"

"Captain, we're being approached and hailed."

Danverse stopped moving and stood up straight. "By who?"

"A military-class cruiser from the Luxorian government."

"Fuck!" He ran a hand through his hair as he let out an exasperated breath. With a final look back at the bed, he could barely contain his anger. "I'll be right there."

LIAM'S ARMS GAVE out, hands sliding forward until his sweating body was flat on the mattress. Hadrian stayed atop him, riding his back, cock buried deep. Liam could feel the cooling wet spot underneath him, but he didn't care. If Hadrian kept sexing him like this, he could die a very happy man.

"You are far too healthy to die from intercourse, my hardy sergeant."

Liam began to laugh. Hadrian tongued and kissed the perspiration from his neck and shoulders. He was in heaven and couldn't prevent himself from purring.

"You have exactly three hours to stop what you're doing."

"I could stop right now if it is too much for you."

Liam could imagine the grin as Hadrian began to pull away. He grabbed his arms and settled him closer still.

"Stay where you are. This is perfect." Liam couldn't stop his satisfied smile. "I want it to be like this forever."

The sheets had never been so luxurious in such a shambles. The scent of sweat and musk permeated the room, heightened by shared body heat. Soft kisses caressed Liam's head and neck as he held Hadrian tighter and poured every ounce of emotion into this intimate evening. Everything was perfect.

Mrs. Claus's digital voice broke the mood.

"An incoming com from Captain Danverse, Sergeant Jacks."

Liam groaned. "This better be important. Put it through." He rubbed his hand through his sweaty hair.

"Liam?" The captain's voice had an impatient edge to it. "Is Hadrian Jamison with you?"

"Yes..." Something was off. "Why?"

Hadrian's grip stiffened. It was fleeting, but the gesture fed a nervous rush down his spine.

"I need the two of you to come down to Cargo Bay Three immediately. We have a problem."

DANVERSE PACED IN front of the cargo-bay entrance. He rubbed his face as his feet refused to stay still. It had barely been five minutes since he'd contacted Liam...and Hadrian...but he was impatient for their arrival.

He heard their voices echoing down the hallway ahead of them. They were walking briskly, but they were so close to each other. He had no place to complain, but he bristled at the sight. He'd known the two of them had become lovers, but it still gave him pause. Even though he shouldn't begrudge Liam a measure of happiness he couldn't offer him.

Liam's stance was oddly protective next to Hadrian. "Marc, what's going on?"

"Can't you hear what's happening?" Danverse's stare was solely for Hadrian. Liam arched his brow as he looked back and forth between the two.

"What are you talking about?"

Hadrian shook his head. "Liam drowns out most of the voices now. It has been very different recently."

Danverse grunted and turned to Liam. "I have a Luxorian military craft docked with my ship. There are soldiers on board."

"What the hell do they want?"

The soft timbre of Hadrian's voice was frightening. "They want me."

And the nervous sound made Danverse unhappy. "Yes, they do. Why is that, Hadrian? What crazy bullshit did you bring onto my ship? They're threatening to arrest us all if we don't give you up. What am I supposed to do about that?"

"No. This is not happening." Liam slapped the control panel. The door wasn't even completely open before he was through. Danverse and Hadrian were quick to follow.

Inside the packed bay stood a small cadre of soldiers clad in sleek, lightweight body armor and helmets with clear face shields. Each man was large, almost Liam's size, and they carried meter-long combat sticks. A few of the guards at the rear, blocking the airlock doorway, carried clear shields. The group looked poised to quell a riot. Danverse gave a small prayer of thanks they weren't packing projectile weapons.

The bay doors closed with a hiss as the soldier with the most rank markings stepped forward.

"I am Master Sergeant Braxus of the Luxorian Guard First Class." His voice was deep, dangerous, and forceful. "We're here to take Hadrian Jamison into custody. If you refuse, we will treat your vessel as an accomplice and seize it in compliance with Interplanetary Cluster law."

Liam was furious. "You have no right—"

"We have every right. That man is a fugitive. He is coming back with us. Peacefully." His menacing stare burned at Hadrian. "If he doesn't, I will blow this ship out of the cluster. That is a promise."

Hadrian stepped from behind Liam, his shoulders sagging. "I will go peacefully. There is no need for any more violence."

Liam spun. "What? No! I'm not letting you go." He grabbed Hadrian by the shoulders. "I don't understand. Tell me what's going on!" Liam was growing frantic, and Danverse could hear the heartbreak.

"I am sorry, Liam. I should not have brought you into this."

Two guards brandishing manacles marched forward, shoved Liam to one side, and grabbed Hadrian. One placed Hadrian in a chokehold while the other tried to get the restraints on his wrists. Hadrian offered no resistance.

Liam pushed forward and seized one guard's arm. "You can't do this!"

A third guard rushed forward and struck Liam hard in the face with his combat stick. Liam's head snapped to the side and he dropped to the floor like a broken marionette.

"Liam!" Danverse ran to his fallen friend. Blood ran from Liam's mouth and nose, and he wasn't moving. Danverse reached to check his vitals but stopped short.

He didn't need to see the rage alight in Hadrian's eyes. It could be heard and felt in the banshee wail. Every corded muscle in Hadrian's neck stuck out in sick relief as the tension mounted in his body. Jagged needles ran up Danverse's spine. He knew what was coming next and couldn't look away.

Hadrian lurched forward, flipping the guard holding him over his head to land on his back. With a savage roar, he stomped the man's throat to the floor as he wrapped the manacles around the second guard's neck. The snap echoed, it was so loud. More guards rushed forward.

Braxus shouted commands. "Protect the ambassador!"

Watching the vid of Hadrian dispatching the raiders had been horrific, but the real thing playing out in front of him was something altogether different. A sickening rush came over Danverse. Hadrian punched through the weak spot of one guard's armor, blood spattering up his forearm. Gone was the artistry of his previous fight. Hadrian was lashing out like a mad animal, with ruthless fury. He was going to kill them all.

Danverse turned back to Liam, who lay unmoving on the ground. He needed to see if he was even breathing. The erupted chaos had interrupted him. As he touched Liam's neck for a pulse, a solid weight slammed into him, rolling with him along the floor. When he stopped, he found himself on his back looking up at a crazed Hadrian straddling his chest, one hand forcing his head to the side, exposing his vulnerable neck as the other blood-soaked arm poised to strike. There was no glint of consciousness in his eyes. Hadrian was in a frenzy.

Danverse knew he was about to die.

"Hadrian, don't."

Hadrian paused.

His deadly strike-hand relaxed slightly, as did his hold on Danverse's skull. The murderous intensity in his eyes flickered out and the rage began to soften.

Hadrian looked shocked at himself.

"Captain...I am sorry..."

"*GUI CHO TOI!*" The shout echoed from the airlock hallway. Hadrian's whole body spasmed and contorted as he fell backward, screaming in agony. Danverse stared as he pried himself out from under the convulsing man. Hadrian's skin flushed a sickly red. His eyes teared and drool ran from his mouth. Every vein in his body seemed to press to the surface as he floundered on the deck.

Danverse looked around. The guards had stopped advancing, and a lone figure stepped through the group carrying the riot shields. He was medium height but with a grace that made him appear taller. His shoulder-length, rich, black hair was immaculate and swept back, groomed as befitted a man of status. He wore a long black coat with contrasting gold trim at the neck and wrists matching his elegant shirt and pants. His youthful face was stunning and reminded Danverse of Hadrian somehow, but there was no honesty or compassion in his eyes.

The elegant man stepped forward and watched Hadrian writhe on the floor. He stood far enough away for safety, but close enough for an excellent view. Hadrian might have had ice-blue eyes, but there was always a warmth underneath. This man had no such quality.

Another man in impeccable dress came out from the airlock. This one was taller and older, with a touch of gray at his temples. The ambassador? His attire was similar to the younger man's but in simple black without the elaborate adornments. He held his head high and his chest out, and spoke with an air of command.

"That's enough, Donovan. I don't want him damaged."

Donovan crossed his well-dressed arms. "But I'm not finished with him yet." He watched with a faint sneer as Hadrian continued to gasp and scream on the floor. Opening his mouth slightly, Donovan played with a tongue piercing. The end of the golden barbell glinted against his pearl-white incisors.

"You most certainly are." The man turned to Hadrian. *"DI NGU!"*

Hadrian stopped thrashing and collapsed, unconscious.

Donovan dropped his arms to his sides, accompanied by a soft huff. He turned to the older man, with an intense stare, his mouth a thin line. His jaw twitched as if he was on the verge of saying something.

"Don't." The older man shot Donovan a glare. "I don't want to hear a word. Go back on the ship. We'll be leaving shortly."

Donovan ground his teeth, then spun on his expensive heel and stormed back the way he'd come. The guards made an obvious point to get out of his way as more men poured from the airlock, rushing around to take care of their fallen companions.

Danverse's pulse was still racing. A wave of anxious heat swept over him, threatening to make him vomit. This was not supposed to happen. They swore it would be a simple arrest and the Luxorians would go on their way. Seeing the power the ambassador and Donovan had over Hadrian made him question the validity of their claim, but he was in no position to protest. They had made it clear who had the superior firepower, and he had the lives of his entire crew to consider.

The ambassador kneeled next to Hadrian. With a firm hand, he stroked Hadrian's unconscious face. It was almost touching. Almost.

"What did you do to him?" Liam raised himself precariously on one arm. His body swayed and his eyes fluttered as if he was trying to keep the world in focus. Blood streaked his face and stained his shirt. A deep welt had risen across his cheek, ending at what looked like a broken nose. Danverse snapped out of his stunned mindset and scrambled over to him.

"Hold still, Liam." Liam pushed him away, refusing his support.

"I said, what did you do to him?" Liam shouted, clearly directed at the ambassador.

The ambassador barely raised his head in acknowledgement and turned to face him.

"You don't think I'd create a dangerous warrior like Ronan here"—he pointed to Hadrian—"without a way to turn him off, do you?"

"His name is Hadrian." The vehemence in Liam's words couldn't be masked.

The ambassador shook his head. "No, it's not. Hadrian was the name of the boy who was his genetic donor. Hadrian died a long time ago. Ronan is my property."

"That's not possible." Liam's face began to sag.

"Oh no." The ambassador raised his brow and smirked. "You didn't fall for him, did you?" He shook his head with a dismissive laugh. "You wouldn't be the first. Ronan's skills are legendary, and I did make him perfect. Even if he did cut off all of his hair."

Danverse was sick of all this bullshit. "Who the hell are you?"

"I am Ambassador Phillip Chien. Ronan calls me Father."

"Why are you taking him?" Liam wavered but refused to collapse.

Chien looked surprised. "You can't imagine I would allow a murderer to escape justice, do you?"

"I don't believe you."

Chien stood and walked over to him. "Of course, you don't. I can see how much you want to believe him. Trust me." A callous smile curled the corner of the man's mouth. "Ronan's sexual skills have made me a wealthy man over the years. I've met few men or women who can resist his charms. He's very convincing." Liam was trying to hold Chien's stare but was beginning to falter.

"To get free, Ronan murdered a friend of mine, Leo Noble. He was the head of one of our most respected data-tech corporations. During his last private session, Ronan murdered him to gain the access necessary to board your ship and escape Luxoria." Chien leaned in closer. "He's been fucking you so you'll help him do whatever he needs. I bet the blow job that started it all was amazing."

Liam's gaze dropped to the floor as Chien stood, regarding Liam with a dismissive snort, and walked back to Hadrian. He motioned to a few of the guards and watched them place the restraints on Hadrian's unmoving body and drag him to the airlock. One man gripped him by the feet while another followed, one hand on his weapon, as if expecting the unconscious man to leap up like a demon. Master Sergeant Braxus commanded the remaining guards to gather up and move out. The men responded, and the cargo bay quickly emptied of their military presence.

Before exiting the airlock, Chien turned back.

"Thank you for your cooperation, gentlemen. You have done the government of Luxoria a great service." He strode through the doorway, followed by the last guard. The airlock door closed with a final hiss, leaving Danverse and Liam sitting alone on the cargo-bay floor.

# Chapter Nine

THE DULL METAL door of room 226 was no different than any other on board, but the thought of touching it sent waves of conflict down Liam's spine. Hadrian's words had him convinced Hadrian was a victim. He wanted to believe the ambassador's barbs were lies, but how could they ring so true? And why was it so easy to believe?

Dried blood stained the clothing he'd refused to change. He had only just left sick bay. Dr. Bosch had made quick work of the damage done by the guard's strike. The fracture in his cheek had been repaired, as well as his broken nose. All he felt was a mild numbness left over from the portable stasis field used during the procedure.

Part of him wanted to feel the pain. If he had been smart, he would have walked away instead of allowing himself to get so close. Hadrian had been evasive about his history from the start. He might not have lied, but the omissions were just as painful. Liam felt used. No doubt Hadrian would have vanished the moment his business on Alpha Centauri was complete. A cement-like weight lodged in his chest at the thought.

How had everything gone so wrong so fast? Hours ago, he had been lying in postcoital bliss, and now he wished he hadn't survived his encounter with the raiders. Damn Hadrian and his mesmerizing eyes. Damn his perfect body and fascinating skin art. Damn his skills at seduction. Damn the perfect man who was now lost to him forever.

He continued to stare at the door. His eyes were as heavy as his heart. No matter how hard he tried, he couldn't bring himself to reach for the controls. Liam realized he had never once set foot in Hadrian's quarters. Dread seeped into him as he imagined what he might find inside now that Hadrian was gone.

A firm hand touched his shoulder and dragged up to the back of his neck. It was strong and familiar, and any other time, it might have soothed him, but not now. There was too much rage and confusion under the surface.

"You don't have to do this, Liam."

Danverse used the tone that would usually help order Liam's errant thoughts. Liam had ignored his presence all the way from the infirmary. It wasn't hard. Danverse had barely looked at him or spoken since he'd helped Liam up from the floor of the cargo bay. Liam was sure Danverse was keeping something from him, but he was too upset to care.

Liam exhaled. "Yes, I do, Marc. I let a murderer on board because I decided to think with my dick for a change."

Danverse squeezed his shoulder, but Liam was beyond consolation.

"None of us knew what was going on. It's not your fault. There's nothing we can do." Danverse sighed. "You just got out of sick bay. It's okay to let someone else handle this."

"I'm the chief of security. It's my job." Liam turned to stare into the captain's sad blue eyes. "This was a colossal fuckup. Let me save face somehow."

"Liam..."

"Marc, I need to do this, or I'm going to hit someone." Liam's gaze traced up the arm touching his neck. "You're closest."

Danverse shifted his shoulders as he relented. Liam turned back to the door. He drew a deep breath and finally reached for the control with an unsteady hand.

"Mrs. Claus. This is Sergeant Jacks. Please open room two-two-six. Security override code beta beta one-four-six gamma." He spoke to Danverse without turning his head. "I'll com you when I'm finished."

Liam stepped inside and reached out to the inner control. The door slid closed, leaving Danverse on the other side.

Liam's presence in the room had a hint of violation in it. Stepping across the threshold had somehow been a profane act. He shouldn't be there. He shouldn't have to be there.

The room looked pristine. Everything was in order, with only the shoulder bag Hadrian had carried on board slung over the back of the desk chair. One by one, Liam opened the storage compartments and found next to nothing. The hooded cloak Hadrian had worn was hanging in the closet, and a few pieces of clothing were in one of the drawers. That was the extent of Hadrian's meager possessions. Not that Liam should have been surprised. Hadrian was on the run from the law, after all.

He opened the drawer attached to the desk. It was empty except for a few sheets of paper. *Actual paper? How often do you see that?* Something caught his eye in the far back corner. He reached inside and pulled out a small, delicate bird made of intricately folded paper. Afraid of damaging it, Liam placed it back in the drawer.

He dragged his fingers along the pristine bedcovers. They never had the chance to make love there. They had always been in Liam's room. Or the locker room. Or the cargo bay. For being so regal in public, Hadrian had a wicked carnal streak.

Of course, he did. He was a whore seeking a willing servant. Sorrow welled in Liam's chest, mixing with the bitter loss.

He scanned the room. The only thing he hadn't touched was the satchel. Picking it up, he caught a faint scent of leather that reminded him of the day Hadrian boarded. It wasn't fair this was the ship he'd booked passage on. Squeezing his eyes tight, he held his breath to keep a tear from falling. Even if it was so close to the surface, he couldn't afford that right then. He gripped the bag in both hands and felt an odd lump.

Reaching inside, he found a small piece of tech. It was metal-surfaced, rectangular, and flat, with a small lens near one end. As he turned it around in the light, the faint impression of a fingerprint could be seen.

Liam placed the item flat on the desk, lens side up, and pressed the pad of his finger over the residual fingerprint. The lens flared red and a holographic image of a man appeared. He was older, perhaps in his sixties, well-dressed and thin. Liam didn't recognize him.

"Mrs. Claus. Secure Subspace Link. Identify the man in this hologram. Luxorian database."

"Facial recognition identifies the man in the holo device as Leo Noble. Head of Magnate Tech Corporation. Deceased."

Leo Noble? Why would Hadrian have a holo from the man he murdered? That made no sense.

The fifteen-centimeter-high man shimmered, a yellow arrow icon floating before his image. Liam touched the icon and Leo Noble came to life.

*"Hadrian. I'm sorry it's come to this, but you have to act quickly. There wasn't time to prepare you better. Phillip has his eyes everywhere, pet. The virus that shut down the security feeds and removed you from his database only allowed a two-hour window, but*

*it's enough. The cloak I gave you is filled with tech to keep him from tracing you. Don't take it off until you're off planet.*

*"No. I will not call him Father. He is possessive and dictatorial. It's a miracle that you didn't turn out like your brother, Donovan. I still cannot fathom how you became such a decent human being in spite of your upbringing.*

*"I've provided you with an anonymous Luxorian bank account to pay for your expenses. It can't be traced and doesn't require a DNA scan to use. It has more than enough to keep you comfortable for a lifetime. And before you say anything, yes, it's a lot of currency, but it's mine to do with as I please, and I won't be needing it anymore.*

*"A few things you need to know: I have made arrangements for you to meet with a Dr. Hajimi Totoyo in the Beta sector on Alpha Centauri Prime. He is the only cybernetic specialist I trust with the skills to remove the subdermal tech that enslaves you to Phillip. Once that is complete, he has no hold on you. It's the only proof of your Adonirati status.*

*"The reason it's the only proof is that you are not a clone, pet. I couldn't obtain a medical scan without raising Phillip's suspicions. All information regarding you is synced to his com at all times. But Dr. Saarken told me everything. You are not true Adonirati. You never were.*

*"Don't feel guilty, Hadrian. It was a mercy killing I demanded of you. I know it was quick and painless. You are far too compassionate to do otherwise. Dr. Saarken identified the Arkarian Syndrome that would slowly end my life, and I will not spend those final days rotting in prison. With his help, we are setting you free, pet. Phillip will discover my involvement in this, and if you hadn't ended me, he would have punished me for sure. I had no intention of dying slowly, incarcerated, with minimal medical intervention, under his vengeful eye. I also had no intention of being able to betray your whereabouts.*

*"Before you pine for my loss, don't. I'm not a decent man, Hadrian. If I were, I would have intervened many years ago on your behalf. But I didn't. I've led a life of decadence that came to an end due to my own excesses. You are my only ticket to a gentle afterlife. I hope it's enough."*

Liam touched the image and it paused. There was more, but it wasn't important right then. His head swam with the gravity of this revelation. He gathered Hadrian's few possessions, dropped the holo device in his pocket, and turned out the lights before walking out the door.

LIAM HAD NEVER woken up screaming like this before. Sad noises accompanied his erratic, half-smothered gasps as he awoke facedown in his bed. In the darkness, Liam was twisted in the sheets, wet with a dense, cold sweat. In his blind attempt to crawl forward, he fell off the end of the bed, crashing to the floor in a painful heap. He lay unmoving as tears ran unbidden onto the thick rug. It was something of a consolation no one was with him to witness his misery.

Long minutes passed before he found the strength to lift himself up. He untangled his legs from the damp sheets and made his way to the refrigerated storage. The door slid open under his shaky touch, exposing the foodstuffs inside. Bathed in the light from the open door, he could see his T-shirt and jock clinging to his sticky skin. The sight only enhanced the sensation. He poured himself some water and closed the door so he might pretend it wasn't happening.

It was 06:14 hours. Hadrian had only been gone for eight hours, and the room's inky blackness refused to whisper any comfort. The sole light in the room was the time clock's dim glow, which was insufficient for much of anything. Liam was fine with that at the moment. The real world offered little respite from the horror of his dreams. He took a long drink in the dark and then took deep, slow breaths in a futile attempt to center himself.

He would *not* go to Danverse. He only wanted to be touched by Hadrian and wouldn't survive the guilt if he submitted tonight. It would be too much of a betrayal. Carefully, he stepped to where he knew the bed to be and took a seat on the mattress. He rubbed his hand over his face and fought to hold back the fresh flow of tears. Every nerve was so raw and overloaded.

Liam had always heard how a bad dream faded once the dreamer was awake. What a load of crap that was. Every moment was burned in graphic detail across his memory. The nightmare had even been different this time. It wasn't enough to relive Belathius Pointe yet again. This time, the dream had one important difference. The boy in his rifle's scope had beautiful ice-blue eyes pleading for help. Even with that change, it still came to an end with the sickening report of gunfire.

Liam couldn't stop thinking about Hadrian. Hadrian's history had a number of holes in it, but Liam knew enough to question what he'd been told up to this point. Hadrian's future was at stake. Ambassador Chien couldn't be trusted. That much he was sure of.

"Lights. Low."

Even at the lowest level, he winced at the soft illumination from the light panels. Sitting on top of the desk, as if taunting him with the truth, was the holo device he'd confiscated from Hadrian's quarters. He had logged the inventory and sent it to the captain, minus the holo.

When he'd arrived in his quarters, he found a message from Danverse with the medical report from Dr. Bosch explaining Hadrian's genetic profile and Adonirati status. Now with Hadrian gone, there was no reason to keep the information confidential. He still hadn't spoken to Danverse since Hadrian's quarters were cataloged. He wasn't ready to face him yet.

He watched the rest of Noble's recording privately after turning in Hadrian's effects to the Security office. The message continued for another five minutes or so and confirmed the shady nature of Hadrian's... owner? A nauseous shudder ran down his spine. With this new information, the horror of his own wartime traumas paled in comparison to Hadrian's history. If Leo Noble could be believed, Hadrian was in serious danger. Liam still had a lot of questions, but he had always trusted his instincts and his gut told him Leo's digital ghost was telling the truth.

The thought of Hadrian enslaved again, after coming so close to freedom, twisted his stomach in knots. He couldn't leave Hadrian to this fate. He wasn't sure what he could do, but he would come up with something. However, he couldn't think bathed in this sea of sticky cloth. Sleep was over. Liam pulled on a pair of shorts and shambled off to the showers to rinse away the physical remnants of the nightmare and try to clear his head.

THE BRIDGE WAS quiet as Danverse looked out the forward viewscreen, leaning against the central command podium. A series of stations lined the hull, with monitors and data displaying the immense vacuum surrounding the ship. Two other officers were on the bridge: Teddy, the communications and navigation officer, and Daveth, the pilot. Both men were kicked back in their chairs, watching the details of a vast area of nothing. Normally, Danverse found the hum of the ship pacifying, and its motley crew with their tattoos and non-military haircuts kept him happy. Currently, the scene before him offered little satisfaction.

Liam had yet to speak to him since submitting the catalog of Hadrian's effects yesterday. This was even worse than when he was spending every available moment with the Luxorian fugitive. Would Liam survive this? Would he?

"Teddy, transfer the com logs to my station."

A moment later, he fingered the touchscreen and surveyed the list in front of him. This far into the voyage, messages were infrequent, even personal ones, but the hail from the Luxorian cruiser taunted him like it was scribed in neon. He touched the entry and a text version of the incoming com shifted into a separate window. How many times had he read this message?

The Luxorian government demanded to board the *Santa Claus* to retrieve Hadrian Jamison, wanted for murder. They weren't subtle about threatening the crew's safety. It was made clear that Danverse would comply or every soul on board would spend the rest of his life in prison under military law. Military, not civilian. The rules were different for the unfortunate people who wound up that way. Most never saw the light of day again.

The military shouldn't have been involved in the first place. This far out, the whole scene should have been out of their jurisdiction, but what could he do? An ambassador wielding the power of the wealthiest armed force in the cluster had the power to do whatever he wanted.

His jaw ached from grinding his teeth so hard. Submitting to Chien, the arrogant bastard, went against his nature, but he did what he had to do to protect his crew; they were his family.

He knew Hadrian was a victim, but there was little he could do about it. It surprised him he didn't want Hadrian caged, considering how close he'd come to being killed in the cargo hold. But he'd seen how the ambassador and his consort had treated Hadrian and Liam. They couldn't be trusted. He found himself not even feeling sorry for the guards Hadrian had killed.

The Luxorian cruiser seemed to have departed without further incident. Even so, he wanted to be sure there would be nothing they could use to harass him or his ship in the future. He never wanted to see another Luxorian flagship again in his life.

"Teddy, are you sure that cruiser is gone?"

Turning around in his chair, Teddy reached back with an ink-patterned arm and adjusted the tie holding his long, brown hair together.

"They're gone, Captain. I've been sweeping sensors since they left and I haven't found a trace of them near us. Not even so much as a trash dump."

"Any chance of a stealthed craft?"

"Doubt it." He shook his head.

"All right. Keep an eye out until I say otherwise. I'll be in the day cabin."

With a quick swipe, he cleared his screen after sending the data to his private station. He pushed off and turned to the anteroom connected to the bridge. A quick DNA ID scan on the palm plate and the door slid open. The room was simply furnished, like most of the quarters on board, except this one was part lounge and part office. Everything was clean and orderly, just the way he needed it.

A portion of the surface shifted upright into a display as he slid into the chair behind the desk. The screen came alive with the message he'd transferred from the bridge. Another quick touch and the bio for Hadrian Jamison came up next to it. He studied the outdated picture. Long tresses of black hair half obscured the face of the man on the monitor. How quickly his appearance had changed. If not for the unmistakable eyes, Danverse would swear the man on the screen was a complete stranger.

"Mrs. Claus. Please compile all security vid data on the whereabouts of passenger Hadrian Jamison since his arrival on board."

"Will this include the restricted data as well, Captain?"

"Yes, everything. Include restricted feeds as well. Captain's privilege. Send everything to my site here in the day cabin."

"Voice print recognized. All data will be transferred in two minutes, twenty-five seconds."

He leaned back in his chair until he faced the ceiling, racked with guilt over bringing the Luxorian government to the ship. When he'd contacted them regarding information on the Adonirati and Hadrian Jamison, they never let on a military vessel would appear ready to blow open the hull with guns blazing. They forced his hand with their threats against his crew and made him choose the lesser of two evils. His men were safe, but he'd handed a man off into the clutches of others who would use him to their advantage. He had nothing to feel proud of at that moment.

Liam would never forgive him. He had no doubt of that. Rubbing his temples, he cursed himself for not having a stash of liquor here in the day cabin.

Mrs. Claus chimed. "Surveillance data is now available, Captain Danverse."

"Begin playback. Mute."

The screen's image displayed Liam escorting Hadrian on board the *Santa Claus*. Centered on Hadrian, the vid followed his movements as he walked down the hall. Hadrian entered his room and left Liam outside.

"Fast forward. Eighteen times." The images passed by at a much greater rate. For the most part, Hadrian didn't do much. He meditated. He ate. He slept. He browsed the Subspace Link. Nothing of notice. Danverse sped the output to forty times normal. There was still a lot of vid to cover to be sure there wasn't anything else the Luxorians could use as an excuse to come back. It was tedious, but he didn't mind. He welcomed the obsessive distraction.

Danverse wasn't sure how much time had passed before the door sounded. He was barely past three days of video and had found little of notice.

"Who is it?"

"It's Liam. I need to talk to you."

His attention snapped away from the screen. "Pause." The vid froze with Hadrian in the locker room shaving his head. "Come in."

The door shifted open and Liam bounded in. His eyes were frantic and his movements twitchy and impatient. Unshaven, his clothes looked like they had been slept in. The guilt grew in Danverse's chest again.

"I need your help, Marc."

"Talk to me."

It was unnerving to see Liam pace back and forth like a caged animal.

"I need him back."

"I know you do."

Liam spun and planted both hands on the desk. "Help me get him back."

"You can't be serious."

"I've never asked you for anything like this before." Liam's glistening eyes were wide and his jaw was rigid as he spoke through his teeth. He had never looked so desperate before. Not even after the nightmares.

"You mean nothing this crazy."

"They're going to torture him!" Liam's volume filled the room. "You saw what happened! He's going to die."

"You don't know that."

Liam pushed off the desk and shook his head. With an outstretched hand, he made an invisible wall between them. "Don't. Don't placate me. You know full well what might happen."

Danverse sighed. "You're right. I do. That man, Chien is running around with the Luxorian military as his personal armed force. Do you have any idea what he'd do to you or me, or this crew, if we tried to rescue Hadrian? Those bastards made it very clear they would kill or imprison us all if they didn't get one hundred percent compliance with their demands."

A sick, shaky gasp made Liam's shoulders tremble. "I can't lose him, Marc."

"I can't save him, Liam." He swallowed to fight back the sympathetic tear. He would not lose control in front of Liam right then. "They have us outgunned and have all the power. I can't risk losing you, too."

"I love him." A single tear escaped Liam's eye.

Sadness pressed into Danverse's shoulders and chest. "I know. I'm so sorry. But I can't risk the lives and safety of everyone on board for one man. Even for you. You know that."

Slumping onto the couch, Liam ran his hands over his face. "I know. I was just hoping you might think of something." Liam rolled his head along the back of the couch, taking long, deep breaths. "Can't we expose Chien? We know he's lying."

"I looked into him. He has huge connections throughout Luxoria. His command of the military could have us nuked out here before anything could be proved. We're lucky they didn't do it after they took off with Hadrian."

"All right, Marc. You can stop now." Liam's body sank deeper into the couch. The frantic manner he'd entered with was becoming dull and flat, his resolve melting as Danverse's words set in.

A tense silence filled the room. Danverse forced himself to bury the shame sitting in his chest. Heartache was etched across every square millimeter of his best friend. It reminded him of what he'd felt when Mac walked out of the mess hall that night. Liam had been through so much. It wasn't fair. At some point, the universe would have to balance things out in his favor.

"I wish there was something I could do. I know I haven't been thrilled with the thought of you and Hadrian, but I want you to be happy. Even if I haven't acted like it." Unsure what else to do, he turned back to his screen. "Continue." The vid started up again at normal speed.

"What are you doing?" Liam sniffled as he sat up.

"Going over Hadrian's activities on the ship. I need to be sure the Luxorians don't have any excuses for a return visit."

Liam glanced around the edge of the screen. "In the shower? The restricted feeds?" His words had a bit of a rumble to them.

"Relax, Liam. I'm not perving on him. I'm fast-forwarding through his time here." Hadrian was shaving his body with a handheld ultraviolet razor while Liam showered nearby. Danverse made a point to hide his reaction as he noticed Liam's cock hardening in the shower.

Liam frowned. "I would appreciate you skipping over any...intimate scenes."

"Are you afraid I'm going to see you doing something inappropriate?" Danverse laughed. "What exactly do you think I'm going to find?" With an arched brow, he smiled. "Does Hadrian have any kinks I should know about?"

Liam shook his head and began to smile back, a blush staining his cheeks. He was clearly embarrassed, which was unusual. Liam had never been shy chatting about sexual conquests before. Hadrian had been the real thing.

"About a week after I got out of sick bay, he found me in the hallway outside of the cargo bay. Skip that."

"In the hallway? You dog! That's not like you, Liam."

"I know. He just brought it out of me." The smile on Liam's face was warm and sad at the same time.

"Hmm...what's this? Pause." The vid stopped as Hadrian left the shower and passed Mac entering. He touched the image of Mac on the screen. "Follow new target. Continue." Since scanning Hadrian was boring as hell, he could perv on Mac for a while. In all the chaos, he hadn't had a chance to talk to him. While he would be much happier watching the tech in his private shower, he could be content with this. The vid continued, with Mac in the center position. Hadrian didn't seem so important anymore.

On the screen, Mac showered next to Liam while chatting away. Danverse wasn't thrilled Liam was still sporting an impressive erection. He paid close attention as Mac began to wash himself and get hard, too.

"What the fuck?"

"Marc?"

There was Mac in the shower. On his knees in front of Liam. And Liam wasn't stopping him.

The furious heat rising in his chest nauseated him. His jaw clamped tight, and the harsh drum of his own quickening pulse filled his ears. Turning from the screen, he burned a stare into Liam that made the big man twist his face in confusion.

The words coming out of Danverse's mouth sounded barely human. "Liam, you...piece...of...shit."

Liam's face lost its color as he glanced to the monitor and saw the scene playing out.

"Oh, shit. Marc, it's not what you think."

Kicking back the chair, Danverse rounded the desk. Liam raised his open hands in defense. "Really? Please explain to me how that's not your cock down my boy's throat!"

"We didn't plan it. It just happened."

"I bet."

"Right afterward, we both knew what a mistake it was." Liam's tone was full of regret, but the possessive beast inside Danverse refused to acknowledge it.

He looked back at the vid and the pleasure on Liam's face. "I can tell how much you were hating it."

"He told me he hadn't been touched in almost a year." Liam's voice was rising. "It was eating him alive! What were you waiting for? Until he was so broken he had no other choice?"

A sudden shove slammed Liam backward into the couch. The shift from sorry to rage that flashed across Liam's face was immediate. The uncharacteristic sight of Liam, fists clenched, leaping forward into his personal space should have made him think twice. But he was far too pissed off to think clearly.

"He wasn't your boy right then. And let's be honest. He *still* isn't your boy! You're too much of a fucking coward to go after him, but you've spent plenty of time keeping me around to satisfy your sick needs."

"That was *you* knocking on *my* door, if I remember correctly!"

"Because I didn't know what else to do! And you took full advantage of it. No wonder you didn't want me with Hadrian!"

"That freak-show whore of yours? Great choice!"

"Because you knew I wouldn't need you anymore and you'd have to go dirty your precious, innocent Mac!" Liam roared as he closed in. He had never challenged Danverse before, and Danverse was too furious to back down.

"Go find Hadrian! You two deserve each other—you're both fucking damaged goods!" Centimeters away, Liam had to feel Danverse's breath on his face. "Here's a tip, Liam: saving Hadrian won't bring the boy from Belathius Pointe back to life!"

Danverse never saw the punch that sent him sprawling over his desk, smashing head and shoulders into the floor. Fire bloomed across his jaw, married to the taste of blood, as he shook his head. Rage welled in Liam's eyes as he stomped forward. Every muscle pulsed as he grabbed Danverse by the collar, pulling their faces close.

For the first time, Danverse shrank. Liam had never been aggressive enough to make him feel overpowered. He had always been the follower, the one who obeyed orders. That was gone now. The alpha dog bowed as the command he held over Liam crumbled.

Liam snarled like an animal. "You fucking bastard. That was low even for you. Well, guess what? I'm done letting people abuse me. You and me, Marc, we're through." Liam's anger couldn't be mistaken even as the tears were poised to fall. "I would rather rot in a sanitarium than ever let you touch me again."

Liam slammed him back to the floor as he released his hold. Jumping up, Liam spun and placed his palm on the reader, opening the door. With a fist, he hammered the door control, cracking the black glass panel. Then Danverse's best friend stalked out, leaving him fuming on the deck.

# Chapter Ten

MAC APPRAISED HIMSELF in the mirror as he smoothed down his chocolate-colored vest. It opened low in the front, showing off his chest, and fit snug around his waist without binding. Freshly scrubbed, not a trace of mechanical fluids stained his skin, and he could still smell a faint trace of soap. His normally wild thatch of hair had been trimmed to an attractive, tamed style that hugged his scalp. Running his hand along his clean-shaven jaw, he hardly recognized himself. He had forgotten the man in the mirror somehow but was determined to keep him.

Cleanliness was one of the few things making him feel centered. Conditions in the orphanage had been squalid, and keeping things tidy helped him forget. Why he didn't keep himself as clean as his surroundings, he couldn't say. Perhaps he valued the ship more than himself.

He loved the *Santa Claus*. It was the only place he'd ever felt at home. Being one of the unfortunate products of the Centauri Civil War, a wartime orphan, he was accustomed to never feeling settled. He grew up without having anyplace to call his own. Becoming the head tech on board was the best thing to ever happen to him. Even with the loneliness, this was far better than what his life had become after he came of age. He'd expected life outside the orphanage to be wonderful, but the reality was overwhelming. It sounded a lot like the stories he'd dismissed as fiction of criminals released from prison. Out of touch with the rest of the world, Mac was nearly swallowed by it. His intellect and skills had kept him from drowning, but only barely.

Finding the close-knit community aboard the *Santa Claus* was a godsend. He'd taken one look at Captain Danverse and known where he belonged. He was useful and wanted, a rare experience for a stray. Being near Danverse brought comfort and order to his world. His thoughts normally raced at blinding speed. Forever analyzing, it often seemed like there were overlapping voices in his head. More than once growing up, he'd been told he was too smart for his own good. If he didn't constantly focus to maintain a stream of linear thought, he would get lost in the overwhelming data. Right then, it was all unraveling.

He'd tried to speak with Danverse yesterday but was refused. Apparently, a fight had broken out between Danverse and Liam on the bridge, and the story had instantly spread through the contained community. Liam wouldn't speak to him either. It only required two seconds of analysis to determine the cause.

The sad weight in his chest made him take a deep breath. He didn't have time to dwell on it. There was work to be done.

"Mrs. Claus. Where can I find Liam Jacks?"

"Security Chief Jacks is in his quarters. Will there be anything else?"

"No, thank you."

Mac was the only person on board with which Mrs. Claus engaged beyond specific requests. It was one of the first things he'd added to the system when he hired on. A surrogate mother had to be capable of more than minimal responses.

His sandaled feet were quiet as he walked down the hall. The only sound other than the engines' hum was the fabric of his snug breeches brushing between his thighs. He rounded the corner and stopped before room 204. After taking another deep breath to steel himself, he touched the door chime.

Liam's voice came through the speaker. "Who is it?"

"Boss, it's Mac."

After a long pause, he heard the door panel beep. Amber text flashed the status on the panel: *Do Not Disturb*. He growled as he pounded the door with his fist.

"Damn it, boss! I want to talk to you!" He leaned against the door but jumped back as it hissed open. Liam loomed in the doorway and invaded Mac's personal space. Deep lines of sorrow scarred Liam's unshaven face as he towered over him. These were the moments when Mac was reminded of how fearsome the sergeant could be. He read the display as an act of intimidation, not aggression, so he stood his ground.

"You shouldn't be here."

Mac looked Liam over. "I'm glad to see you're dressed. I want to talk to you."

"If Marc finds out you're here—"

"He'll what? Stop talking to me more?"

"Mac...he found out about us in the shower."

Mac nodded and huffed. "Of course he did. Why else would he shut us both out? How did he find out anyway?"

"He was following Hadrian on the privileged security vids. I guess he stopped following him when you came on the screen. And there we were."

"Lovely. I don't know if I should be flattered or offended. Either way, I'm not here to talk about him."

"Then why are you here?"

Not wanting the door closed in his face, he ducked under Liam's arm and took a seat on the corner of his ridiculously large bed. With a raised eyebrow, he cast a dubious glare over the rumpled sheets but stopped himself because it wasn't why he was there.

"I wanted to see how you were doing, boss. I don't have a lot of friends. I need to take care of the ones I have."

Liam walked back to his desk and faced away, sifting through the files on his monitor. Several data pads were online and scattered on the desk. Personal ID files of the raiders and a Subspace Link to Luxoria were visible on the screen.

"What are you doing?"

"Researching." Liam grumbled as he thumbed through the files on his screen, refusing to look Mac's way. It was not like the boss to be this dismissive. He had to be in bad shape.

"I'm sorry about what happened to Hadrian. I know he was really special to you."

"He still is. I haven't given up on him yet." Liam continued to work without pausing.

"What do you plan to do?"

"I'm going to get him back."

Mac climbed off the bed. "Boss, that's crazy. You can't even get back to Luxoria."

"The raiders' ship has faster-than-light engines. Most of the details I can figure out on the way."

"You can't just bull your way in there. You'll get yourself killed."

Liam looked back over his shoulder. "I'm a sniper, Mac. I don't storm the beach. I sit back and wait for my chance."

"Have you asked the captain for help?"

"He already said no, right before we got in a fight."

"Then what are you supposed to do?"

Liam shrugged as he dug deeper into his information. Mac thought he probably should be pissed at the whole scenario but couldn't find it in himself. All he felt was a growing sense of guilt. No matter what complications had been thrown his way with Danverse, they were nothing compared to what Liam was experiencing. Life sometimes was unfair. An orphan understood the reality all too well.

Liam began mumbling as he scoured the monitor data. "I'm so close. I just need to find a way to shut down…"

The odd way Liam drifted off was unnerving, and even more so when he pivoted his chair to face Mac. Liam's piercing eyes burned a strange menace. Being in this room at that moment seemed like a bad idea.

"Um, boss? Why are you looking at me like that?"

Liam stood. "Do you still have that scrambler from the raiders?"

"Yeah. It's in my quarters." His suspicions grew like wildfire as Liam closed the gap between them, a manic tension in his eyes.

"And you have all the specs for the raiders' ship, right?"

"I haven't cleared them from my data pad yet."

Liam was so close, Mac could feel the heat from his body. "You turned off my equipment that one time for maintenance."

"It's part of my tech clearance." He became quieter and quieter with each response.

"Go back to your quarters and get that data pad and scrambler. You're going to show me how to use it. Then you're going to turn off the docking protocols and tractor beam."

Mac swallowed. "Why am I doing all this?"

Liam paused for a moment. "Because I'm taking the raiders' ship and getting Hadrian back one way or another."

"You can't ask me to do this, boss." The shock made his eyes feel larger than possible.

"I can't stay on board knowing I had a chance to save him. I love him, Mac, and I need him. Hadrian told me once that he would do anything to be with me. I'd like to believe he'd do the same if the situation were reversed."

"You're asking me to blatantly go against the captain. You know what he means to me, right?"

Liam gave him a sad nod. "The same that Hadrian does to me. You'd sacrifice all of us if you thought you could save him, wouldn't you?"

"That's not fair, boss." Mac turned away. The truth struck too hard.

"No, it's not. But what's happened to Hadrian isn't, either. I don't know why I didn't say something sooner—maybe I blamed Marc for Hadrian's arrest—but I have evidence he's innocent. I just can't go through their government to prove it. I have to do something more drastic, and I have to do it now."

Sighing, Mac ran a nervous hand through his hair. "You better come back, boss. Don't make me regret this."

"Oh God. Thank you, Mac." Liam swooped in, snatching him off the ground in a crushing hug.

"Cap'n's going to kill me." Squeezing his eyes tight, he pressed his face into Liam's neck.

"No, he won't. It may get his attention, though."

"I already had a plan for that, thank you very much."

Liam pulled back with a wicked grin. "Does it have anything to do with this nice outfit and cleaned-up look you're sporting?"

Mac smiled and ducked his gaze. "I was going to find him after I checked in on you."

"You still can. It would have worked, Mac. I hope this doesn't make it harder." Liam turned his head and looked him in the eye. "Give him a chance. He loves you. On this ship, you don't get that pissed off over a blowjob if you're not completely hooked on a guy."

Releasing him, Liam ran his hand along Mac's neck and head. Rubbing his palm across his eye, Mac pushed back a threatening tear. This was going to be a stressful day. He hoped he was up to the task.

"All right, Mac. Go back to your room and get that stuff. The faster I head out, the better my chances."


MAC TURNED AND headed for the door as Liam began rummaging through the room behind him. Now that he'd brought Liam everything he'd asked for and showed him how it all worked, he had been forgotten, but that was fine. Once the door closed and he was alone in the hall, he fell back against the hull and exhaled in a violent rush. Body shaking, he struggled to stay upright, a tight grip on the satchel slung over his shoulder.

Mac couldn't believe he'd found the courage to perform a flagrant act of insubordination. It wasn't like him at all. His own nature always had him following orders or doing tasks to make others happy. The captain's presence had heightened his need to submit, but this was not the time. Taking the initiative like this scared him witless. He needed to find the strength to follow through. He'd come this far, hadn't he?

When the captain found out, he was going to be livid. Now Mac was an accomplice in spacecraft theft. Liam was going to rescue Hadrian. Hadrian was captured. Was it hot in there? Travel to Luxoria at cruising speed would take approximately 2.45 days. The hum of the engine sounded off. His tech manual was open to page 345. The fibers in his shirt were a synthetic poly-blend.

Mac palmed his temples and hissed. "Stop it!" Anxiety made his thoughts race in random directions, and he was losing focus. Gritting his teeth, he chanted one word in his head over and over. *Danverse.* The one person who always brought sanity when his mind ran rampant. He repeated the thought, louder and louder, until it began to drown out the scattered voices.

"Oh God, I need you." Mac had never been more thankful there was no one in the empty hallway to hear him.

With great effort, he ordered his thoughts. Once he was no longer in danger of hyperventilating, he continued around the corner, heading for the locker room. He splashed cold water on his face and shot a determined stare into the mirror.

"You can do this." He challenged his reflection until it looked like he might believe it.

Pulling his personal data pad from the satchel, he checked the time. He estimated he had roughly six minutes before Liam left the ship. He needed to get moving.

"Mrs. Claus. Is Captain Danverse on the bridge?"

"Yes, Mr. Smith. Do you require anything else?"

"No, thank you."

He trotted to the lift and, moments later, was heading for the bridge. Pausing at the door, he took a deep cleansing breath, straightened his clothes, and placed his hand on the black access panel.

Teddy and Daveth were chatting at their posts while the captain stood at his station. Danverse looked stressed, quite like Liam did earlier, with a startling bruise along his jaw. The gossip about the fight was true.

Danverse checked random items on his screen with little interest. Mac scuffed his feet on the floor to get his attention.

"Mac?" Danverse turned in surprise and wasted no time surveying Mac's new look. His gaze hovered at the point Mac's vest exposed his chest. "You look good."

"Thanks. You're looking a little rough."

Daveth was turned in his chair. "Nice outfit, Mac." He nodded and apparently lingered too long.

Danverse whipped his head around to face the pilot. "I'm gonna be really pissed if we crash into something because you're not paying attention." The warning made Mac more at ease. There was still something between them. Mac hoped it would still be there after the next few minutes. Glaring, the captain waited for Daveth to return his attention to the main viewport. Daveth stole a glance over at Teddy, who returned an eye roll and went back to his task. Looking at Mac, Danverse seemed to soften.

"What brings you up to the bridge?"

"I came to see how you were doing. Find out if you're willing to talk to me yet."

Danverse began to fidget. He cut a glance over to the other crew members and back. Mac knew he didn't want to have this conversation in front of them.

"You caught me at a bad time, is all."

"I can understand—"

Teddy's voice rose above everyone. "Captain?"

"What?" Danverse didn't appreciate the interruption.

"The raiders' ship. It's disembarking."

Anxious heat rose in Mac's chest as it all began.

Danverse snapped to face Teddy. "What do you mean, *disembarking*? I didn't release anything."

"The engines are powering up."

"Who the fuck's on board?"

Teddy checked his screen. "Uh...it's Sergeant Jacks."

"Fuck! Put a docking override on it and get him back here!"

Teddy touched a series of controls at a frantic speed. An icon on his monitor flashed red, and he repeated the commands.

Danverse began to shout. "Hurry up, Teddy! Get that docking override online!"

"I can't! They're disabled!"

Mac stood quietly as the crew realized they had no control over the situation. Teddy and Daveth were both scrambling at their stations to complete the captain's orders with no success. Danverse glanced over at him, his eyes narrowing in curiosity.

Danverse slammed his fist on the console. "Get them back online!"

As Danverse ground his teeth, a wave of unease rolled over Mac. It would only be moments before everything boiled over.

"Mrs. Claus! Who turned off the docking system?"

"The docking system protocols were disabled for maintenance by Mackenzie Smith's personal override authorization, Captain Danverse."

Mac shrank as he glared at him, both hurt and angry. Danverse's face reddened as the veins in his neck stood out in sharp relief. Flooded with guilt, Mac struggled to keep from tearing up. His mouth clamped thin, trembling with guilt, regret, and other unfamiliar emotions.

Teddy broke in. "Captain, I have the docking systems back online. Initiating tractor override."

"Stand down."

Teddy spun in his chair. "What?"

"I said stand down. Let him go."

"You can't do that."

"Last time I checked, I was in charge. Liam has work to do. And so do you."

Teddy gawked at the captain, confused. Danverse stared him down, and he relented. As Teddy resumed his position, Danverse squeezed his knuckles white on the console's edge. He closed his eyes and took a deep breath. When he exhaled, he turned on Mac.

"My day cabin. Now." He stalked forward and clasped the back of Mac's neck. His hand twitched, making Mac flinch. When the door closed behind them, the pressure intensified, and then Danverse snapped his hand away.

The exasperation was thick in Danverse's anger. "Do you have any idea what you've done? Do you understand the kind of danger you've put us all in?"

"What are you talking about?"

Danverse rounded on him. "Mac, if they trace that ship back to us, they will put all of us in prison—if they don't kill us outright."

"If they wanted to kill us, they would have done it by now. It's in the boss's hands now." His shoulders sank in shame as his justification in aiding Liam began to fray. Somehow prison didn't factor into his calculations.

"Why would you do something so *stupid*?"

He flared at the insult. "Because he asked me to!" He stepped forward, challenging Danverse's humiliating comment. "It's not stupid. Risky, yes, but I can't just sit back and watch Liam melt down when there's something that can be done."

"It's not risky; it's reckless! He could be killed!"

"Killed out there making an effort, or wasting away on board?" He closed in farther as Danverse's stare bore into him. "You can already see it happening, can't you? Which option do you think he would want?"

Danverse's chest rose in dominance. "That's beside the point."

"He needed to do something about it."

"And he already asked me. I told him no."

Frowning in disgust, Mac stepped back. "So you don't want him to save Hadrian?"

"Of course, I do! But I wouldn't tell him to do something this dangerous. And I sure as hell wouldn't want him dragging the crew into it. You most of all."

"He can do what he needs to as long as he does it your way?"

"To protect us all, yes. And as long as you're on this ship, so will you."

His eyes narrowed. "Or what? You'll chain me to the wall and whip my ass until I beg you to fuck me?"

Danverse's eyes bulged and his skin flushed a deep crimson. No words came out of his mouth as suffocating silence bathed the room. Mac crushed his eyes shut to hold back the brimming tears. Covering his mouth with his hand, he raked his skin with his fingers as he turned away.

Mac couldn't stop himself from sobbing into his hand. "You're a fucking hypocrite. You're all pissed off over something stupid I did in the shower that meant nothing, while you've been involved with the boss all along."

"That's what you meant in the mess hall when you said you'd seen the security vids. How did you get access?"

"There's nothing I can't get into on this ship if I want to."

"So you've been spying on me."

"Only you. You're the only one I gave a damn about. Every time I tried to get you to notice me, you went hot to cold and I didn't understand. You didn't leave me a choice. Thanks to you, no one wanted me."

"That's not true, Mac."

"I broke into the security history days ago and watched your nights with Liam. It scared me at first, but I saw how you took care of him after. It's part of who you are. I know I shouldn't have, but I needed to know more about you and you weren't talking to me. Look, I don't want to talk about all the dumb shit we've done to each other… I feel stupid enough as it is."

"Please tell me you didn't help Liam to get him out of the way."

Mac shook his head. "No. He's my friend and I know how much he's hurting. He needed my help. Everything else was for you." Reaching into his satchel, he drew out a small box and placed it on the desk. It was wrapped in black satin paper with a blood-red bow. "This was supposed to be for your birthday."

"You remembered?" Danverse's voice was a whisper, his brow furrowed.

Tears began to fall down Mac's cheeks. "I would do anything for you. Every day since that stupid night in the mess hall has been torture." He sniffed hard through a sob. "I can't stay on board and watch you live your life without me."

He stared hard and long at Danverse, who stood dumbfounded. He waited for a response and nothing happened. Danverse's eyes were glassy, his shoulders slumped. His slackened jaw and open mouth issued no sounds. No words.

With a sharp gasp, Mac pivoted on his heel and headed for the door. Heart pounding, he reached for the cracked control but was stopped short by Danverse gripping his wrist. The captain's body heat warmed his back.

"You will not leave me because I'm a stupid jackass without giving me a chance to apologize." Danverse wrapped his free arm around Mac's chest and pulled him closer. An uncontrolled shiver ran down Mac's spine as Danverse's words ghosted along his ear and neck. "I waited a long time for you, Mac. I was afraid you wouldn't accept my kinks, and I couldn't handle the idea that you'd think I was some kind of freak. So I kept you at arm's length, like a coward." He tightened his grip and his voice roughened. "But losing you would be worse. I love you too much to let you go, boy. Stay. Please."

Mac turned in his arms and locked eyes, searching for a hint of deceit. All he could see was need. They both moved forward, crushing their lips together as he snaked his arms around Danverse's neck. A forceful tongue demanded access to Mac's mouth, which he granted without resistance. Greedy, devouring kisses were better than any words and spoken apologies. This must be heaven, pressed between the unyielding door and the hard man in front of him. When they finally parted, out of breath, Danverse stared at his lips with lidded eyes.

"You wore these clothes for me?" Danverse ran his fingertips along the open neck seam of Mac's vest, dipping into the chest hairs.

Mac blushed. "Yes. I thought you'd like it." He could barely speak through the lusty haze crashing to the surface.

Danverse slid his hand inside to caress Mac's fuzzy pec and pinched a hardened nipple. "I do." After another wet kiss, he pulled back. "Are there any other surprises for me?"

"I'm wearing the jock as requested, so I'd be ready for you."

A wolfish grin paired itself with Danverse's rising brow as the memory came clear. Diving forward, he attacked Mac's neck and shoulder with biting kisses, making Mac moan. His eyes closed as he clutched at Danverse's head, trying to drive him harder for more. Danverse wrapped his muscled arms tighter around his waist while he sucked and bit until Mac's feet left the ground, sandals dropping one by one to the floor. When he finally bumped into the edge of the desk, Mac's eyes opened and his bare feet found the ground once again.

Danverse's gaze was needy and forceful as he reached down and stripped open Mac's breeches. A happy hiss blew through his teeth when he was greeted by a red jockstrap, tented obscenely by Mac's aroused flesh. The touch of his strong hand kneading the hardened organ through the fabric was almost too much.

Mac gasped. "Please. I love you so much, Marc. Make me yours. Now."

Danverse nodded, eyes lidded, and spun Mac at the waist, bending him over the desk. There was no fight in him as Danverse's heated hands opened his backside. Then his world changed when Danverse's thick, writhing tongue snaked inside him. Mac's eyes attempted to roll to the back of his skull. He nearly cried out in protest when the pleasure stopped.

Danverse pressed his body against Mac and whispered in his ear. "You're already wet. You came here to get me to claim you, didn't you?" A clothing-covered erection settled between his buttocks. So sensitive in anticipation, he could almost feel every ridge and vein against his exposed bottom.

"You're goddamn right I did."

Danverse's chuckle, along with the sound of his buckle coming undone, echoed in the room. Mac fought off the urge to come as soon as he felt the touch of the searing, blunt cockhead prodding at his opening. Silky and solid at the same time. Danverse enveloped Mac's torso with his strong arms. Mac whimpered as he tried to push back, but Danverse held him from moving.

"Stay still. This is mine." Danverse tightened his grip as his mouth returned to Mac's neck. Biting down, Danverse breached him at a gradual, steady pace, the bite's intensity distracting Mac from the pain of the entry. Mac huffed, trying to press back to make the penetration deeper, but to no avail. This was completely at Danverse's speed, and the slow burn was driving Mac out of his mind. He sighed in satisfaction once Danverse's hips crushed his backside, his cock as deep as it could reach.

Danverse's words were raspy and sharp. "I've waited too long for you, boy. This first time is going to be hard and fast. Hang on."

He barely had time to nod before Danverse pulled back and slammed into him. A harsh rhythm ensued and he held onto the desk as Danverse's cock beat the hell out of the spot inside him that turned his brain to mush. Wordless noises filled the room as he lost control. His rushing orgasm soaked his jockstrap's pouch, and he gave a haggard shout in time with each thrust. Danverse's thrusts became erratic and he rammed home full force, one last time, bottoming out. Mac could feel the heat and warmth flooding inside him with each animalistic grunt and pulse.

Both men were panting as Danverse's weight pressed him into the desk. Stroking the side of Mac's head, Danverse kissed the trails of sweat along his temples. Mac shifted slightly.

Danverse gasped and tried to nudge himself deeper still. "Don't move. I want to stay inside you as long as I can. Are you all right? I didn't hurt you, did I?"

"Trust me. I'm okay." Completely sated, he couldn't hold back the grin. There were no random thoughts colliding in his brain. No clashing noise of ideas. Just simple, clean bliss.

Eventually, Danverse softened enough to slip out, and he lifted Mac to his feet, and then helped Mac straighten his hair and clothing before they'd have to be seen. Neither one could stop smiling, and both kept glancing away like schoolchildren caught crushing on each other.

"I can't believe you're finally mine." Danverse stroked Mac's face with a look of wonder and disbelief. "I have so much I want to teach you."

"Like what?" Mac ran a finger in circles over Danverse's chest.

"Like who's in charge." Danverse raised an eyebrow. He found the favorite spot for his brawny hand, along the back of Mac's neck. Mac couldn't help the shudder that chased down his spine. "Someone needs a lesson after being involved in vehicle theft with another crew member. That's a punishable offense."

He looked up at Danverse. The pressure of Danverse's hand was already reigniting his arousal. The power of youth.

Mac prayed Danverse could keep up, but doubted he needed to. "Any chance of a bribe with services rendered for a lessened sentence?"

Danverse answered with a dirty grin. "I think we can both have fun and still teach you some discipline. I have a feeling you'll respond well to it."

# Chapter Eleven

*"YOU CANNOT BE serious, Leo."*

*"I'm afraid so, pet."*

*"I have never killed a man without cause. You cannot ask me to do this."*

*"Hadrian, you have no choice. Everything is already in motion. Phillip will ultimately discover my hand in your escape and torture me for revenge."*

*"Then I will not leave."*

*"Then he'll know I tried to free you and torture me regardless. Are you going to allow that to happen?"*

*"That is not fair."*

*"No, it's not. But neither is this situation. I will no longer sit back and watch this sick game play out."*

*"Why now, Leo? Why, after all this time?"*

*"Let's just say the time is right, pet. It's time for you to run. It's time for you to be the person you always should have been."*

*"What am I supposed to do?"*

*"Run. Take this."*

*"What is this?"*

*"This holo pack will explain everything in more detail, but now you have to go."*

*"But only if I end your life."*

*"Yes."*

*"That is murder."*

*"No. You will be doing me a service. Once Phillip knows what I've done, he will show no mercy in trying to discover your whereabouts. I will not risk the chance of betraying you."*

*"Father will not—"*

*"Yes, Hadrian, he will. Don't lie to yourself. You know better. I am not a man with the fortitude for his brand of persuasion. You know this."*

*"But, Leo..."*

*"But, nothing. Time is precious. You must fly, pet. Live your life, but end mine first."*

*"Leo..."*

*"You know I'm right. No. No tears. Go now. Just make it quick, please."*

*"Forgive me, Leo."*

*"DO IT!"*

Hadrian awoke with a start, facedown on the rug. Wet salt stained his cheeks and soaked the fibers beneath him as his hands clenched open and closed against his will.

"I failed you, Leo. Please forgive me."

With a wince, Hadrian lifted himself off the floor and onto his knees. The guards had been especially harsh with him on the trip back to Luxoria and Father had turned a blind eye. Further proof the man saw him as nothing more than a possession, a favorite plaything at best. He would heal quickly, but he refused to look at the bruising hidden under his clothing. It's not as if he could blame the guards' hatred. He'd killed three or four of them in the cargo bay before Donovan's command filled him with blinding pain, shutting him down.

Hadrian didn't feel sorry in the least.

When they'd struck Liam, he couldn't hear him anymore. The sound of Liam filled him anywhere and everywhere since they had joined, and at that moment, it was replaced by shocking silence. They had killed him for no reason. Horror had buried its ugly claws in his chest and tore his self-control into tatters. Every one of the soldiers had expected a killing machine—he'd heard the overlapping fears—and by damn, they had gotten one. He couldn't believe he'd nearly killed Captain Danverse as well.

New tears slipped down his face. No other man had ever piqued his genuine interest, and now Liam was gone. Once he had seen the doctor on Alpha Centauri, he'd planned on following Liam to whatever corner of the universe could keep them both.

Now...now it was too late.

He scrubbed the moisture from his face with tense hands. The cleansing breaths sounded like a wild animal's hiss through gritted teeth. Neither years of discipline by combat masters nor battles in the arena had brought him to tears since he was a child. Now he struggled to restrain the bleeding in his chest that came from no physical wound. He was in foreign territory.

Unfortunately, the room he was in was all too familiar.

Sumptuous carpet lined the floor in reds and golds. Gray-striped wall coverings hid the construction materials behind them, softening their appearance. In stark contrast to the décor, metal doors, one at each end of the long wall, served as the only entrances. Doors on the two shorter walls connected to his lavatory and closet, and the opposite wall was filled with floor-to-ceiling windows showcasing the city skyline. The ground could not be seen from this height. The bed was thick and luxurious, with ornate posts running to the ceiling. All the furniture was exquisite, with no expense spared for Father's favorite. The spacious room was an exercise in opulence. Despite this, it was still a prison.

Hadrian knew where each camera was hidden, watching him every moment. Echoes of the guards on the other side of the wall had taught him. He had been comfortable there once, ignoring the truth, but this small taste of freedom left him bridling. It wasn't his home anymore.

What would he do now? He could fight. He could cut a bloody swath through the men there, but every future path he viewed ended without even a hope of success. Father's building was too well-guarded. There were too many opponents. Also, Hadrian's education had included little technology information. There was no way he could disable security systems and other surveillance. Only Leo's involvement made it possible the first time, and that escape had been from Leo's home, not there.

But why bother? Without Liam, what was the point? Freedom had no meaning without him.

With a sigh, Hadrian resigned himself to his fate. What choice did he have? He would be a good Adonirati. He would do what he was told. Somehow, he would learn to be happy again in this silk-swaddled hell. If he ever was. A lifetime of lessons couldn't be undone in a few short weeks. He could tamp down his feelings and be the man he was trained to be.

Standing with an aching slowness, he found his balance and moved to the bedside table. With a gentle touch to the corner, a drawer slid open, whisper quiet. He shuffled the contents until he could reach the back. Cupping his hands, he kept his treasure hidden from the security feed. Opening them slightly, he peeked inside.

A folded paper bird a few centimeters long sat sheltered in his palm. With a single fingertip, he stroked the delicate neck and wing while keeping the tiny item shielded from view. More paper animals lay at the rear corner of the drawer, a tiny parchment zoo. Whoever Father had search his room after his escape apparently hadn't seen them as important.

The antique origami was from one of his few unblocked Link sources. It was a part of an ancient Earth history lesson. The artistry was precise and elegant, and Hadrian excelled at it. He learned to keep them hidden from the time Father caught him making one when he was twelve. Father had crushed the paper trinket under his heel, saying it wasn't a useful skill for his profession. Yet he never made an effort to block the information. That night, Hadrian had spent long hours straightening and refolding the damaged item. It was never the same, so afterward, he made them in secret and hid them, changing their location periodically so they wouldn't be found.

Carefully, he placed the little treasure back into the drawer, hiding it again behind the boxes of balm and first-aid tech. He knew someone was coming.

The left door slid open and Donovan stepped forward with a lone armed guard at his side. Impeccably dressed, as always, he looked as if he'd come over straight from the salon. Hadrian met his cold stare and knew what was coming even as the smile curled Donovan's cruel lips. A wave of disdain washed over him.

"*DUNG NHU DA!*"

Hadrian gasped as he felt the electric surge race from the base of his skull, down his spine, and out to his fingertips. Every muscle flexed and his entire body seized, refusing to release. Unable to move, he fell over, unable to cry out as he landed on his tender side.

"Not so frightening now, are you, Ronan?"

Hadrian could only stare as Donovan stepped forward and used his foot to flip him onto his back.

Stooping low, Donovan slapped Hadrian's face with the back of his hand a few times. "Not frightening at all."

Donovan spoke over his shoulder. "You can go. He's useless right now." The door slid closed with a smooth swish as the guard left the room.

Fortunately, the paralysis wasn't absolute, but Hadrian could only take shallow breaths. He certainly wasn't comfortable but wasn't in pain. And he knew from experience it wouldn't last. It would only be a matter of time before Donovan became bored...or angry.

Leaning over him, Donovan studied him with undisguised contempt. He opened his mouth and clicked his tongue piercing against his teeth. It was a crude habit Hadrian found exceptionally annoying.

Donovan sneered. "How could you have been caught halfway across the cluster? You should've stayed hidden."

He tapped his teeth with the piercing a half-dozen times as his derision grew.

"I was so happy you were gone. Father could finally stop fawning over you because you weren't so perfect anymore." Frowning, he slapped Hadrian's frozen face. "But you couldn't stay gone."

Donovan stood and began pacing. His elegant demeanor frayed further with each step. "He made you strong and beautiful, while I've done everything at my disposal to make him happy." A fine spittle began to wet the corners of his mouth, his voice becoming shrill. "*I am his consort*! But still, he runs to collect you the moment he found a wisp of information on your location. I will always be second to you. *And you're nothing but a glorified whore!*"

Rage twisted his features. Donovan's beauty was a facade at best. True ugliness sat at his core. Which swelled with each passing moment. Unable to move, Hadrian cringed inside. He knew what was coming next.

"I'm going to make you miserable. I'm going to make you suffer. You're going to wish for death before I get bored of you, brother."

Donovan kneeled and turned Hadrian's face to ensure eye contact. His cold blue eyes burned into Hadrian's.

"Father won't protect you. You're not in favor anymore." The air from Donovan's angry whispers fell mere centimeters from his lips as he stroked Hadrian's cheek with manicured fingertips. A single lock of Donovan's well-kept hair fell forward, touching the edge of his cruel smile.

Hadrian braced himself.

*"GUI CHO TOI!"*

Every raw and open nerve was flash-dipped in molten metal. Pain seared each square millimeter of his flesh, burning his mind and eyes. If Donovan was watching, Hadrian couldn't know. Even the paralysis couldn't stop his writhing convulsions on the floor. Tears spilled down his cheeks, as he was unable to open his mouth to scream.

LIAM DOUBLE-CHECKED the route back to Luxoria. The navigation monitor calculated his location in the planetary cluster on its monochromatic display. The faster-than-light engines were functioning normally, but from this point, it would still take almost two days to reach the planet. He hoped he hadn't lost too much time.

The raiders' ship—which he had renamed *Hadrian's Hope*—was a sturdy little craft. She wasn't much to look at, but she could do the job. So much of the tech had been spliced together from other sources, the inside had a strange patchwork quality. *Hadrian's Hope* was a small, silent, maneuverable craft with stealth capabilities that were beyond illegal. Liam was convinced the full visual camouflage and sensor cloak meant he could hover and fly between buildings during the night without ever being spotted.

The ship was small, more the size of a shuttle than a spacecraft. Liam shook his head trying to imagine seven grown men holed up in there for two days straight. He was feeling boxed in already and it had only been a few hours.

Settling back in the pilot's chair, he browsed the data pad Mac had given him. The weapon inventory was still in its storage compartment along the back wall, and Liam's eyes had gone wide over the insane artillery stash the raiders traveled with. Military-grade machine gun, incendiary grenades, surveillance tech, dozens of handguns, thousands of rounds of projectile ammunition... Who carries all this shit around?

Not that he minded. He planned to use any tool at his disposal to either rescue Hadrian or avenge him.

"Please let him be alive."

Liam shook his head. Now was not the time for caving in to despair. He didn't know Hadrian's status, and speculating was useless. A lot of planning needed to be done before nearing the planet. He couldn't go barging in and get them both killed.

Unfamiliar with the control panel, Liam scanned the surface until he found the button to activate the voice command. A green light flashed as the computer chirped at him.

"Secure Subspace Link to Luxoria. All data on Ambassador Phillip Chien."

A few moments passed and data began flooding the screen. There was a lot to work through, but Liam had time. He had just begun to read when the communication system beeped.

He was being hailed. Recognizing Mac's encrypted signal, he answered the transmission and his spine went rigid. Danverse looked back at him from the screen, sitting shirtless at his desk in the dark, the dim monitor providing the only light in the room. His dirty blond hair was disheveled, and Liam prepared himself for an angry tirade. Only, the rage wasn't there.

"Liam, are you all right?"

"I'm fine. How did you get this frequency?" Liam eyed the captain with suspicion. With the last words they'd spoken to each other, he hadn't expected to hear from Danverse any time soon. In fact, he hadn't expected to speak to him until the whole affair was done, one way or another.

"Mac gave it to me once he was sure I wasn't pissed off anymore."

Liam's eyebrow cocked in doubt. "So you're not mad?"

"Not anymore." Danverse shook his head. "And I shouldn't have been in the first place."

Liam said nothing. This apology, if that's what it really was, would have to be good.

On the screen, Danverse fidgeted and grimaced.

"I know I said a lot of shitty things, Liam. I was out of line. I can't even really be mad at what you said back, because it was all true." Danverse rubbed his face, struggling to get his words out.

"I was jealous when Hadrian came along. I admit it. The second you saw him, I could see us coming to an end. I didn't have any control over what was happening, and it rubbed me in all the wrong ways. It still does, a little, but only because I'm not as important to you anymore.

"I love you, Liam. You and I have been through a lot together and I wasn't ready to let you go. Don't get me wrong—I'm not in love with you, and I'm not going to say I love you like a brother because, with our history, that's all kinds of creepy."

Liam snorted. "Who knew you had boundaries?"

"Part of me was happy he was gone, but after I saw how hurt you were, I knew it was more than a fling with a passenger. I think I knew it was more than that from the start." Settling his weight back in the chair, Danverse looked to the ceiling. "For fuck's sake, he saved your life and probably all of ours too. I should have given him some credit."

Sighing, he looked back at Liam. "As captain, you know I can't officially tell you to go out and save Hadrian, right? You've always been a follower, Liam, and this is big. Bigger than anything you've ever been involved in. There was going to be a point where I couldn't back you up. You had to be able to do this on your own.

"I wanted you to come up with something that wouldn't implicate us all. I definitely wasn't happy you involved Mac. Even so, I probably would have handled it better if I hadn't seen that vid of you and Mac in the shower. I couldn't see straight after that. Mac makes me a little crazy."

"Only a little?"

The edge of Danverse's mouth began to curl. "Maybe more than a little."

"You know there's nothing between us, Marc."

"Yeah, I know. Mac made it very clear to me."

The tension in Liam's back began to dissipate. The anger and frustration in Danverse was gone. His eyes seemed to sparkle even in the transmission's dim light. Despite the bruise and swollen jawline, he would swear Danverse looked...happy.

Movement in the background caught Liam's eye. A faint shadow. A body—a man—rolling over in the captain's bed? It was hard to tell, cocooned by the thick blankets.

"Marc. Is that Mac?"

Danverse rubbed the back of his neck and shifted his gaze away. A beaming grin bloomed across his face. If happiness were light, Liam would have gone blind. Danverse nodded like a fool. Liam knew he couldn't get the words out.

"From the look on your face, I'd say it was all good."

"Yeah. Really good. I wish I'd gotten over my shit sooner. We wasted a lot of time, but now that I have him, I'm going to treat him right."

Liam felt a slight pinch in his chest. He was happy for his best friend but wished for his own luck as well.

Danverse leaned forward. "Liam. I want to help. I can't risk the crew's safety, and especially not Mac's, but I'll do what I can. I want you to get Hadrian back. You still have a home on the *Santa Claus*, but this can't follow you here. You know what I mean?"

Liam gave Danverse a grim nod. "Yeah. Leave no trace. Leave nothing alive to follow you home."

"This could get bloody, Liam. Are you ready for that, Sergeant?"

Determination swelled Liam's chest. "Yes, sir."

"That's what I want to hear. Mac tracked down some information that may be useful. The first contact is a genetic engineer, Dr. Victor Saarken. He's been connected with Phillip Chien and the Adonirati program for decades. He may be the man responsible for modifying Hadrian."

"Saarken? That's the name Leo Noble mentioned on the holo."

Danverse's brow furrowed. "What holo?"

"I found it in Hadrian's effects. It was from Leo Noble, the man Hadrian was accused of murdering. He mentioned a Dr. Saarken and said he had a hand in freeing Hadrian. If what you're saying is true, he may have information I can use. I'll hack his DNA ID file in the government mainframe and put a locator on him."

"Be careful with that."

"Don't worry. This isn't the first target I've tracked."

Danverse sighed. "I know. No matter how long we've been out of the Marines, it all comes back to you, doesn't it?"

"Looks like it. By the way, why isn't Mac telling me any of this?"

Danverse blushed as he gazed back over his shoulder at the sleeping man behind him. The glowing smile came back as he wet his lips.

"He's a little worn out." For the first time in the conversation, Liam recognized a hint of sated exhaustion in the captain. Faint circles were visible under his eyes as he took a drink from a cup of water.

"And you're dehydrated, I see." Liam laughed. It had been a long time since he'd seen Danverse so content.

"We made up for lost time"—his gaze slid to the side—"and then there was the matter of overriding my protocols to deal with. I have to admit Mac takes to discipline a lot better than I expected." Danverse looked back over his shoulder again. "I couldn't ask for a better mate."

Liam stiffened as a pang of jealousy shot through him. It made him feel guilty. Danverse was just as entitled to happiness as he was.

"I'm happy for you, Marc. I really am. For both of you."

"Thanks, Liam. Now let's work on getting your man back."

THE NEXT TWO days were excruciatingly slow. If not for the encrypted coms from Danverse and Mac to ease the monotony, Liam might have gone mad. Hours passed in pure molasses as he pored over the data on Chien and *Hadrian's Hope*'s specifications. Understanding the craft's details would be as invaluable as being intimately familiar with the weapons cache aboard.

He was still no closer to a rescue plan but knew he had to start with surveillance. Finding Dr. Saarken would come first. Liam's gut instincts screamed that the doctor would have the information he needed. Saarken knew how to find Hadrian. He had to. Liam told himself over and over that Hadrian was still alive. He had to believe that.

When the proximity alert went off to indicate he was nearing Luxoria, Liam's heart gave a start.

*Just another sniper stakeout.* On earlier missions, he'd waited longer for a target. This was no different. Sleep had been fractured at best, but at least the nightmares seemed to be on hold.

Chewing a dry ration bar, he sat in the pilot's seat, waiting for night to fall in the city where Dr. Saarken lived. The bar was tasteless, the consistency of recycled plastic, and made him wish for Gamin's Bandish stew. When he found Hadrian, that was what he was going to do first: take him out to eat. On a real date. After the most amazing kiss that proved he'd never let him go again.

*Hadrian's Hope* sat in synchronous orbit, fully cloaked, unseen by any. The face of the emerald-and-azure globe faded into black with the lethargic swallowing by the sunset. This final delay was the worst. At night, he could be sure the cloak would get him planetside and that much closer to Hadrian.

Once he'd hacked the doctor's DNA scan, Liam tracked down his luxury apartment in the Prime District. The coordinates were programmed into the ship's navigation and the handheld com Mac had provided. Liam stared at the planet's positioning map indicator representing the Saarken home. Step one in finding Hadrian was only a few hours away.

With time to kill, his mind fell into an awful swell of loneliness. He missed Hadrian's touch. It wasn't fair. Their time had been too short and he wanted more. Did Hadrian feel the same way?

The alarm chimed at 21:00 hours in the Prime District's time zone. Liam double-checked the cloak, which was functioning at peak efficiency. He couldn't throw the ship into drive fast enough.

An hour later, he'd found a remote rooftop where he could park the camouflaged ship.

Using the com's directions, he wove his way through the city, keeping to the shadows and trying to be as innocuous as possible. Periodically, he would duck into an alleyway to avoid well-dressed people strolling by. He swept through the streets until he came to the right building. Wealth oozed from the polished white stone making up the sleek facade. Rows of pristine windows were embedded into the exterior with perfect precision. In the dark, the skyscraper's height seemed endless, like most of the architecture in this district. The sky was almost missing, blocked by spires of construction on all sides. As impressive as it was, Liam wanted nothing to do with it. He was bringing Hadrian home to the *Santa Claus*.

With a quick check of his com, Liam calculated where the doctor lived, slipping in the front door as another tenant walked out. He reached into the shoulder bag he was wearing and palmed Marley Keyes's scrambler. It was slightly warm, as it always was when turned on. Liam was determined not to be seen on any security feed.

The elevator was blissfully empty, as was the immaculate, finely appointed sixtieth-floor hallway. Population schematics noted the doctor as the only occupant on this floor's wing. That would help keep things quiet. He pulled a firearm from the discreet holster under his arm as he approached the front door, turning slightly to keep his weapon hand hidden behind him. Pulse quickening, he touched the door chime with his knuckle to prevent a fingerprint.

A rough male voice squawked through the door. "Hello? Can I help you?"

"I'm looking for Dr. Saarken."

"Who's there? The vid is full of interference."

"I'm a friend of Hadrian Jamison."

Silence. Liam's grip on his weapon tightened as he pressed the chime again.

"Please, I need to speak with you."

Liam jumped back as the door lurched open. Standing before him was an impossibly huge, muscular man wearing only a pair of tight black shorts and matching bands on his wrists and ankles. He scanned the man for a weapon other than his chiseled mass, yet found nothing obvious. Eyebrows appeared to be the only hair on his flawless physique, and Liam had to look up to find them. Was he Adonirati? Behind the hulk stood a smaller man, looking older than Liam knew he should, and behind *him,* Liam could see the muscle man's identical twin. This had to be Dr. Saarken sandwiched between his bodyguards.

Saarken scrutinized Liam, eyes drawing into a scowl. "Sergeant Liam Jacks?"

Liam froze. "How do you know who I am?"

"Why are you here? You should be over halfway to Alpha Centauri by now." The doctor's voice lashed out, making Liam feel like a scolded child. Saarken stared him down with a frightening intensity.

"What happened to Hadrian?"

Liam was so taken aback by the man's forcefulness it took him a moment to respond. "Phillip Chien found him. Brought him back here. I need to find him."

Saarken's jaw went tight, unmistakable anger rolling off him. A shaky hand slapped the shoulder of the behemoth shielding him. "Zero. Move aside." The large man shifted, obeying the doctor's order. With a trembling finger, he pointed at Liam.

"You. Jacks. Put your gun away and get in here. We need to talk."

# Chapter Twelve

BEFORE LOWERING HIS weapon, Liam assessed Dr. Saarken. Chestnut hair with highlights of golden blond framed a handsome face that was etched prematurely, making him appear older than the stats on his ID file. He was frail and unsteady. The tremors in his movements could not be hidden. A slender mechanical framework was strapped to each leg, from thigh to ankle, to support him. Medical crutches were attached around his upper arms, and he had a tight grip on the handles.

Saarken huffed. "Sergeant Jacks, if I were in danger, Zero and Orez would have dismembered you by now. Trust me. I bred them to be faster and stronger than you on your best day." He rapped his crutch along the shin of the bodyguard behind him. "Orez, get out of the way. Jacks, get the hell in here."

Liam slowly holstered his weapon as he followed Saarken's shambling gait into the apartment. He glanced at the bodyguard, Zero, as the door closed behind him. Orez was standing next to him and keeping out of the way. Carbon-copy men, they were so exact it made Liam want to stare. They hadn't shown him any malice in manner or expression. Were they capable of expressing themselves? Or were they simply breathing dolls waiting for instruction? Liam felt no real hostility toward Saarken or his men, just rampant curiosity.

Exiting the foyer into the main room was painfully slow. Saarken's walking speed was hampered by his obvious need to stabilize each step before proceeding to the next. It seemed inappropriate to walk in front of him.

"Orez, prepare a guest room for Sergeant Jacks. Zero, make us some tea." Both Adonirati immediately set off, presumably on their tasks, leaving Liam alone in the sitting room with Saarken.

"I didn't say I was staying."

Saarken shook his head. "Of course, you are. It's late and we have a lot to discuss, and you shouldn't be running around too much in the daylight. Even with whatever tech you have that's hiding you from my systems. Very clever."

Liam followed the doctor across the luxurious carpeting until Saarken reached an exquisite armchair upholstered in a rich, supple leather. The doctor edged in a circle and started to lower himself into the seat. Liam stepped forward and reached out to help. Saarken slapped away the offered hand.

"Don't touch. I'm not an invalid."

"I'm sorry. May I ask…?" Liam motioned to the crutches and leg braces as Saarken carefully sank into the chair.

"I have multiple sclerosis."

"That wasn't in your dossier."

Saarken narrowed his eyes at Liam. "I have enough clout for data keepers to respect my vanity, I suppose."

"Don't they have a cure?"

Saarken's mouth became a thin line. "I'm so glad you mentioned that. As a medical doctor and genetic engineer, I had never thought of taking the cure."

A shamed heat rose in Liam's face. "I guess I deserved that. I'm not used to seeing anyone disabled. It's not very common."

"You're right. It's not. I happen to be one of those poor souls who are deathly allergic to the cure. I'm too sensitive to even have the allergy suppressed." Saarken paused and took a calming breath. "This is a good day. It's often much worse than this. I have to settle for being smarter than everyone else." Zero appeared, placing a tray carrying a teapot and two cups on the small table next to Saarken. "Thank you, Zero. Collect Orez when he's finished and go to our room. I'll call for you if I need you."

The obedient Goliath exited the room without a single word.

"You're not going to keep your bodyguards nearby?"

"No. Would you pour the tea?" Saarken disconnected the crutches from his arms. "You're not here to kill me, and I don't want to kill you. We need each other, I would say. Plus, I'm betting you'll be more comfortable without the twins looming over you."

Liam poured the tea and sat in the adjacent armchair. He had to control the sigh that nearly escaped him. Two days in the pilot's seat of *Hadrian's Hope* had not prepared him for the luxury he was now enjoying. Aware of the holstered weapon under his arm should he need it, he waited for Saarken to take the first sip.

The corner of Saarken's mouth curled. "See? Not poisoned."

"You can understand why I might be a little paranoid. You seem awfully ready to help me."

"I don't like my work coming undone. A lot of effort and planning went into setting Hadrian free. I'm not capable of fixing it myself." He held up a quaking hand. "As you can see, I'm hardly the man for the job."

"You're a genetic engineer. There's nothing you can do?"

"My condition didn't present itself until I was in my twenties. Somehow it had stayed hidden from standard scans. A winner in the cosmic game of impossible chance. Normally, it wouldn't matter. A cure exists, after all. Unfortunately, drastic genetic manipulation has to be done before puberty sets in. When done afterward, the body seems to try to correct itself. With sometimes-disastrous results."

"That's why you altered Hadrian so young."

"Yes." Saarken took a long sip from his tea and frowned. "I will never forgive Phillip for selecting those two boys from the orphanage."

"Two boys?"

Saarken nodded. "Hadrian and his brother, Donovan."

"That shit Donovan is Hadrian's brother?" In shock, Liam nearly dropped his cup of tea.

"Ah. I see you've met the snotty bastard."

"Did you enhance Donovan, too?"

"Only cosmetically. Donovan was intended as Phillip's consort, Hadrian as his Adonirati." A snarl curled his lip. "Although he treated both boys as his sexual playthings."

"Please." Liam raised a hand as he struggled to control the grinding of his jaw. "I don't need any more encouragement to shoot that man through the head. Why take the boys? Why go to all the trouble of the elaborate cloning story?"

"Because Phillip is an arrogant man who doesn't believe there are limits in his own life. He wanted the greatest Adonirati of all and believed a clone wouldn't suffice. I think he simply wanted to break the rules and get away with it. He took one look at those two boys and refused to give them up."

"But you helped him. You helped him get exactly what he wanted."

Saarken sighed, his voice trailing off in reflection. "Times were different then. I was much stupider than I am now."

"Tell me about Hadrian. What kind of enhancements are we talking about?"

A small smile graced Saarken's lips as he lost himself in thought. He took another sip of his tea, and Liam swore the man looked prideful.

"I made him as strong, fast, and beautiful as possible without making him inhuman. He is a living work of art. None of my creations have ever been so perfect. I have made many Adonirati in my years. My fortune is based upon it. But it saddens me to know my greatest creation wasn't mine originally. I was, however, especially proud of his other enhancements."

"Other enhancements?"

"I played in his cerebrum a little bit and brought out his psionic potential."

"Hadrian is a psi?" Liam already knew the answer. All the oddities surrounding Hadrian he'd taken for granted or dismissed were suddenly clear.

"A para-human, yes. Nothing too drastic. I brought out his empathic talents. I wouldn't be surprised if he displayed some form of telepathic skill as well, picking up thoughts as well as emotions. He also seemed to develop some kind of precognitive skill. I hadn't expected that. It explained his ability to outfight his opponents in the arena. He could see what would happen ahead of time and hear their thoughts and strategies."

"Or take on seven men in the cargo bay without a scratch." Liam's voice drifted as he recalled the incident that nearly cost him his life. A shiver ran the length of his spine.

Saarken nodded. "I was never able to test his skills. I didn't tell Phillip about them, so I couldn't be sure if he was aware of them or not. From what I've been able to observe over the years, I'd say most of it comes instinctively to him."

"When he fought the raiders, he walked between gunshots as if he knew where they'd be beforehand."

"It appears he's learned to focus it when necessary, but he would be largely untrained."

"Why did you add those enhancements if Chien hadn't requested them?"

"Empaths have a natural tendency to bond with an appropriate mate when they meet. It compels them to forsake all others. They aren't even aware of it. It comes at them in a love-at-first-sight fashion."

"Does it affect the potential mate?"

Saarken nodded. "Hadrian's mate would be affected as well."

"So Hadrian would force someone to fall in love with him?" Liam's breath stalled as his pulse began to rise. Was his attraction to Hadrian a compulsion brought on by his empathic bonding? He knew his interest in Hadrian was sudden, but was it *his* interest?

"No, Sergeant." Saarken's face brightened with awareness. "It can only stoke an attachment that would have formed on its own. It may have heightened your attraction, but it can't force you to love someone. Hadrian's not that powerful."

"Why make that addition?"

"To ensure Hadrian's defection from Phillip. However, he never found anyone suitable in all the unfortunate liaisons Phillip subjected him to." Saarken's gaze roamed over Liam's body. "Apparently, we needed an off-worlder."

"Your part in this was blatantly illegal. Aren't you worried I might turn you in?"

Saarken held up his shaking hand. "What would they do? Put me in prison? Make my life miserable?" His laugh lacked humor. It didn't seem like the first time he'd had this discussion.

"Sergeant Jacks, my condition is treatable but not curable. When it flares up, I can't hold a cup of tea and the numbness in my legs keeps me from being able to walk even with these braces on. Some days, I can't take care of myself in the simplest of ways. That's what Zero and Orez are for. They also provide companionship. No one wants to make love to a cripple in this corner of utopia. I already am in prison." Saarken closed his eyes for a moment. "Now, ask me something useful."

"Tell me about Leo Noble."

Saarken took a shaky sip of his tea. "Leo was one of my patients and a friend of Phillip's, if that's what you want to call it. He was also completely besotted with Hadrian." Saarken rolled his eyes. "Oh, he would never touch him. Hadrian was too perfect. Leo liked to worship him from afar. He told me he used to purchase time with Hadrian to keep him from the lecherous rabble. They would simply have dinner and conversation with his allotted time. It was quite ironic."

"How so?"

"Leo suffered from Arkarian Syndrome, a debilitating combination of sexual infections he acquired from one of the infamous orgies he'd orchestrated. He was resistant to the cure and it failed. When I diagnosed him, I saw an opportunity. He wasn't difficult to enlist. Hadrian had yet to bond with anyone, and Leo's time was limited.

"Leo had the expertise to place the tech virus that would shield Hadrian long enough for him to get to the spaceport. His guards were easy to distract. Hadrian's visits to Leo were regularly scheduled and without incident. A simple prostitute was enough for them to ignore their duty. A prepaid transport and Hadrian was on his way. I had already researched the *Santa Claus*. The crew's background and the ship's safety standard made it an ideal choice. Hadrian should have been able to travel in relative anonymity."

"He made us suspicious. His biography was too simple, and we ended up alerting the Luxorian government when we started looking into the mystery."

"I suppose it was a bit arrogant on my part not to have all the pieces better prepared."

"We tend to be extremely thorough in our background checks. It was hard for us to ignore. If it's any consolation, most people wouldn't have noticed."

"I suppose that's something."

"Did you know Leo would have Hadrian execute him?" Agitated, Liam had to suppress the accusation.

Saarken looked away. "I may have suggested something to him. Leo would never have survived the interrogation once he'd been found."

"Chien used the murder charge to justify tracking Hadrian down in midflight. They threatened our crew's safety to get the captain to comply. Then, when the arrest went bad, they tortured Hadrian. With some kind of odd phrase. How did they do that? Was it the subdermal tech?"

"I'm afraid so. It's the security measure built into all Adonirati. It's also the primary method of identification. A simple scan identifies it and marks the ownership. It's nanotechnology that's bonded to the brain and nervous system to make him respond to certain voice commands."

"What kind of commands?"

"Sleep. Stay. There's one for punishment. One to provide pleasure. I doubt that was used very often. They're for training and control."

"What keeps other people from using them?"

"They're coded to specific voiceprints. Hadrian's will only respond to Phillip's or Donovan's voice. I programmed all their commands from a bastardized version of an ancient Earth language so they couldn't activate them by accident. Not that it stopped them from using them on purpose."

"Can you remove them?"

"I'm afraid not. The nanotech needs to be deprogrammed by a specialist. I know how to activate and perform the setup on them, but not shut them down. The manufacturing protocols are proprietary."

"That's why you were sending Hadrian to Alpha Centauri. Dr. Hajimi Totoyo is the specialist."

"Yes. And I still intend to get him there."

Liam paused and stared into his cup. "Do you think Hadrian's still alive?"

"Without a doubt. Phillip would never go to so much trouble if he meant to kill him. He would simply have had the military destroy your ship. Besides, he's not going to give up his favorite toy."

"Do you know where I can find him?"

Saarken nodded. "I can help you find Phillip's primary residence, where Hadrian lives. He's likely there."

"I'll need to do some reconnaissance so I can plan my next move."

"You can do that tomorrow evening. It's very late. We'll get you settled in, and I'll help you with any supplies you might need. You can get a proper meal and rest before it all begins. Don't worry, Sergeant. Hadrian will be all right." Saarken returned his cup to the serving tray. It rattled as his trembling hand refused to be calm.

"Doctor, I still don't know why you're doing this. Why are you going to all this trouble?"

"You wouldn't understand."

Saarken strapped the crutches to his arms and raised himself from the chair.

Restraining himself from helping, Liam sat back to process the conversation. Hadrian was likely alive and once again the slave of Ambassador Chien. Every instinct told him Dr. Saarken could be trusted, in spite of his involvement. Little things like the soft derision in Saarken's voice whenever he said Phillip's name stood out. A sudden realization swept over Liam.

"This is about Phillip, isn't it? He was your lover, wasn't he?"

Saarken froze. For the first time, he seemed surprised. He stood perfectly still, staring at a blank spot far away on the wall.

Saarken's voice was barely audible. "The MS presented itself not long after he found Hadrian and Donovan. The first flare-up was severe and debilitating. He lost interest in the freakish cripple rather quickly afterward."

Liam goggled. "You must be joking. All this—from the very beginning—is to get back at your ex?" It took everything he had to contain his outrage at the architect of this whole affair. Saarken began an awkward shuffle toward the hallway.

"Hell hath no fury like a lover scorned." Saarken continued without even looking at Liam. "Come, Sergeant. I'll show you to your room."

HADRIAN WALKED DOWN the hall with his guard escort not far behind. Leather bands adorned his wrists and ankles, the mark of the subjugated. Bare-chested, he was clad only in a red-and-gold-patterned sarong made from fine Luxorian silk tied at the hip. The sheer fabric hugged his lower half in a decadent fashion and clung to every curve and muscle. The uniform of the Adonirati at rest. His feet made no sound on the plush carpet as the silk trailed behind him.

His face was as stoic and impassive as it had been throughout the late dinner he had been subjected to. Expected to be quiet, Hadrian was the perfect Adonirati. He did not speak, except when spoken to, as he'd been taught. He did not laugh at the superficial jokes or join the vapid conversation of the elite guests surrounding the abundant table. He did not recoil from the salacious touches of greedy men and women. Father was watching, and Hadrian was intent on returning to his good graces.

Throughout the meal, he could feel the wealthy guests' wanton urges. They danced close to the dangerous Adonirati beast in some rite of passage that would not be spoken aloud. With enough money, they could purchase their opportunity to walk over the flaming coals, convinced their status would protect them.

The whole dinner had been hollow and lifeless. He ate the artfully prepared meal laid before him on handmade ceramic, which was almost unheard of in this region, but it might as well have been rotted garbage. He wished for a bowl of Bandish stew. The simple entree, full of glorious flavor, was Liam's favorite.

But Liam was dead, and there was no point to that enjoyment anymore. Or any enjoyment, for that matter.

Was this what his life would be from now on? Is this what it had always been? His few weeks of freedom aboard the *Santa Claus* had given him experiences he couldn't forget. On the ship, he had marveled at being treated as an equal. He had not been a servant to anyone's needs but his own. Amazing how such a short period of time could rewrite a person's sense of self.

The crew of the *Santa Claus* were good, decent people who lived honest lives. They took pride in their accomplishments and weren't mired in the moral corruption surrounding him this evening. He missed their little off-planet world terribly.

Since returning to Luxoria, he had resolved to fall into his station in life and move on. How fragile his resolve had proven to be. One dinner filled with people who regarded him as nothing more than a slave had undone it all. Hadrian could hear the condescension they didn't utter in words. He knew what they really meant when their gazes traveled over the exposed flesh of his body, feel their untamed desires as their unwanted fingertips brushed his skin.

He paused in front of the door to his quarters. The guard reached for the control pad, and his DNA scan unlocked the portal. Hadrian thanked him and entered. The door closed and locked behind him, like every other doorway they walked through.

The room looked the same, but there were small differences. Slight wrinkles were visible on the pillows and duvet. Not everything was the way it had been left. Guards had searched his room during the meal, as they often did. Hadrian was used to it by that point. He checked the bedside table and opened the drawer, pushing aside the contents to reach to the back. The paper menagerie was missing.

Hadrian's shoulders sagged as hopelessness beat him down. This is the way it had always been. Why did he care so much now?

Every precious folded animal that helped tether his sanity was lost. Just like Liam.

Liam's death had been in the back of his mind all night. It was as if Liam's spirit drifted in the background, mocking him, reminding him how much he ached inside. Liam's echo was not bringing him any comfort. It threatened to eat him alive, reminding him of all that was gone.

This was Hadrian's future. His life would be one of servitude until his usefulness passed. Then what? He had never heard how Adonirati were retired. It usually happened in an unfortunate loss in the arena. Outside of that, what else? At what point would his fate be sealed?

Hadrian moved to the large mirror mounted to the wall. Glossy ice-blue eyes lined in red looked back at him.

*"I am Adonirati. I am not my own man. I do not have a say in my destiny, Leo. There is no alternative."*

The face in the mirror began to tremble as his mouth pulled tight. A single tear slid down his cheek.

Hadrian finally understood what he had always known, yet somehow buried the reality of: the concept of a slave. That was what he was. Property. He would always be subject to the whims of others. Abused by others. A plaything to Father's and Donovan's cruelty.

Never again would he know another's loving touch. No more genuine affection, only the desires of affluent degenerates. Hope had died along with Liam.

Tears streaked his face as he gazed down. He opened his left hand, revealing the knife he had hidden under his wristband. It had taken several bottles of ale to lull the guests enough to be able to hide it. It was a considerable risk. He wasn't allowed anything resembling a weapon. Lethal when unarmed, a blade in his possession was unthinkable.

He pulled the knife free and examined it as carefully as he could with wet eyes and trembling hands. It was a simple dinner knife. Lightweight designer metal rolled in his touch. It was not particularly sharp, but it would serve its purpose.

Crying freely now, streaks of tears dripped off his chin and spattered along his bare chest. His body quaked with suppressed sobs.

Hadrian gasped. "I would have followed you to the ends of the universe, Liam. I am so sorry. Without you, it is not worth it."

Somber sounds filled the room as Hadrian lifted the blade and pressed it to his throat.

# Chapter Thirteen

THE LAST FEW hours had been excruciating. With Dr. Saarken's help, Liam found the skyscraper Phillip Chien lived in. *Hadrian's Hope*, in full stealth mode, drifted between the buildings, hovering outside the immense window wall of Hadrian's bedroom.

When he first arrived, Liam had the fortune to watch Hadrian dressing to go out. Through the monitor, he savored the image of Hadrian's naked body, fresh from bathing. Liam ached to touch. The indecent cloth tied around Hadrian's hips would give him fevered dreams for weeks.

Alas, the show ended too soon. One of the two doors opened and a guard led Hadrian.

Even with such a short sighting, Liam was alight with energy. Hadrian was alive!

The next two hours, he'd spent waiting. It was nothing new to stay hidden until your target finally presented itself. Sniper school 101. Seeing Hadrian again gave him the hope he needed.

In the dark of the night, he managed to attach a surveillance device to the corner of the window before the two guards came in and searched the room. The sound transmitted perfectly as the men went through every corner and storage place, trying to put it all back the way it was. At one point, one guard found something in the bedside drawer. Liam couldn't see what it was, but he crumpled it up like paper, placed it in his pocket, and continued the search.

There didn't seem to be any urgency about their activities, so Liam guessed they either weren't in a hurry or were performing a boring routine.

Eventually, they left, and Liam had to be content with waiting again. He considered trying to track Hadrian through the building, but thought better of it. Being in front of the window when Hadrian returned would be a better option. It was unfortunate he didn't have a way to send a message to Hadrian inside, but given what he knew of Chien and if the guards were any indication, the room was most likely monitored.

So he waited.

Another hour passed and Hadrian returned. He was beautiful, as usual, but looked sad. Liam stroked the image on the screen as he watched. Hadrian stood in the middle of the room, gazing around. Had he noticed things out of place? He slid open the nightstand and reached deep into it. When his shoulders deflated, Liam knew he'd discovered the missing item. Whatever it was meant a great deal to him, enough he didn't bother to close the drawer. Anger rose in Liam's chest on Hadrian's behalf. His stoic beauty was gone, replaced with a despair that tore at Liam's heart. Hadrian walked to the mirror and Liam watched the man he loved start to cry.

A knife appeared, apparently hidden in Hadrian's hand and wristband. Liam's palms were pressed on either side of the monitor as he watched. Something was wrong.

Hadrian gasped. "I would have followed you to the ends of the universe, Liam. I am so sorry. Without you, it is not worth it."

Liam stared as Hadrian lifted the knife to his own throat.

Liam screamed as he beat his hands on the display. *"No! Hadrian, no!"*

Startled, Hadrian dropped the knife. It bounced on the expensive rug and under the bed.

Liam froze and watched Hadrian stare out into the open. Hadrian's shaky voice came through the speaker.

"Liam, is that really you?"

Hadrian couldn't have heard him. The surveillance was one-way.

"I can feel you out there. Are you alive?" The hope in his voice pushed a tear from Liam's eyes. Why would he think Liam was dead?

"I can hear your voice in my head again!" Hadrian slammed himself against the window to gaze out into the darkness. "When they struck you in the cargo bay, everything went silent. I thought you were dead. When I asked Father if you survived, he said no."

What Liam wouldn't give to stroke that perfect skin and show him how alive he was. If only he could wrap Hadrian in his arms and take him home right that instant. Tears of relief washed his cheeks as he brushed his fingers over Hadrian's image.

Liam spoke to the screen. "I'm outside. Watching. I'm going to find a way to bring you home." He knew the tech had nothing to do with how Hadrian could hear him, but Liam had zero experience with psi-talents or para-humans and this he could understand. Speaking out loud made sense. Trying to think at his mate did not.

It was hard to tell if Hadrian was laughing or crying. "I could not live without you. I am so sorry."

"Don't be. I can't live without you, either. Dr. Saarken is helping me and we'll find a way. Please be patient."

"Dr. Saarken?"

"There's a lot to explain. I haven't been here long enough to come up with a plan, but trust me. I'll be out here in the evenings to watch over you. I can hear everything in the room, so you don't have to speak too loud. Are you being watched?"

Hadrian nodded. "Yes, but they do not listen. I learned that long ago, as well as the places they cannot see clearly."

"I don't want to risk them finding me out here. Can you hear me okay?"

"Your thoughts are like sunshine. I can hear and feel you more clearly now than ever before."

"Good. I only have the one device, so I can only hear you in this room. We can use that to plan, but be careful. Don't do anything to arouse suspicion. I don't want anyone to think anything's out of the ordinary. We'll need the surprise."

"All right. I trust you. How did you get here?"

"The raiders' stealth craft. It looks like they were worth something after all." Liam paused. "Hadrian, it's so good to see you."

"I wish I could see you. But I can feel you as clear as daylight. It is very warming..." Hadrian's face lost its joy as his head tilted to the side. He seemed to be seeing or hearing something unpleasant.

"Liam." Hadrian was suddenly panicked. "You have to go."

"What's happening?" Liam couldn't hold back his growing alarm. This was the tone Hadrian used right before the raiders' attack.

His words were rushed. "Please, whatever happens, I need you not to watch or listen. You cannot save me tonight. Come back tomorrow."

"Why?"

"We will both be killed. You have to go!"

"What's going to happen?"

"I don't want you to see what's coming. Promise me!"

Liam swallowed. "I promise."

Hadrian turned his back to the window as the door opened. Donovan and a small cadre of large men pushed into the room as Hadrian pressed against the transparent wall. Donovan's malevolent grin sent chills down Liam's spine.

"You promised," Hadrian whispered.

"*DUNG NHU DA!*" Donovan shouted.

Hadrian went rigid and fell over. He didn't move a muscle as one of the men grabbed him by the arm and dragged him to the center of the room. Liam could see the particle weapon holstered under the guard's arm. All the men were carrying identical armaments. Even if he could get inside, he would likely be killed. Liam inhaled a ragged breath. He had to trust Hadrian. *Please let him be right.*

Donovan knelt next to his paralyzed brother, clicking his tongue piercing along his teeth as he spoke.

"I know you can hear me, Ronan. You're not unconscious." He slapped Hadrian's face. "These men are from the military troop that helped arrest you. You killed some of their men, and they asked me for a chance to discuss it with you. I couldn't see any reason to say no." The ice in Liam's spine was spreading.

Donovan stood and turned to the men. "Security vids are down for maintenance for ninety-five minutes. Don't use weapons, and do nothing permanent. He has a match in two days. He heals fast, but if he can't be in it and win, you'll take his place. Have fun." Spinning on his heel, Donovan strode out the door and was gone.

The group of men circled Hadrian's crumpled form like a pack of wolves. The alpha reached out and rolled Hadrian face down on the carpet. His rough hand tore the fragile sarong from Hadrian's waist and tossed it aside. Hadrian's limp body offered no resistance. When the alpha began to unbuckle his belt, the others followed suit.

Liam's hand quaked as he punched the control to turn off his monitor. He couldn't watch or listen. He had promised. Trust Hadrian. Hadrian would be all right. He said so. An anxious rush twisted Liam's stomach and he raced to the lavatory. His system was empty long before the crying heaves subsided.

He could barely see through the tears as he sat in the pilot's chair and began maneuvering back to Dr. Saarken. No matter how much it pained him, there was nothing more he could do there. *Hadrian's Hope* slid between the skyscrapers while Liam desperately tried to quell the rage in his chest.

If he had to, he would kill every one of those motherfuckers to get Hadrian back.

THE RELENTLESS RAINSTORM pounded the wall-sized window. Lightning flashed in the distance, but at this elevation, he was surrounded by it. Hadrian reached out into the night with his feelings, but found nothing. No sign of Liam. No love beaming back at him for support. Just the storm's rage and the cold thoughts of the men there with him.

Father examined the bruises on Hadrian's skin. His touch was gentle, but not warm, as he probed his naked Adonirati without a shred of interest in his dignity. Standing at rigid attention in the middle of the room, Hadrian wore only the requisite wrist and ankle straps. He made a point not to wince as Father reached between his ass cheeks with two fingers and prodded his tender opening. The guard observing the procedure turned away in discomfort.

Father checked his fingers, perhaps for blood. "Are you damaged from last night?"

"No, Father." Only a lifetime of training kept him from showing his revulsion at the examination. Previously, Father's touch had been accompanied by some form of parental admiration, but that was not the emotion rolling off the man now.

"If those bruises remain tomorrow, you are to cover them before the match."

"Yes, Father." It wouldn't be the first time. A slew of cosmetic devices sat in the drawer to hide the damage inflicted by yet another form of abuse. Father liked his prize possession to be perfect at all times.

Hadrian inwardly cursed himself. How could he stand there after the night before and seem so unaffected? He had been treated like less than an animal and was expected to show no reaction. Curling up in the corner or dismembering a random guard seemed like the proper response, but he knew better than to succumb to his needs. Doing so would only lead to more correction.

"You understand why I'm being so firm with you, don't you?"

"Yes, Father." Of course, he knew. Father was reestablishing his rule over the wayward child. It was amazing how such a short period of freedom had changed his view. Before, he would have blamed himself for being insolent, and Father would have blamed him too.

"I was very wounded when you ran away."

"Forgive me. It was a moment of poor judgment. I allowed myself to be swayed by Leo Noble. It will never happen again."

"I would hope not. You damaged our family greatly, but we will recover. Rumors spread in your absence, and there is talk that you are no longer my faithful Adonirati. I do not enjoy being laughed at behind my back." Father walked over to the bed and retrieved Hadrian's blue-and-gold sarong. The red-and-gold garment had been ruined the previous night. He wrapped it around his pet's hips and secured the knot, then stepped back to survey his efforts.

"You were always my favorite, Ronan. You understand that, don't you?" Father's gaze roamed over Hadrian's body. "I'm not sure if I approve of you shaving off all your hair. I preferred you as my tamed barbarian with a cultured demeanor. I'll have to see if this new look grows on me or if I'll require a change."

Coming closer, Father ran his hand over Hadrian's head and gripped the base of his skull. It could have been an endearment, but Hadrian could only read domination in his touch.

"You have a chance to make me proud again, Ronan. You're going to win that fight for me. Isn't that right?"

"Yes, Father." Hadrian showed no emotion as he flinched inside once again at his assumed name and Father's possessive tone.

"Of course, you will. Your opponent is strong, but the odds are being placed not for if you will win, but when."

"I don't understand."

"Because of your skill, most bets are being placed for the fight to end within the first five minutes. Mine are being placed for after fifteen. The odds are longer for that time frame. I have a great deal of currency placed on your return bout and stand to make a small fortune when you win."

"I did not think you needed the money."

Father tilted his head. "It's not about the money. It's about winning, and showing those naysayers you're still mine."

"Yes, Father."

Father's gaze darkened. "Under no circumstances are you to allow the match to end before fifteen minutes have passed. Even if you are bleeding to death. Are we clear?"

"Yes, Father."

"Good. Your life will be much easier if you remember to do what you're told. Once the match is over, those cretins will be falling over themselves for a night with you. They'll pay another small fortune for the opportunity. I'll recoup the past month's losses in a single appointment. And you will make it worth every piece of spare change they pour into my accounts. Are we clear?"

"Yes, Father." Hadrian was surprised he managed to maintain his composure. Father was already planning an assignation? His pulse began to rise. No one but Liam would ever touch his body again like a lover. He couldn't bear the thought of submitting to anyone else. But how would he stop them? The night before had proved how vulnerable he really was.

"Good. Now rest. I want you at full strength for the bout."

Hadrian refused to move a centimeter until Father and his guard exited the room. He refused to even turn his head until he heard the locks engage. A flash of lightning filled the room with unrecognizable shadows. His eyes began to water. Spreading his hands along the transparent wall, he looked out into the storm. He reached out with his thoughts into the night for a glimmer of Liam but was granted nothing but the sounds of weather. As he slid to the floor, he curled himself as small as his muscled form would allow.

"Hurry, Liam. I do not know how much more of this I can take."

"STOP PACING, SERGEANT. It's getting on my nerves and disrupting my music."

Liam whirled and glared at Dr. Saarken, who sat in his comfortable chair sipping a cup of tea, crutches leaning against the nearby end table. A quiet concerto played in the background through unseen speakers. Lightning flashed in the night and the rain beat against the window.

"I need to make sure he's all right." A sickening mix of anger and anxiety flooded Liam. It clawed under his skin and made him want to hit something. He focused on the doctor, the designer of all this insanity, and considered his options. Then he took a quick glance at the towering twins, Zero and Orez, and thought better of it.

"But you can't. I'm glad we stored your craft before the storm arrived. Even on the rooftop, a stealthed ship would be discovered in this kind of rain. You can't risk discovery at this juncture. It's too dangerous. For everyone."

Liam ran his shaking hand over his scalp. "I know, Doctor. I know." He ground his teeth and closed his eyes. "I had to walk away while that group of men—"

"Shh. I know you don't want to hear this, but that is probably not the first time something like that has happened to Hadrian. It's amazing he hasn't been broken, considering all he's endured over the years." A soft chime distracted the doctor and he carefully set down his teacup.

Liam slumped onto the settee. He rubbed his face in a vain attempt to calm his nerves. Abandoning Hadrian the previous night had been the most painful thing he'd ever done, short of pulling the trigger at Belathius Pointe. A nightmare had ended what little sleep he'd attempted afterward.

"I need to know he'll be all right." Tremors burned in his hands as he ran his palms along his thighs. He had to keep it together. Hadrian needed him. If he fell apart now, he would be useless.

"Of course, he's all right. He probably foresaw how it all played out. He just didn't want you to witness what was about to happen." Saarken picked up a data pad sitting next to the teapot and read the message scrolling over it.

"How can you be sure?"

Saarken snarled. "That cheeky bastard." He raised the pad so Liam could see it. "This is my invitation to tomorrow night's Adonirati match. Hadrian, or should I say Ronan, is the top-billed fight."

"Donovan said as much last night."

Saarken dropped the data pad in disgust. "It's part of what he was bred for. Phillip is trying to make a grand entrance. There's been a lot of unseemly talk since Hadrian ran away. It's unheard of. I imagine his self-esteem was bruised, to say the least."

"So he's putting Hadrian into a match? For what?"

"To prove he's still in charge. The man's ego has no boundaries."

This conversation was not assuaging Liam's anxiety. He stopped tapping his foot when he realized how closely Saarken was observing.

"You're stressed, Sergeant. Do you require the services of Zero or Orez?"

Liam snapped his gaze to the doctor's. "Excuse me?"

"They are trained Adonirati. They could help ease your tension if you needed."

"You're not suggesting…"

Saarken sighed. "Don't be coy, Sergeant. I'm a doctor. Are you still using rough sex to combat your postwar anxieties?"

A furious blush reddened Liam's skin and he was unable to speak. Though Saarken was right, he had never heard anyone say it so bluntly before. If he'd had the stomach for tea right then, he would have sprayed the carpet with it in surprise.

"That would be a yes." There was no humor in Saarken's tone or expression. It reminded Liam of the clinical responses he'd received from the military psychologist after Belathius Pointe. Those responses were what drove him to leave therapy when he and Danverse were released from their military contract.

"How did you know?" Liam was shocked at how coarse his voice seemed.

"You're not the only one who can do a thorough background check. I previewed everyone on board the *Santa Claus* before planning Hadrian's trip. Granted, your psychological profile ended when you left the Marines."

"Those are privileged military files."

"I have a great deal of money." Saarken tilted his head. "You didn't answer my question."

"I don't appreciate you invading my privacy."

Saarken's voice grew harsh. "Since you arrived on my doorstep, everything has become far more serious. I need to know if you're up for the challenge. A great deal rides on your ability to see this through. It's not only your safety at stake now. It's mine as well. I may not be afraid to go to prison, but I'll be damned if I'll make it easy on them.

"I'm not asking to entertain myself." Saarken huffed. "I'm checking to see if you need help. I heard you before you woke up. It sounded like night terrors. Look at you. You're trembling worse than I do and you look ready to detonate. I can arrange a session for you if it will help. You can use either one of my Adonirati. Or both."

If Liam had been uncomfortable before, he was way beyond that point now. He glanced over at the behemoth twins. Both of them sported identical rippling muscles, still covered in nothing more than minimal, formfitting black shorts. The bulges hidden in those shorts gave Liam pause. Zero and Orez were capable of holding him down and having their way with him. Punishing him for all his sins, past and present. There would be nothing he could do to stop them. Liam could feel the sweat begin to trickle down his back while his jock grew restrictive. Even one would be enough, but both of them...

A flash of lightning broke his train of thought. Guilt flooded his chest. How could he even entertain the idea of this inappropriate version of therapy? He'd gone this route with Danverse and where was he? It didn't fix his troubles. It was pure avoidance. No. Nothing was important until Hadrian was safe. Hadrian was all that mattered.

Liam looked away and shook his head. "No, thank you. I need to find a better way to cope. That's not how I want to handle things from now on."

"If you're sure."

"I'm not." Liam shifted on the couch and wrapped his arms around himself. "But I'll never forgive myself if I lay hands on anyone but Hadrian. As long as he's alive, he's the only one."

A quiet smile graced Saarken's lips. "You'll do fine. Hadrian is very lucky." Saarken's shoulders dropped as he peered down at his unsteady hands. It didn't require an empath to read his mood.

Liam's unease became less significant as he looked at the doctor. The frail man had to be painfully lonely. Harboring that kind of jealous anger for so long, did Saarken know how to connect properly with anyone? With his physical limitations, he had little hope of happiness in his social circle. Liam still had Hadrian. As strained as the connection was right then, it was far better than the isolation Saarken must have experienced. That reality helped to ground Liam and soothe the quaking under his skin.

"I need to see Hadrian." Liam stared, pleading, into the night storm. "I want him to know I'm still here. If he's fighting tomorrow, there's no way for me to contact him."

"Don't worry, Sergeant. I may have an idea."

# Chapter Fourteen

"WHAT'S TAKING SO long, Sergeant? I'm not getting any younger."

Dr. Saarken stood, bearing his weight on his crutches, in the guest room Liam had been staying in. He stared at the adjoining bathroom door where Liam was prepping himself for the evening. This had been a good day. His legs felt stable in the braces, and the numbness was less pronounced. He'd finished his morning tea without a spill and holding himself steady was less of a chore for a change.

Liam groused through the door. "I can't believe I let you talk me into this."

"This is the only way for you to lay eyes on Hadrian tonight."

"Why not after the match?"

Saarken was silent, unsure how to respond.

"Doctor? What happens after the match?"

"If Hadrian wins, and he no doubt will, he will be in great demand." He breathed deeply before continuing. "Phillip will be looking to capitalize on that. Hadrian will bring a great price for the evening."

This time, it was Liam who was silent.

"I'm sorry, Sergeant. There are aspects of the Adonirati existence that are unsavory, to say the least." Saarken felt fortunate he couldn't see Liam through the door. The more time he spent with the sergeant, the more guilt he felt over his hand in this. How did it all get so far out of control?

"Hadrian shouldn't be an Adonirati."

Saarken winced at Liam's anger. It was well deserved.

"I'm trying to undo that."

Saarken stood alone in the lavish guest room. Ever since Liam had declined the offer of Zero and Orez's services, he'd kept them away from the sergeant as much as possible. Liam might have said no, but there was a marked conflict in his eyes. It was better to keep him from temptation. If he succumbed, he might lose his nerve for the coming trials.

They needed to rescue Hadrian soon. There wasn't the benefit of months of preparation again. This time around, they would need to take advantage of a moment's opportunity. From what he had been told and witnessed, neither Hadrian nor Liam would survive an extended campaign.

Lost in his thoughts, Saarken started when the bathroom door opened.

"I feel ridiculous." Liam grimaced.

"You look perfect."

The fetish garment of black leather straps, forming a harness, fit Liam well. The straps gathered to a codpiece of matching material, finishing in a thong. Leather Adonirati bands encircled his wrists and ankles. He ran his hands over his now-smooth skin, completely devoid of hair including the top of his head and beard. Zero and Orez's little brother.

"How did you get your tailor to make this getup and the other clothes so fast?"

"As I've told you before, I have a great deal of money."

Liam frowned and rubbed his bare head. "Did I really have to shave off everything?"

"It is well-known that my Adonirati are clean-shaven at all times. They will believe you are a new creation of mine that fits through doorways better than the twins. Or they'll think you're an Adonirati role-player."

Liam threw him an irritated glance. "I hardly think someone's going to reach in and check for pubes."

His crutches thumped on the carpeted floor as he lurched forward, narrowing his eyes at Liam. "You are on Luxoria now, Sergeant." He was annoyed he had to explain this. "The affluent elite here have no boundaries when it comes to the Adonirati. This is the only way to get you into the venue without anyone asking questions or performing a DNA scan on you. Everyone must believe you are my faithful servant, or we're all at risk.

"You will be quiet unless spoken to. You will nod and be polite at all times and do whatever I ask of you. If someone decides to reach in and size up your endowment, you will nod and accept it. Anything else and they will be suspicious. No one will believe I'm being possessive enough with my escort to object."

Saarken's stare pierced Liam until his shoulders dropped and his gaze drifted to the side.

"Hadrian got to wear a sarong, at least. I feel weird with my ass hanging out in public is all." Liam practically pouted as he checked himself in the wall mirror.

"Your assets are better protected in this outfit than some Adonirati. Besides, it's what is expected of my escorts. I saw no need to deviate."

Liam arched an eyebrow. "And you're not getting anything out of this, are you?"

"I would be lying if I said I didn't enjoy the view." Saarken grinned as he stepped back. "Allow an old man his few pleasures in life."

Liam did look incredible. With his body hair removed, every muscle stood out in stark relief, dancing with every movement. He wondered if Liam realized what a fantastic physical specimen he was. What a magnificent Adonirati he would make. If the circumstances were different, he might have called for Zero and Orez so he could watch as they took turns on the sergeant.

"You're not an old man."

"I feel like one." A bitter tang came over him. He'd thought he had the perfect mate in Phillip. Everything would be joy and rapture forever. Then came the first flare-up. While his desire was unimpeded, the MS affected his sexual function with numbness and occasional impotence, making intimacy inconsistent at best. Phillip had taken little time to move on.

The slightest thought of Phillip Chien was a jagged shard leaving bloody slices along his spine. It had been so long since he left, but he was unable to make peace. His condition was a constant reminder of what he'd lost. He had wanted to move into another district to create some distance, but Phillip kept him close all these years, threatening to expose his part in Hadrian and Donovan's acquisition. Now he wanted nothing more than to undo Phillip's utopia. With Liam's help, he could save Hadrian and ease his conscience, while slapping Phillip from a distance.

"Remember, Sergeant. This is not an opportunity to rescue Hadrian. It is simply the chance to see him and assess his fitness. The more you understand about his life, the better you'll be able to plan his escape."

"How close will we be able to get?"

"Close but not near enough. However, you will be able to see everything. I have excellent seats." Saarken moved toward the door. "Now finish getting ready, as I instructed. The driver will be here soon. Your introduction to Luxorian society is about to begin."

LIAM STEPPED BAREFOOT from the transport onto the runway leading into the arena. Not used to walking around without shoes, he breathed a sigh of relief at the carpet under his feet. A slight breeze caressed exposed skin that had not seen the light of day in years. If he stayed calm and composed, he might avoid the all-over body blush.

The outside of the building was massive and as opulent as everything else he'd seen of this district. The facade stretched in all directions and was the only structure on the block. Stone polished to an impossible shine framed out the elaborate carvings in gleaming red and gold. Unseen uplighting created dramatic shadows, emphasizing the designs. No windows were visible from the outside.

A soft clearing of Dr. Saarken's throat brought him back to his role. He turned to the doctor and carefully helped him from the vehicle. He was not to aid him when they started walking. Saarken insisted.

Saarken's black knee-length tailored jacket conformed so smartly to his body, his crutches barely marred the fit of the sleeves. Elegant black pants covered the braces he knew the doctor wore beneath, and a chemise of black-and-opal-patterned silk finished the ensemble.

As the doctor began his slow trek to the entrance, he held his head high with an air of arrogance. Saarken walked more smoothly this evening, but still required the mechanical aids. Liam stayed one step behind, as he'd been told, and took in the other well-dressed spectators from the corner of his eye. Several people clad in expensive couture glanced the doctor's way. Some gave a sad look. Others showed haughty disdain. If Saarken noticed, Liam couldn't tell. The doctor simply moved forward, no doubt daring any of them to say a word.

A pair of elaborate doors swung open as they approached. The design and pattern along their surface reminded Liam of an ancient gate to a lost land. The walkway dipped down into the darkened foyer, allowing them to be swallowed alive by this den of iniquity. *Welcome to the first circle of Hell.* If any hair were left on the back of his neck, it would have been standing tall.

Just inside, stood a colossal man checking in patrons. The doorman wore little more than pierced nipples, decorative tattoos, and a jockstrap made of dark chain-link with a seductive sheer pouch exposing every curve of his generous package. Coupled with the requisite manacles on his ankles and wrists, Liam recognized him as Adonirati. A simple ID scan of Saarken confirmed his private invitation, and the pair moved into the grand hall.

Strategically placed illumination kept the darkness of the space under control. Rich fabric lined the walls in blood red, evoking a decadent luxury. A crowd of aristocracy milled around in the gallery, gossiping and admiring one another while waiting to enter the amphitheater. Dressed in a gown of the deepest scarlet, a raven-haired woman with an elaborate lace hat sidled up to Liam and stroked his chest and arm. She traced along his skin with gold-accented lacquered fingernails.

"Victor, it seems like it's been ages since I've seen you here." Her voice rolled through her ruby-painted lips with elegance and insincerity. Standing perfectly still, Liam worried where her hand would go next.

Saarken barely looked at her. "Good evening, Marchella. If I only come occasionally to these events, it makes them more special."

"If you say so, dear." She raked her gaze over Liam as her touch roamed closer to his codpiece. "I love your new toy, Victor. He's a much better scale than the other two." Brazen in her exploration, she brushed the edge of the only part of his outfit keeping Liam decent. He tried not to tense at the unwelcome contact.

"Would you like to swallow his cock here in front of everyone?"

Marchella dropped her hand and frowned at Saarken's jibe.

"How droll."

"I remember how you vanished with Isomoff's Adonirati last year. I'm hardly going to let you drag him off into a private suite and leave me standing by myself. I need my escort. Perhaps another time." Saarken dismissed her by turning his attention to nothing in particular on the other side of the room. In a practiced huff, Marchella spun on her high-priced heels and found another socialite to intrude upon.

Liam shifted close so only Saarken could hear. "Thank you."

"You did well, but I didn't want to test your limits before we'd barely gotten inside. Now do you believe me when I speak about the decadence of the wealthy here?"

"I'll never doubt you again."

"Good. Let's make our way to my booth before I have to work through a crowd."

He followed Saarken through the next door, which brought them to a glass-enclosed platform. A simple touch to a small panel near the door and the enclosure slid sideways to a fixed point, then dropped below the ground level. The entire auditorium could be viewed from this transport.

Circular rows of opera booths stacked on top of each other along the cylindrical room to dizzying heights. A sumptuous, hollowed-out skyscraper. At the bottom, Liam could see what had to be the arena. An open round space with matte-black flooring, it had several doors along the high walls surrounding it. Large vid panels hung like some grotesque chandelier down the center of the immense space. No one would have a bad view. Like every other aspect of the building, the theater dripped in unrestrained expense.

The lift came to a stop at the bottom tier of booths. Following Saarken, Liam noted how good the vantage point was. If this weren't such a serious matter, he might be looking forward to the event.

It wasn't long before the other booths filled with blood-sport fans. The murmur of noble voices echoed and layered upon themselves. Not standing in a swarm of people he couldn't trust eased Liam's mind some. An Adonirati waiter brought a tea service to the booth before moving along.

"So, what are the rules?" Keeping in character, Liam poured a cup for Saarken.

"The contestants enter, and when one is left standing, the fight ends. It's as simple as that." Saarken reached forward and activated the touchscreen attached to the balcony wall. A program of the night's event scrolled across the monitor. "There are five fights scheduled tonight. Hadrian's is last."

"Is anyone ever killed in the arena?"

Saarken threw an amused look at Liam. "You've seen Hadrian's skill set. Would you care to ask a less-stupid question?"

"All right. How often has Hadrian killed someone in the arena?"

"Every match. Phillip demands it. He's always believed in manipulating or crushing the opposition."

The lights dimmed and the vidscreen chandelier came to life, announcing the first match. The fighters entered the floor from opposite doors and squared off. A wave of cheers expanded as the fight grew more aggressive. Eventually, the match ended with one fighter lying unconscious on the ground. One match down. Liam couldn't give a damn about the program. After watching the fight with unfocused eyes, he could barely remember any details. He was only interested in Hadrian.

"Have you ever sent Zero or Orez into the arena?" Liam watched two large Adonirati clear the unmoving loser from the arena floor in preparation for the next bout.

"Never."

Liam studied the doctor. "Why not?"

"Even though they would excel, that's not what I have them for." Saarken paused. "They are my companions. I may be willing to share them, but I will not risk losing them over money or glory. They're all I have."

The second fight ended as one fighter broke the other's spine. As the maimed contestant writhed on the floor, the crowd roared its depraved approval. A nauseous chill ran down Liam's spine. What would he do if that were Hadrian mortally wounded on the ground?

The third fight was well under way when Saarken leaned close.

"It appears his highness has finally graced us with his presence."

Liam followed Saarken's gaze to a booth across the arena, which had previously been empty. Chien and his consort Donovan were taking their places. Anger swelled in Liam's chest as he gripped the armrest of his chair.

Saarken reached over and covered his hand with his own.

"Stay calm. The two of them never miss one of Ronan's matches."

Liam realized how clearly he could see the pair. "Is there any chance they'll recognize me?"

"Unlikely. Your appearance is radically different from when they met you. And from what you told me about the incident in the cargo bay, Donovan barely saw you, and Phillip doesn't pay attention to any Adonirati except his own." Saarken picked up his tea and nodded to the couple across the way. Phillip smiled, gave a brief nod in return, and resumed his smiling conversation with Donovan.

Saarken patted Liam's hand. "See? We're fine. Try to enjoy the match."

Keeping his stoic face was becoming difficult. The sight of Phillip and Donovan made Liam wish for a weapon. For some reason, he had known but hadn't acknowledged the idea they would be present. The excitement of seeing Hadrian had blinded him. Saarken looked over as Liam took long, slow breaths.

"Steady yourself, Sergeant. You'll serve no one if you give us away."

Liam exhaled and stiffened his back. "Sorry."

"You're doing fine. No one's the wiser. Once we see Hadrian, we'll begin planning how to remove him once and for all."

"I'm a sniper. I'm used to sitting back in the shadows and waiting. Hidden intelligence, not this public spying. It makes me very uncomfortable."

"Learn to adapt, Sergeant. Quickly."

The third fight dragged on, and he wondered if the eventual cheers were for the winner or because the match had finally come to a close.

He kept Phillip and Donovan in sight, without direct stares that might draw any attention, through the intermission and the fourth bout. They socialized with other well-dressed aristocrats and sampled hors d'oeuvres and drinks. They laughed amongst themselves and whispered in each other's ears. It was as if they were on a date. The idea infuriated Liam, but he refused to let on.

Distracted by the couple, he barely noticed the fourth match ending. A surge of spectator noise broke his preoccupation. He turned his attention back to Saarken and found the doctor perusing the program.

"A warning, Sergeant. Hadrian's match will be bloodier than the rest."

"You already said he's under orders to kill his opponent."

"No. I said bloodier. This match will feature weapons."

Liam frowned in confusion. "All the rest of the fights were hand-to-hand."

"This one is different."

It was difficult for Liam to restrain his disgust. "I don't know how you can be so calm about all of this. It's sickening."

"Only because you're not used to it." Saarken sighed. "I did some checking earlier. Phillip has placed a substantial bet on Ronan's victory tonight."

"Your point being?"

"Current bets on Ronan's matches are made based on how long it will take for him to win. Not *if* he will win. The majority have been placed for a quick fight. Phillip's bets are marked for anything beyond fifteen minutes. He expects Hadrian to drag the fight out."

"Why would he bother?"

"To reestablish his dominance. Either Hadrian does as he's told and makes fools of everyone who gossiped over his defection, or he's maimed or killed in the ring. When it comes to winning, Phillip has no limits."

A sense of dread filled Liam as he settled back into his chair. The more he learned of Luxorian society, the more treacherous Hadrian's removal was becoming. The hope of a silent rescue in the dark was eroding fast.

The crowd erupted as the vidscreens came to life, Ronan's image splayed across them in garish color. His match was close at hand. Even the sight of Hadrian larger than life on the screens brought a tightness to Liam's chest. It was an effort to maintain the calm facade his disguise required.

Saarken's eyes gleamed. "That's a striking look for Hadrian. The hair removal is very appealing."

Liam's brow flattened. "Don't get any ideas, Doctor."

"Sergeant, now that Hadrian's appearance is in my known realm of interest, it would not be suspect if I purchased him for the evening." Saarken smiled when Liam gasped. "It would give you a chance to plan."

"You'd do that?" Liam tried not to sound too hopeful.

"I think it would be a good idea. I'll contact Phillip after the match and make the arrangements."

Sitting still became difficult as Liam's excitement crested. An evening with Hadrian was more than he could have hoped for. He wanted to grin but had to show restraint. The theater's volume rose in a deafening arc, and Liam had to remind himself to breathe as Hadrian stepped out into the arena floor.

Liam feasted on the sight of his mate dressed only in a leather kilt and the requisite Adonirati manacles. The view was so good the fine details of Hadrian's tattoos were visible. A chant of "Ronan!" arose as Hadrian turned, eyeing the vast number of spectators. Hadrian's gaze spiraled skyward over the endless stacks of seats, searching. Hadrian stood tall, but his poise was off. A fracture in his confidence seeped through his Adonirati demeanor.

This was dangerous. If Hadrian was unfocused, he risked injury or worse. Worry gripped Liam at the prospect.

Even thought he couldn't possibly hear him, Liam whispered him a prayer. "You can do this, Hadrian."

Hadrian froze, spun, and locked eyes with Liam. He beamed and his chest rose, his determination renewed. Fresh and invincible, Hadrian turned to face Phillip's booth. Donovan sneered and looked away, while Phillip gave Hadrian a commanding nod. Hadrian bowed, then strode over to the weapon rack rising out of the wall. He selected a well-balanced sword. It rolled in his practiced hand as he moved away, taking his place on one side of the floor.

Signaled by the crowd's roar, the opposite door opened, letting Hadrian's opponent into the ring.

"For fuck's sake, he has to stay in for fifteen minutes with *that*?" Liam gaped in shock.

The menacing fighter easily stood four meters tall, dwarfing Hadrian. His size and musculature placed Zero and Orez as sad second cousins. The fighter was barely covered by a loincloth that left little to the imagination, including his green skin and blue spotting down his back and limbs. His blue-black hair ran in a long, thick braid down to his buttocks.

Saarken paged through the program information. "It appears his DNA donor was a Tharrasian native. They are wild, savage humanoids that live in a tribal setting. They are known to be aggressive and brutally raided the first surveyors to their planet until the military pacified them."

The Tharrasian walked to the weapons cache and picked up a huge bladed staff. Every footstep echoed, even over the noise of the theater, as he took his place opposite Hadrian. Hadrian appeared unfazed, taking a moment to glance at Phillip and back to his opponent.

Liam's pulse pounded in his chest as he listened to the rhythmic chimes count down to the start of the match. The Tharrasian dug his feet into the floor and gripped his weapon with both hands, every muscle tensing, waiting to strike. Hadrian stood perfectly still. Liam couldn't breathe. The crowd was louder than ever before.

A loud siren flared and the Tharrasian sprang from his stance. His jade flesh blurred as he swung the pole arm overhead, then down at Hadrian. Hadrian narrowly sidestepped as the blade embedded itself in the floor. Like in the cargo bay, Hadrian's eyes were glazed and unfocused.

Hadrian whirled, stepped onto the weapon's shaft, and ran up its length until he was face-to-face with his opponent, who was still holding on. One quick, sudden thrust and Hadrian sank his sword hilt-deep into the Tharrasian's throat, just above the collarbone. The giant's eyes flared wide and his face went limp as he fell backward. Hadrian stepped onto his chest and surfed his torso until it crashed to the ground. Then he jumped to the floor, withdrew his sword, and tossed it to the side.

The crowd lost its mind.

Fist raised, Hadrian met the cacophony of cheers with a defiant stare. Rotating, he addressed the entire amphitheater, until he settled on the booth of Phillip Chien and Donovan. As a final motion, he threw a sharp nod at them both. Donovan's face was a mask of shock as he turned to Phillip, who rose from his seat. His stoic eyes gazed down at his slave with the faintest hint of a scowl. The emperor was displeased.

Liam grabbed Saarken by the arm. "It's time to go."

"I agree." Saarken was stunned, his words barely audible.

"I guess it's safe to say we won't be purchasing Hadrian tonight." Liam helped Saarken to his feet and slipped his crutches over his arms. It struck him that Saarken wasn't objecting. Liam's pulse began to race.

"That's an understatement." Saarken's grim face added to Liam's worries.

"Doctor, you know Phillip." Supporting Saarken, he pushed him along to the lift. "How bad is this?"

The lift doors slid open and the pair stepped inside. Saarken activated the control and the enclosure moved upward.

"It's disastrous. Hadrian's usefulness is coming to a quick end."

"Over losing a bet?"

Saarken closed his eyes. "Phillip can't abide being embarrassed. It's part of why he left me. Now not only has Hadrian escaped him, but he's defied him in public."

"We have to hurry. I'll gather my gear as soon as we get back."

Saarken shook his head and pierced Liam with a stare. "I hope you're good at improvising, Sergeant. Hadrian's run out of time."

# Chapter Fifteen

HADRIAN WONDERED IF he was screaming. He couldn't hear or see anything, only feel the scorching knives stabbing every square centimeter of his flesh inside and out, peeling him apart. Even his vision was useless. Everything was violent color splashes made up of nothing in particular. Was it possible to bleed from every pore?

"*GUI CHO TOI!*"

With those words, the torture stopped. It was unfair the same phrase was used to start and end the agony, making him beg to hear it again after dreading its use.

His whole body felt damp. Cool air on his skin raced a shiver through him. The pungent scents of sweat and urine were most likely his own. Even the carpet crushed against his face felt wet.

With a herculean effort, he rolled over. Every muscle screamed at the task, his weakness was so profound. His head lolled and his vision spun. He was laid out on the floor of his suite. Father and Donovan were here. As he tried to catch his breath, he began to remember.

They'd left the amphitheater in silence after the match. He was escorted to his room and had the opportunity to shower and dress in his favorite sarong before they entered. He'd seen what was coming. There was no path to avoid it. Father and Donovan had taken turns using the pain command on him for what he thought must have been the last hour or two. It might have been longer. His sense of time was shattered.

Every muscle spasmed in the aftermath of the correction. His breathing was labored and rapid. Despite his attempts to move, his leaden limbs refused to budge. One session with the pain command would leave him as weak as an infant. He didn't know how many times it had been. He'd lost count some time ago.

Donovan stepped forward and knelt over him while Father poured himself a drink from a bottle resting on the occasional table between the two doors.

"You're disgusting." Donovan clicked his tongue piercing along his teeth. "Drooling into the carpet. Sweating like a day laborer. You've even soiled yourself." He shook his head. "You're pathetic."

"You have never punished me so much before." So exhausted, his words were slurred.

Donovan sneered. "You've never required it before. It was only a matter of time."

When Hadrian attempted to move his arm, Donovan jumped back, kicking at the flailing limb as if it had the strength to harm him.

"Don't touch. I don't want you to dirty me."

Hadrian's voice was as listless as his arms, yet it didn't stop him. "You do not need me for that." Donovan's backhand was faster than he thought his brother was capable of.

"Do you see?" Donovan shouted at Father while gesturing at Hadrian. "This is your favorite? This is what I've played second best to for all these years?" He stalked over to Father and invaded his personal space. "You can't trust him anymore. He defies you at every opportunity." Donovan's anger was taking hold and his words were strained. "You need to put him down. Retire him. *Now*."

Father rolled his shoulders back. He set down his drink and stood tall. "No."

"You can't be serious! He's dangerous! He's not like the others. Every day, he becomes more likely to try to kill us all." Donovan's voice became a growl. "Either you put him down or I will."

The glint in Father's eyes was the only sign that betrayed his rage. "You will do no such thing."

"Phillip, you can't be serious!"

"*I said no!*" Father's roar startled Donovan, who cowered. "I will not hear another word of this. Are we clear?" When Donovan stayed silent, Father grabbed a fistful of his perfect hair. "*Are we clear?*"

Donovan's volume was a shade of itself. "Yes, sir."

Father seemed satisfied with the response. He relaxed the hand in Donovan's hair and caressed his cheek. "This is not to say he won't be dealt with."

Hadrian could see and feel Donovan's murderous glare. Father had never made him submit publicly before, and now Hadrian of all people had witnessed the scene. He could taste the shame and hear Donovan's furious plotting. He would never be safe in his brother's presence again.

Hadrian allowed his head to loll so he could look around the room. It was pitch-black outside the wall-sized window. That meant it was probably still the same evening. It was only the three of them. No guards. Did they not want observers? Did that mean no one was watching from the security station? The knife from his suicide attempt was under the bed. It might as well have been several kilometers away, he was so weak.

Even if he could reach the knife, he doubted he could defend himself. His body had betrayed him, fragile and helpless.

Father clutched Hadrian's jaw and jerked him back to face him. He crouched over Hadrian while Donovan crept forward. The man was a master at stoic grace, but waves of disdain emanated from him. Father appeared calm but was far from it.

He gave Hadrian's head a shake. "Look at me. You were perfect. The pride of the social scene. My champion." His teeth ground softly. "Now, you're worthless."

His hand tightened on Hadrian's jaw. "You never openly disobeyed me before you ran away. Now you have made me a laughingstock. Again." Father shoved Hadrian's face away. "You used to obey me without question."

Rising to his feet, he looked down in contempt. "And you will again."

Walking back to the small table, he poured a second drink and handed it to Donovan. As he took a long sip from his own and admired the flavor, he stroked the glass. Ignoring Hadrian for the moment, he turned his attention to the amber liquid. The moment was far too short.

"You behaved perfectly until you escaped."

Donovan added fuel to Father's fire. "I still don't believe he did all of this without help. He can barely use the most basic tech around here."

Father took a sip. "You're probably right. I'd be willing to bet Leo had you kill him to keep him from revealing everything. It's too bad. If he were still alive, I'd make him suffer forever for his hand in this."

Hadrian refrained from commenting. Staying silent was a better option than risk antagonizing them. He wasn't sure how many more pain commands he could survive. It had happened so many times this evening, he was a pale imitation of himself. Better to say nothing and assess the danger he was in. Which, as far as he could tell, was immense.

"You were the greatest Adonirati. I took great pride in presenting you to dignitaries and leaders of industry, knowing they would never own one as unique as you. Now you're drooling into the carpet because you can't follow a simple order." Father sipped his drink. "You've changed, Ronan—"

"My name is Hadrian."

Father pointed at Hadrian with the drink in his hand. "This is exactly what I'm talking about. You were never that willful until you spent those weeks on board the *Santa Claus*." Father went silent as his features brightened with an epiphany. He downed his drink and strode back over to Hadrian. He got down on one knee and leaned forward.

"I should leave you to Donovan's tender mercies. You might last the night in his care. But I have a better idea." A cruel shade of glee came over Father. "Since the crew of the *Santa Claus* broke you, they will be responsible for fixing you."

Fear crept into Hadrian at the malevolence he felt beneath Father's visage. Donovan's dark smile broadened, privy to some private joke between them, as he knelt, taking his place at Father's side. Hadrian looked behind them at the twin doors, wishing someone would come in, but he couldn't sense any presence in the hallway.

Father stirred a new chill over Hadrian's skin. "You will be yourself again, Ronan, or I will have Master Sergeant Braxus commandeer that vessel and arrest every member of the crew for aiding and abetting a fugitive. I will have him destroy the ship and bring every one of those degenerate reprobates back to Luxoria for the rest of their lives.

"I will have them punished, one at a time, until they beg me to put them out of their misery. I will make you watch as I personally execute each one, and then move on to the next. There are some thirty-odd members of the crew? That could take a while to get through. I hope you have the stomach for it.

"I will not tolerate insubordination in my house. Your compliance may be the only thing that saves them all. Every single man on that ship is guilty, from the lowliest deckhand to that poor fool sergeant you wrapped around your finger. Granted, I may do it all for my entertainment, regardless.

"Remember, Ronan, if I follow through, it will all be your fault."

Hadrian felt sick. There was no option anymore. No matter how well Hadrian behaved, Father had every intention of assaulting the *Santa Claus* to make an example out of them all. The thought shined so intense, he couldn't block it out.

"I think that's a wonderful idea, Phillip." The antagonizing click of Donovan's tongue piercing inflated the dread flooding Hadrian. He marshaled his strength for what was coming next. Father turned to Donovan. Smiling, Father reached up to graze Donovan's cheek with the backs of his fingers.

Hadrian's words were listless. "I am afraid you are right," he whispered. Both men paused, staring at him in confusion.

Father squinted. "Ronan, who are you talking to?"

"It has to be now. I am ready."

The bullet pierced the window, burrowing through Father's skull. Blood exploded in all directions as his body slumped to the expensive carpet. Donovan shrieked and snapped his attention to Hadrian on the ground. Using all his strength, Hadrian lurched forward.

"*GUI CHO T—*" Donovan's shout was cut short. His eyes bulged as Hadrian gripped his piercing in his right hand, using the barbell to pull his tongue into the air. Grasping at Hadrian's arm, he slapped at it, screaming incoherent utterances while trying to free himself. Grotesque inside and out. Hadrian's hand was weak, but he held firm. Dragging Donovan close, Hadrian spat a seething omen.

"You and Father will never torture me again. Goodbye...brother."

Hadrian extended his arm, pushing Donovan's head as far away as possible, refusing to allow him to speak. He had no intention of ever hearing the command to inflict pain, paralysis, or anything else again.

"*Do it now, Liam!*"

Donovan's head burst in a shower of crimson as another bullet came through the window. Hadrian pushed the body away, and it fell to the floor. Exhausted beyond compare, Hadrian collapsed.

Gasping in exhaustion, Hadrian knew time was short. "Hurry, Liam. I can hear them. They're coming."

LIAM SET DOWN his rifle where he stood in the open hatch of *Hadrian's Hope*, hovering mere meters away from the building. Snatching up the preloaded rotary cannon, he threw the carry strap over his shoulder. He palmed the support grips and released the safety with his thumb, his finger ready to squeeze the trigger.

"*Hadrian, stay down!*"

Orange fire leapt from the barrel as the spinning chamber fed the weapon, and Liam held tight to control the recoil. A deafening hail of bullets ate the window until it had the consistency of lace. It took little time to exhaust the ammunition, but even as damaged as it was, the plexiglass-hybrid wall refused to come down.

Howling in disgust, Liam threw down the gun and scrambled to the pilot's chair. With hurried hands, he tapped the control panel and the ship tipped, sliding sideways toward the building. *Hadrian's Hope* burst through the tattered window, sending chunks of glass in all directions. Another quick press of the controls, and the ship hovered half in and half out of the skyscraper. Liam leapt from his seat and raced into the building. Liam wore a full military jumpsuit, and his heavy boots crunched over the sea of broken window that was once a lush carpet. Weapons confiscated from the raiders hung from multiple holsters and utility belts strapped to his waist and hips.

He rushed to Hadrian's side where he lay sprawled on the floor, limp. This wasn't the moment to feel guilty for not arriving faster. He'd lost a great deal of time getting out of the amphitheater and throwing his gear together. Blood spray marred Hadrian's features, but he couldn't find any open wounds. It had to be the remnants of Chien and Donovan. Hadrian appeared otherwise undamaged.

"Hadrian, can you walk?" He knew the timer was counting down. In a house like this, that level of noise would be investigated immediately.

Hadrian's head dipped. A weak nod. "I will try."

Liam was reaching down to help him when Hadrian froze and grabbed his arm. He stared at nothing as he gasped.

Alarm edged Hadrian's voice. "The house guards are coming. From both doors. Now."

From his hip holsters, Liam pulled a machine pistol with each hand as both doors to the hallway slid open. He fired at both entrances where large men in civilian clothing tried to rush the room. The guards were armed but unprepared for the controlled bursts of gunfire that shredded them in the doorways. They fell in graceless positions, leaving the entrances blocked open.

"More are coming. They are ex-military." Hadrian struggled to get upright.

Holding steady to provide support, Liam kept his weapons trained on the twin doors. "We have to hurry. There's no cover here."

Seeing movement at the right door, he fired a warning shot. He breathed hard and kept a tight focus on the doorways. Hadrian needed to hurry. Liam didn't think he could carry him and protect them at the same time.

A man swung into the doorway with his weapon drawn. Liam fired without remorse, removing the threat. Or was he the distraction?

Liam barely saw the particle weapon flare from the left door as Hadrian leapt up in front of him. Hadrian's eyes went wide in shock as the beam flash-burned his left arm off halfway between his elbow and shoulder. The severed limb landed on the floor with a thud. Liam whirled and put an indecent number of bullets into the gunman while managing to catch Hadrian before he fell to the ground.

It was like being at war all over again. The stench of bodies and gunfire singed his nostrils. Luxuries like panic couldn't be afforded. Completing the mission was all that mattered. Liam grabbed two small cylinders from the strap across his chest. Flipping the tops, he pressed buttons on each. A quick flip of the wrist sent them bouncing into the hallway through both of the open doors. Dropping Hadrian to the ground, Liam covered him with his body.

Twin explosions rocked the hallway as debris and screams rained down.

Liam crawled to his feet as clouds of smoke and dust billowed into the room. Hadrian wasn't moving, and he couldn't waste any more precious seconds. He had to risk it. He rolled Hadrian until he could pick up his rag-doll body and position it over his shoulder. The weight was more difficult to manage than he expected. Reaching into his belt, he armed two larger grenades. He threw them into the room and hallway, then struggled to carry Hadrian to the ship. He slammed the controls, and the hatch had barely begun to close when the ship lurched out of its window perch from the explosion. Bright flames surrounded the ship, licking at the sealing door, throwing Liam and Hadrian into the opposite wall. Liam quickly untangled himself and clambered to the pilot's chair. A few deft taps to the panel had the ship banking and lifting into the night sky. The side viewport gave Liam a glance at plumes of flame washing through that floor of the building, spilling out the window and up into the sky.

"Hang on, Hadrian. We're getting out of here." He hoped Hadrian could hear him. Liam checked the ship's cloak was intact and then punched the engine to escape the planet. The internal dampeners were working as well as could be expected, but the launch was rough. As soon as he cleared Luxoria's outer atmosphere, Liam activated the return path to the *Santa Claus* and engaged the faster-than-light drive.

The stars ahead blurred as he turned on the autopilot and charged back to Hadrian. Now that the gunfire was over, real panic set in. Had they gone through all this for nothing? Staring at the burned stump, Liam fought the urge to retch. Hadrian needed him now.

"Hadrian, can you hear me?"

No response.

Leaning closer, he sighed in relief when he found a pulse along Hadrian's neck and felt the faint breath from his mouth and nose.

He jumped up and pulled a couple of blankets from one of the storage compartments. Once he used them to sweep the debris from the area, he laid out more comfortable bedding. From behind another panel, he extracted the medkit.

He opened the kit and pulled out the handheld scanner. It was old but functional. He passed it over Hadrian, looking for any internal injuries or other damage. Finding none, Liam pulled a combat knife from the sheath at his shoulder, cut loose the foul sarong and the leather manacles, and tossed them aside.

"You will never wear those again."

Hadrian might not have been able to hear him, but Liam swore to keep the vow.

Liam shifted Hadrian to the blankets and continued. Scanning over the amputation, he steeled himself for the readout. The skin was charred at the end, but there was no blood loss. The phaser beam had cauterized the wound. The device flashed its first-aid instructions, and Liam reached in and unwrapped a hyperclean pad. It absorbed the sweat and grime, sterilizing the skin as he swiped it over the surface of Hadrian's arm.

Double-checking the triage list, he wrapped a mesh bandage of fiber-optic filaments over the stump, using the attached tech ring to fasten it around Hadrian's upper arm. A few quick touches to the ring's controls and the bandage activated, allowing air but no contaminants through its miniature field.

After checking the instructions again, he attached another device to Hadrian's shoulder, much like the ones he'd woke up wearing in sick bay after the raider attack. They were easier to use than he'd expected. Activating with a hum, fluids and pain meds began synthesizing to be transdermally fed to his patient. Once that was in motion, he went through three more hyperclean pads as he cleaned every millimeter of Hadrian's flesh.

According to the scanner, Hadrian was stable, so he covered him with another blanket, and turned the atmospherics up a notch to keep him as comfortable as possible. Then Liam lay down next to him to witness the rise and fall of Hadrian's chest. He needed proof they'd survived.

Desperate for his touch, he curled forward until his forehead brushed Hadrian's bare shoulder. Only then did he allow himself to feel the full weight of what had happened. They had done it. But at what cost? Tears broke free as he lay next to his unconscious partner.

"Please wake up, Hadrian. I need you." The adrenaline high wearing thin, Liam cried himself to sleep on the hard deck of the ship.


DR. SAARKEN STOOD numb as the emergency newsfeed played. They had hurried back after the match. Hadrian's defiance would make everything go so wrong. He hadn't even had a chance to say goodbye and been far too alarmed to consider sleep once Sergeant Jacks flew out of his home, not that Liam didn't have good cause. But Saarken had been starting to enjoy Sergeant Jacks's company.

Now he stared blankly at the vidscreen as fire suppressors struggled to put out the blaze belching from what used to be Hadrian's suite.

Terrorists have attacked the home of Ambassador Phillip Chien. Explosions and gunfire were reported this evening before what seem to be multiple incendiary devices ripped through the floor, burning everything in sight. Suppression units are having difficulty controlling the fire, as it appears to have been started with a device that fuels it, keeping it burning longer than usual.

While it will take time to get an accurate casualty count due to the intensity of the flames, at least sixteen people are missing and presumed dead, including the ambassador and his consort as well as guards, staff, and the ambassador's Adonirati, Ronan, who'd just won the title fighting bout earlier this evening at the Grande Hall Amphitheater.

Terrorists are being blamed due to a security vid from an adjacent building that captured the explosion and revealed the shape of a small, cloaked ship before it jumped skyward without a trace. At this time, no one has claimed responsibility.

Saarken turned off the screen. He couldn't watch anymore.

The escaping ship proved Liam had been successful in liberating Hadrian. If Hadrian had died, Liam would no doubt have killed himself in the hell he brought down on Phillip and the others. Saarken admired Liam's devotion. Now the pair were on their way to a happily ever after. A lovely thought. Some people deserve such things.

They had all been successful, hadn't they? After so many years, Saarken had his revenge over Phillip. Phillip would no longer hold him in his thrall. He could hurt no one any longer. Saarken told himself he should celebrate.

Phillip was dead.

His legs struggled to hold his weight as the first tear ran down his cheek. His arms shook and the crutches threatened to give way. Zero and Orez, ever the dutiful servants, swept him up and cradled him between them as his sobs unhinged him.

He pleaded through painful gasps into one of his companions' chest. "Please, take me to bed."

The twin giants stroked, nuzzled, and kissed him as they walked down the hallway to the master bedroom. Zero turned down the oversized bed while Orez undressed the grieving Saarken with careful fingers. After disrobing themselves, they lay him between their hulking forms, protecting him as he exhausted himself. He knew they could stay there for him as long as he needed and never break his heart.

LIAM AWOKE FROM a soft touch on his cheek. His eyes fluttered open to the sight of weary ice-blue eyes.

"You have been crying." Hadrian's voice was dry and cracking.

"Shh, don't speak." Liam jumped to his feet, found the cold storage, and pulled out a bottle of water. He opened it and helped Hadrian sit upright to drink, keeping the blanket wrapped around him. "Sip slowly."

"Where are we?"

"On board *Hadrian's Hope* en route back to the *Santa Claus*. We're on our way home."

Hadrian cocked a brow. "*Hadrian's Hope*?"

"I had to call it something." A warm blush seeped into Liam's face.

"So we are free?" Hadrian's eyes glistened in concert with the hope in his voice.

"We still have a few things to take care of, but I think we are." Liam returned Hadrian's slow smile. It was as if they were both having a hard time believing it was true. He reached up and stroked Hadrian's face to make it as real as he knew how. "I love you so much, Hadrian."

Hadrian began to laugh and cry. "I love you, too, Liam."

Leaning forward, Liam pressed his lips to Hadrian's in a gentle, affirming kiss. It was long and slow and full of a lifetime's worth of promises. When he pulled back, Hadrian's eyes were glassy and he looked content.

"How are you feeling?"

The light left Hadrian's eyes. "As if I was tortured all evening and then had my arm burned off."

A rush of sadness enveloped Liam. "Hadrian, I'm so sorry…"

"It is not your fault. I saw the path. It was a choice of my arm or your life. I would do it again in a moment. It was a small price to pay for our survival."

"Are you in pain?"

He shrugged. "Some, but it is very tolerable. The medication seems to be working. I doubt I would be conscious without it right now. The odd thing is, I would swear I can feel a sharp itching in my left hand."

"The medkit says phantom pains are normal. It's not really there."

Hadrian shifted his gaze away and pulled the blanket higher up his left shoulder. "I know. I have already looked. I do not want to see it right now."

"That's fine. I'll take care of everything."

"How far away are we?"

Liam stepped up to the pilot console and checked the display. "It looks like we're about another day out from catching up to *Santa Claus*'s flight path. You're stuck in here with me until then."

"That sounds like a perfectly fine way to recover for now."

"Do you think you can eat? It's just rations, but you need to keep up your strength until we can get you on board with a proper doctor. I'll contact Mac and Danverse and fill them in when we get closer."

"I think I can."

Liam pulled out food packets and more water for each of them. An odd picnic on the blankets. They whispered and joked and sat as close as they were able. Hours later, Hadrian had enough strength to sit next to the pilot's seat where they could watch the stars go by in the vastness.

"I did not get to tell you—you make quite a handsome Adonirati."

"Oh I do, do I?" Liam laughed. "The shaving took some getting used to."

"Given Dr. Saarken's aesthetic preferences, I am surprised he let you go."

Liam shook his head. "He tried to talk me into a threesome with his bodyguards at one point." He caught Hadrian's quick, unhappy glance. Was that a hint of jealousy? "I think the outfit and shaving were payback for me saying no."

"If you are asking my opinion, I think you should grow the body hair back. I like the feel of it against me when we sleep."

Liam's shoulders sank in relief. "Oh, thank you. I was afraid you'd want me to keep it all smooth." His hands motioned across his body. "I'm a big guy. That's a lot of work."

"I particularly liked the outfit Dr. Saarken dressed you in." Hadrian smiled as he fixed his gaze out the viewport.

"Really?" Liam grinned back. "I was a little hurried getting to you after the match."

Hadrian rolled his head to face Liam. "You are still wearing it under that jumpsuit."

Unzipping his front, he exposed the leather harness underneath. "I kind of like it. Is that going to be okay with you?"

Liam looked up through his brow with the practiced gaze he'd used on his mother as a child to get his way. It was so blatant it had to work.

Hadrian began to chuckle.

"When we get home, my love, and I am feeling better, we will play the game where *you* are the Adonirati and *I* am the rich gentleman."

"Will I like this game?" Imagining what the game would entail gave Liam rushes under his skin. He began tracing the edges of the leather bands surrounding his wrists with his fingertips. They matched the ones still on his ankles. He wondered if Hadrian could feel how aroused the thought made him.

Even through his exhaustion, Hadrian's eyes smoldered. "Yes, I can. And from what I have seen, you will most certainly enjoy it."

# Chapter Sixteen

"HOW ARE YOU holding up, Liam?"

Danverse poured two whiskeys from a storage cubby behind his desk as Liam sat in the day cabin.

The *Santa Claus* cruised quietly along on its cargo run to Tharrasia after a week's leave on Alpha Centauri. Liam rubbed his scalp, his hair barely more than stubble. It was taking a long time to grow back. He cursed Dr. Saarken for not telling him how effective the ultraviolet razor was.

"I'm doing all right. I'm just worried about Hadrian." He accepted the offered drink, took a strong sip, and balanced it on his thigh.

"Doc Bosch is taking good care of him."

Liam nodded. "I know. But we've been through a lot. I guess I'm a little overprotective these days."

Danverse sat on the other end of the couch and saluted with his glass. "Well, it's not like you haven't had things to worry about."

"Ain't that the truth. We're lucky we found each other, but it didn't come free." Liam settled back and looked up at the ceiling. All of Hadrian's connections to Luxoria were gone. The new identity files and bio Mac introduced into the Link looked solid. Hadrian was happy to become a citizen of Alpha Centauri and relieved he didn't have to change his name. He was just getting used to it. "It looks like we're in the clear, but we've kept a lookout for the authorities."

"Well, you did engage in 'terrorist activity' on Luxoria." Danverse finger-gestured air quotes for emphasis.

"Ha. Ha. I will not feel sorry for anything that happened that night."

Danverse smiled. "I was just surprised it was so huge. I expected something more subtle."

"Desperate times. Desperate measures." Liam took a strong pull from his whiskey.

"You know, with all the craziness, we've barely had a chance to talk. Be honest with me. He looks fine, but Hadrian can be a hard read sometimes. How's he really doing?"

Liam shook his head. He couldn't believe how fast time had passed since his last night on Luxoria. It had been almost a month since he freed Hadrian.

"Hadrian took losing his arm in stride, but I think he hides a lot. He's very practiced at putting on a brave face."

"Doc Bosch said you did a nice job of patching him up on the trip back."

"I just read the triage manual." Raising a hand, he stopped Danverse before he could say more. "No, seriously. Dr. Totoyo did all the hard work." Once on Alpha Centauri, some serious luck had fallen in their laps when Totoyo told them he could fabricate a replacement arm. A gift to honor his friend Leo Noble's sacrifice. It wasn't cheap, but they couldn't pass up the opportunity. Not many doctors would risk their careers on that kind of unlicensed work.

"But it's all fine now, right?"

Liam nodded. "Yeah. It is now." It hadn't gone perfectly, though. Shutting down and removing the transdermal tech was more complicated than anyone had expected, including Totoyo. So was attaching the cybernetic arm. Hadrian's body nearly rejected the addition, making for a rough recovery. If it hadn't been for Hadrian's modified constitution... Liam hated to think how it would have turned out.

"I'm glad to see Mac was able to make the final adjustments to the arm."

"Oh yeah." There was no way Totoyo could be available for any of the follow-up, considering everything. He couldn't risk being linked to all the legal debris of Chien's fall any more than he already was. Plus, it wasn't safe for Liam and Hadrian to stay on planet. "Thank God, Mac's a fucking genius."

"If the doc gives Hadrian the all clear, do you think he's ready to become part of the crew?"

"He doesn't have much choice, does he?" Leo Noble had left Hadrian an insane amount of money, but between the costs of the transdermal tech removal, an illegal top-of-the-line prosthetic, and restitution for the loss of the raiders' ship, it was mostly gone. "He's nearly broke. Who else would hire him?"

"I told you that you didn't have to pay us back for the raiders' ship." Danverse took a healthy swig of his drink. "I almost shed a tear when you autopiloted into the Sun, even if it was the smart move."

Liam couldn't screw the crew out of their salvage bonuses after the scare everyone got when the raiders had come on board. There was also far too much risk of someone tracing it back to them by letting it be sold. The Luxorian newsfeed about the fire and Chien's demise had reached the entire cluster even though few world leaders appeared overly outraged. Sympathies and prayers abounded across the Link.

"I had to make amends somehow. The money was Hadrian's idea."

A satisfied grin stretched Danverse's lips. "The men and I really loved the bonus."

"I bet they did."

Danverse laughed at Liam's deadpanned response as he took another sip of his drink. Then he sat back in his seat and became serious once again. "Seriously, Liam. How are *you* holding up?"

Liam looked away in reflection. "Pretty good, believe it or not. There's been a lot going on, but I haven't felt this in control of my life in a long time. I haven't had a nightmare since we got back."

"Really?"

Liam's voice dropped a notch. "I killed a lot of people that night, and I don't feel sorry for any of it. To save Hadrian, I'd do it all again if I had to. But I feel like pulling the trigger was my choice this time. And I didn't have to sacrifice an innocent to save anyone."

"Who knew that blowing up a building was good therapy?"

Liam shrugged. "Well, I tried rough sex, but it didn't take."

Danverse let out a deep, resonating laugh. "Don't say that too loud. Mac has gotten a little possessive lately."

Liam frowned at Danverse, confused.

"Oh, don't get me wrong—when it's time to play, he's the perfect sub and it's so fucking hot, Liam. It's better than it's been with anyone before. Um...no offense."

"None taken." Liam chuckled.

"But if it looks like I'm being too friendly to certain crew members, he's all attitude."

Liam rolled his eyes. "Oh yeah, because you're nothing like that at all."

"Hey, don't make fun of me. I'm sharing here!"

"Ha! That's what you get for making a crew to expand your dating options."

Danverse's eyes lost focus as he spoke. "Yeah, but Mac's all I need. Liam, I haven't wanted or touched another man since I kissed him in Engineering on the way to Alpha Centauri."

Knowing his best friend, Liam was sure he was replaying the last several weeks of sex in his mind.

He smiled at Danverse's happiness. "I think Mac's perfect for you, Marc. It's about time for both of us."

Danverse slugged back the remainder of his whiskey and rose from his seat. "Speaking of our other halves, we'd better head down to sick bay. They should be finishing up soon."

Liam killed his drink and stood up to leave. As he stepped toward the door, the captain's hand on his biceps turned him back. Danverse's brow creased as he paused for a second, mouth open. He forced himself to speak, struggling to find the right words.

"I'm so glad you guys are staying on board. Life is a lot harder without your best friend."

Stepping forward, Liam pulled Danverse into a crushing hug. When Liam placed a friendly kiss to his temple, Danverse returned the embrace in kind.

Closing his eyes, Liam absorbed the welcome contact of his closest confidant.

"Where else would we go, Marc? This is home."

THE SICK BAY doors opened to reveal Hadrian, shirtless with medical tech attached to his shoulder and chest, sitting on one of the beds while Dr. Bosch checked his vitals. Mac stood on the other side of the bed scanning Hadrian's new left arm. The sight of Hadrian spread warmth through Liam's chest.

"Is he going to make it, Doc?" Danverse asked.

Dr. Bosch smiled. "I'm feeling pretty confident. His body's adjusted to the cybernetics and he's not showing any signs of rejection anymore."

"It appears I can keep it." Hadrian glanced over at Liam and looked truly content for the first time in weeks. Liam didn't need to be empathic to feel the relief radiating from his mate.

"He's also recovered ten times faster than any of us would have. I still want to do checkups every month to make sure there aren't any surprises, but I think we're good."

Liam climbed up on the bed and sat next to Hadrian. "Hey, mister." They leaned into one another, lacing their fingers together, and weeks of tension evaporated in an instant as Hadrian nuzzled against Liam's neck and shoulder.

"This tech is amazing." Oblivious to anything else, Mac stared transfixed over Hadrian's new arm. The synth-flesh-covered limb was indistinguishable from the real thing, the seam hidden by a metal armband below his deltoid. The only visible giveaway was how the tattoo disappeared underneath the band without reappearing. Otherwise, it was a seamless transition.

Mac was giddy and awestruck. "Dr. Totoyo is a fucking genius. I've been going over the specs for this arm, and I'm still getting wet over the tech. The synth-flesh skin and musculature can be adjusted to the appropriate density and size to match the owner. The nanotech neural grid servos are all bound to the nervous system, giving complete sensory feedback. It has an internal heating and cooling system to maintain a natural body temp. It's fucking amazing. And since I'm the only one on the ship qualified to do the maintenance, Hadrian and I are going to be seeing a lot of each other." Mac bounced on the balls of his feet, a broad grin spreading across his face.

In contrast, Danverse was wearing more of a scowl.

"Seriously, Cap'n?" Mac flashed him a look of disbelief. "You're really going to flash me attitude over spending time with Hadrian?"

"This is not the time, Mac."

"You are such a fucking hypocrite." Mac stalked around the bed to one of the monitor stations along the wall. "Mrs. Claus, transfer my security feed to station sick bay number three, please."

Mrs. Claus was polite as always. "Will there be anything else, Mr. Smith?"

"No, thank you."

The screen came alive with an image of Danverse chatting with Liam in the day cabin. The feed was recent, from several minutes ago. Dr. Bosch hid his face behind one hand and turned away. Liam tried to make his bulk small and unnoticed, realizing where this was headed. Hadrian simply sat watching the exchange. Mac touched the screen controls and sped the vid ahead until the moment the men hugged. He froze the scene.

"BOOM!" Mac stabbed a finger at the screen. "What the fuck is that? You're gonna give me shit for helping Hadrian? At least I don't have a history with the man I'm laying my hands on."

"When were you laying your hands on me?" Hadrian asked, and Liam motioned him to be quiet, shaking his head.

"I told you I didn't want you spying on me anymore, Mac." Danverse crossed his arms and seemed somehow taller in his petulance. The alpha male was coming to the forefront.

Mac's eyebrows went up. "What do you expect? If you hadn't slept your way through the crew at one time or another, I wouldn't have to." Liam probably shouldn't have been watching, but how could he not? He could swear Mac was having the time of his life challenging Danverse. From the set of his jaw, it was clear Mac struggled to restrain a grin.

Danverse appeared less pleased as he growled. "Mac..."

Mac looked up at Danverse like a penitent child, which everyone knew was utter bullshit. "How else am I supposed to keep an eye on you and watch you shower while I'm working?"

When Danverse didn't respond, Hadrian did. "Um...you could take a break from your work and join him."

The entire room went still and everyone slowly swiveled their heads in his direction. Liam snorted, trying to contain his laugh. The doctor started cackling, and Mac's composure went down in flames next. Danverse's displeasure melted as he turned away, mouth tight, trying to keep from laughing out loud. Hadrian was amused.

Danverse shook himself so he could speak. "Doc, is Mac done here for now?"

"His scans are all finished for today. As far as I'm concerned, he can move on to something else."

"Good." The captain's smile turned lecherous. He stalked over to his boy and heaved him over his shoulder, to Mac's delighted protests. Danverse clamped a firm hand to Mac's buttocks, ending Mac's struggles with a gasp. He walked to the exit and touched the control.

As the door slid open, he twisted to look over his shoulder.

"Don't need us for a few hours. And don't need Mac for the night. He'll be off duty."

Liam waved goodbye as the door hissed shut, and the pair were gone. Dr. Bosch removed the diagnostic devices from Hadrian's shoulder and chest and began switching off monitors.

"Does this mean that I am finished as well, Doctor?" A flicker of hope edged around Hadrian's question.

"Yes, Hadrian. You're all set for now. I'll message you later to schedule your follow-up, but for now, get out of my office."

Liam was first off the bed. He handed Hadrian his shirt, took his hand, and led him out of the room. Hadrian's warm hand squeezed in a fierce gesture that made Liam's heart soar. If they weren't already in space, he would go out to see if he could fly.


DANVERSE WATCHED AS Mac slept, nestled into the thick pillow under the minimal light. His gaze followed the line of Mac's back as it rose and fell, finishing at the meaty globes of his buttocks. Almost invisible, fine, downy hair graced his skin, still carrying a sheen of sweat.

He couldn't sleep. Some nights, he was smothered by the fear of Mac not being next to him when he woke. He knew it was irrational, but he'd lost Mac before. It made him more possessive of his boy, but he loved him so much. Thankfully, Mac didn't seem to mind his dominant nature.

Mac's challenge in the infirmary aroused him enough he had to leave before his cock embarrassed him. In such a short time, Mac had learned how to trigger his need to claim his boy, and he did it well. They had missed dinner, but that was all right. They could eat after Mac rested. Fine lines of redness were still showing on Mac's back from the first touches of the lash on his skin.

Danverse had been gentle. Mac was a natural submissive in the bedroom, but Danverse needed to introduce things slowly so as not to spook him. No matter what, it would never be as severe as it was with Liam. That was a lack of control he would never inflict on Mac. He planned to keep Mac for as long as the boy wanted him. Hopefully, that would be forever.

With his fingertips, he traced the swell of Mac's bottom, grazing the flesh with feather-light touches. Twice tonight, Danverse had spent inside him. His caress dipped into the valley and found the tender opening still wet with sweat and leaking fluids. Even asleep, Mac responded by shifting his legs apart. Danverse's cock began to fill yet again.

"Look what you do to me, boy. Climbing over Mac, he poised himself for the start of round three, unable to resist the unspoken request. He was moments away from applying a new bite mark to those tempting globes of flesh when Mrs. Claus interrupted him.

"You have a private, encrypted call from Luxoria on a secure channel, Captain Danverse."

Looking down at Mac, he half whimpered and half growled at the interference. He would have preferred to ignore the call, but coming from Luxoria, he had no choice. With a herculean effort, he crawled out of bed and covered Mac's slumbering form with the blanket. Annoyed, he sat at his desk without even bothering to dress. Besides, he could only be seen from the chest up at this angle.

"Put it through, Mrs. Claus."

The monitor came alive and he tensed. In what must be his private home, firm muscles spilling out of his simple sleeveless undershirt, sat Master Sergeant Braxus of the Luxorian Guard First Class. Without the helmet and uniform, Danverse could see the man was about his age, with close-cropped dark hair. To say Danverse was confused was an understatement.

"Master Sergeant Braxus."

"Good evening, Captain Danverse. I wasn't sure you'd recognize me."

"I remember everybody. Is there a problem?"

"No, there's no problem. I just thought you'd appreciate a personal update."

Danverse's brow creased. "The last time I saw you involved the threat of prison for me and my crew and the destruction of my ship. Your arrest of one of my passengers ended with my security chief in sick bay after an assault by your men. Call me suspicious."

Braxus shifted in his seat and his broad shoulders slackened. The gesture was strangely disarming. Danverse wouldn't have expected the man to show any vulnerability.

"I wanted to apologize for that. Ambassador Chien had a practice of strong-arming his way through things. I was under strict orders to bring an end to the situation. I had hoped you wouldn't call my bluff. Thankfully, you give a damn about your men."

"So you were just following orders?"

Braxus's sigh was filled with regret. "Captain, you have to understand. As charismatic as the ambassador was, he preferred to intimidate and manipulate his way into power. Everyone of any importance who worked for him was under some kind of blackmail. Some were subtler than others."

"Even you?"

Braxus paused. "We all have secrets. Chien made a lot of enemies. Now that he's dead, there aren't many people willing to take up his cause. The *Santa Claus* and her crew are no longer of any interest to the Luxorian government. The aiding-and-abetting charges the ambassador was holding for leverage have been dropped and purged with prejudice."

"All because the man's dead?"

"The explosions and the incendiaries made a mess of the place. There were barely enough remains to do the DNA scan that made the list of casualties. Everyone on that list is assumed dead. That includes the Adonirati, Ronan. The case is closed. No one really cares what happened to the ambassador."

Danverse spoke slowly to be clear. "So they're going to wash their hands and move on, Braxus?"

"Yes, sir. And please, call me Noland."

"All right, Noland. Why are you telling me this?"

"I was pretty sure it was your security chief I saw at Ronan's match that night with Dr. Saarken, dressed as an Adonirati."

Danverse's mouth flattened as he shook his head. "I wouldn't know anything about that. But why didn't you say something then? Some of the men who died were military, weren't they?"

"I went into the military to do my duty, not to be under the control of the corrupt and rich. The men who stayed close to the ambassador had no such ethics. Something bad was bound to happen eventually. If not that night, it would've happened some other time. My obligation to Ronan's arrest ended when he was returned to Luxoria. I wasn't under orders to keep the ambassador apprised of any other information regarding him.

"But I'm not in the military anymore. I resigned last week after making sure the legal matters surrounding you and your crew were quashed. Feel free to continue to do business with Luxoria. If you keep out of trouble, they won't be looking in your direction. And if you do come to Luxoria, you should let me know. I would love to meet up and maybe have dinner." A cocked brow and sly grin. "Or lock us away in a hotel room."

Danverse was so taken aback he nearly laughed. He knew he must have looked like a stunned animal.

"After all this, you're asking me out?"

Braxus squared his shoulders, making his thick chest rise. "I've spent the last several years under the thumb of a man whose intentions couldn't be trusted. You learn to go after what you want when the leash is finally off."

"Fair enough. I won't say I'm not tempted, but I have to say no. But feel free to visit us. There's about thirty men on board. I'm pretty sure you could find someone to keep you entertained for a vacation." A fierce grin and heat filled his chest as he spoke the next words. "I'm spoken for. *Very* spoken for." Looking over his shoulder, he gazed at his sleeping boy. A wistful sigh escaped him.

"Hmm. Maybe I will see about spending some vacation taking a trip with you the next time you come around. It's not a bad idea. Even if you and I are only going to be friends. Your man is a very lucky guy, Captain."

Danverse turned back to the screen with a predatory gleam in his eye. "He's about to get even luckier." He rolled his chair back and stood tall, giving Braxus a full view of his state of undress. He reached down and cupped his swelling cock.

"Aww...that's not fair," Braxus complained.

Danverse leaned over the desk, a wolfish grin spreading over his face in the glow of the monitor.

"Good night, Master Sergeant." He switched off the screen and returned to the better offer.

LIAM SAT IN his and Hadrian's suite, going over security logs on a handheld data pad. The quarters adjacent to his were unoccupied, so Danverse had given permission to add a door between them during their last port—another of the expenses that had drained Hadrian's funds—since they would be living on board. One room now served as a study and living room, while the other would stay as the bedroom. Considering the scale of Liam's bed, this was a perfect arrangement.

The week in port had been chaotic. Mac had set up the room with a couch and chair and a few odds and ends until they could decide on something more permanent. It gave them a home to come back to. Liam was fine with the suite the way it was, but Hadrian was already poring over shop catalogs on the Link, fixating on luxurious furniture he couldn't afford. Teaching Hadrian how to manage finances would be very important. Hadrian was accustomed to a level of finery that would be in short supply for the foreseeable future. He would have to learn to adjust.

Reaching for his water on the end table, Liam was greeted by a number of graceful folded-paper animals he had found hidden away in several storage compartments. He thought they were beautiful. Hadrian's ability to create something so delicate always amazed him. Lethal hands graced with the skill of an artist. It made him wonder if Hadrian had ever had the opportunity to paint. He filed the thought away under "future gifts."

Now that Hadrian was cleared to work, he would be starting out as part of the security team. Liam was making a to-do list for Hadrian's first day as a *Santa Claus* crew member. There was a good chance that with the worst behind them, they might be able to live a happy, normal life together.

The door hissed open, and Hadrian walked in with his bag slung over his shoulder. Wearing nothing more than a sheer, knee-length sarong tied at his hip, his skin still glowed from the heat of the shower. Liam would have loved nothing more than to join him, but the sight of Hadrian being sprayed with water always gave him a raging erection. Which wasn't a bad thing, but it would be awkward if someone walked in. And someone was *always* walking in when Hadrian was out in public. It was the price he paid for having a partner this attractive on a vessel full of horny men.

"That's an awfully sexy piece of fabric you're wearing." Liam's pulse quickened at the mere sight of Hadrian's bare flesh.

"Yes. I particularly enjoy how it shows everything yet nothing at the same time."

Liam set down the data pad and strode up behind Hadrian. The shoulder bag slid to the floor as Liam wrapped Hadrian in a pair of loving arms. Liam couldn't hold back his pure joy at having him there and sharing their lives together. It wasn't so long ago such a thing didn't seem possible. Even so, there were still one or two nagging doubts.

"Are you happy?"

"Why do you ask?" Hadrian held tight to Liam's arms.

"I found a number of origami animals hidden in various drawers. I told you, I love them. You don't have to hide them like I'm going to take them away."

Hadrian sighed. "I know, Liam. I think it is simply a habit that will be difficult to break."

"I just want to be sure that being here on board will be good for you. You've been through so much and gone through so much change. I want you to be sure."

Hadrian turned in his arms and placed his hands on Liam's cheeks. "Life here with you will be different, but it will be good. There are some adjustments, but I have felt more at home in this small time on board than I ever felt on Luxoria. I am finally getting to experience what I felt in so many others over the years. And you made it happen.

"Never doubt how much I love you, Liam. I plan to spend the rest of our lives learning how to make each other deliriously happy." Hadrian rose on his toes to kiss Liam's waiting mouth.

Liam's eyes drifted closed as their lips caressed each other, while a skillful tongue slid alongside his own. It was lazy and loving, not consumed with need, but no less gratifying.

"You know, I'm supposed to be on duty tonight, since Marc is working Mac over."

Hadrian laughed. "Is that really how you describe their lovemaking?"

"With Marc's particular kinks, yes."

"You did not seem to have a problem with it." Hadrian's smirk teased.

"How did you... I never told you about Marc."

"I may not be hearing others very well anymore, but your feelings are always there for me. And sometimes, I get flashes from you. There have been a few of Mac replacing you in Marc's bedroom and life." Dr. Bosch had told them both that between his bonding with Liam and the trauma of removing the subdermal tech from his nervous system, his empathic nature had dampened.

"I don't want Marc like that. Believe me."

"Shh...they were not sad flashes. More like happy wishes for the two of them." Another kiss greeted Liam's lips. "Besides, I'm pretty sure I can beat any man who tries to take you from me."

Liam pulled back, his eyebrow quirked. "Excuse me...you just said 'I'm.'" Hadrian stared at him. "I've never heard you use a contraction before. Maybe hanging around all us roughnecks is corrupting you, Mr. Jamison."

"I happen to like the way you corrupt me, Mr. Jacks." Hadrian's seductive chuckle went straight to Liam's groin.

He stepped backward to gain the room he needed to peel his T-shirt off without losing eye contact. Hadrian licked his lips as Liam's pants fell away. He hooked his thumbs into the waistband and stripped away his black jock, his aching cock already at full mast.

Hadrian snapped his fingers and pointed to the floor. "On your knees."

Like a trained animal, Liam sank to the floor, waiting for Hadrian's next command.

"Stay."

Liam kept his eyes forward as Hadrian stalked around him. The heat from his appraising gaze threatened to scald his skin. He must have liked what he saw, because the sheer sarong tented over his hardening cock and he didn't seem to care. Ultimately, Hadrian stopped in front of Liam, his proud member pointing at its target. Liam knew what he would soon be doing and shivered in anticipation.

"Untie me." Hadrian's command was soft but bore a dominance that pushed the first drop of dew out of Liam.

He reached out for the simple knot that held the delicate fabric together. Lust made his fingers tremble. He didn't want to risk ruining the garment, because Hadrian needed to be able to wear this again, but only for him. There would be an assortment to choose from in the future. Yes. Yes, there would be. The fabric parted, drifting to the floor, and Liam's mouth went dry.

Hadrian's skin was impossibly smooth and every muscle beautifully defined. He followed the slablike chest and rippling abdominals down to the prize. Surrounding the base of the most perfect cock he had ever been fortunate to know sat a metal ring matching the band around Hadrian's arm. A sex-god made flesh stood before him, and he planned to worship.

Hadrian shifted forward. Liam's hand rose, but his mate took a frustrating step backward.

"Don't touch."

Liam immediately dropped his hands to his sides.

Satisfied, Hadrian stepped forward once again. "Don't move."

While Liam stayed perfectly still, Hadrian rubbed his swollen glans along Liam's bottom lip, spreading the slickness. He shuddered at the contact as Hadrian wet his own lips, his eyes locked on his supplicant.

"Taste."

Liam snaked his tongue out, tracing the spongy plum sitting on the edge of his mouth. He moved with care, not wanting Hadrian to steal away his present. When Hadrian didn't move, Liam kissed the head and his eyes closed at the salty flavor. Growing bolder, Liam wrapped his watering mouth around Hadrian's flesh. The soft groan that followed did not come from Liam.

Hadrian's hand wrapped around the back of his head as the silky, hard shaft slid deeper into his mouth. He pressed his tongue flat along the skin as it drifted in and out. Hadrian's cock was gentle and hesitant, at first, but built in intensity and depth. Before long, the metal ring grazed Liam's lips in a welcome rhythm.

Liam was lost. The only thoughts in his mind were smeared in lust: the obsessive urge to taste, fill his mouth and throat with his mate's meat, and the growing moans that were driving his senses into overload. He lost track of how long he knelt there. It didn't matter.

Hadrian's thrusts lost their cadence and his hand began applying pressure to Liam's head in spasms. Rasping breaths filled his ears as Hadrian's cock swelled. Liam whimpered as he awaited the inevitable. Hadrian cried out as pulses of fluid bathed Liam's eager tongue and filled his mouth through the final, staggered thrusts. When the crescendo abated and the shaft withdrew, Liam licked his lips clean and looked up at his mate with lidded eyes.

A light coating of sweat glossed Hadrian's skin. He maintained a devilish smile, while his cock still stood proud and unflagging.

"Stay."

Liam remained kneeling as Hadrian positioned himself behind him. The still-hard organ brushed the open valley between Liam's willing haunches. The sound of Hadrian spitting into his hand was all he heard before the wet head breached his opening. Without instruction, Liam spread his legs wider for better access as Hadrian circled his arms around him.

Liam tipped his head back, finding Hadrian's shoulder. He couldn't resist an urgent bounce as Hadrian's magnificent piece worked its way inside him. It was difficult not to force himself down to the base, but this wasn't about punishment anymore. Once he was fully seated, he was given a moment to adjust before Hadrian snapped his hips back and forward.

Hadrian tightened his arms and pounded into Liam, making him grunt happily with each plunge. Gripping Liam's steely cock, Hadrian stroked him in a matching rhythm. A heated sweat broke out over Liam as Hadrian masterfully battered his internal button; he couldn't last much longer.

"Hadrian! I can't... I'm coming..."

Liam grasped the arms around him and lost control. Semen sprayed out in thick jets as his muscles quaked around Hadrian's tool. He shouted out loud, amazed at how Hadrian could drag him to the edge of ecstasy so easily. Not wanting to be left out, he clenched his ass. Hadrian yelped and buried himself to the hilt one last time, unloading again with equal intensity. Eventually, their heart rates and breath patterns calmed. Hadrian carefully withdrew as he kissed and stroked Liam's temple.

"Are you all right, love?"

Liam wet his lips and cleared his throat. "Better than all right." He squeezed Hadrian's arms in response. It was the closest thing he could manage to returning the embrace.

"I would say work is done for the night."

Liam had rarely felt so sated. "I agree. You know, when you start working tomorrow, you'll be under my command for a change."

"That should prove interesting." They shared a weary laugh.

Hadrian helped Liam to his shaky feet and the pair ambled to bed. Neither of them cared about cleaning up. The mattress was calling. After commanding the lights off and burrowing in, they wove their arms and legs together, sharing body heat. Neither appeared to be done touching the other. Hadrian nuzzling into his chest was soothing and made him want to press closer.

"I can feel your love so strongly, Liam." Hadrian's exhaustion was taking quick hold as he began to drift. "I didn't believe anyone could care for me as deeply as I do for you. I waited for you for so long. Sometimes it doesn't seem real."

Liam kissed the top of Hadrian's head, smiling because he caught another contraction in Hadrian's speech. "It doesn't get any more real than this." He held back a joyous tear. "I've waited a long time for you too. Now sleep. Tomorrow is the start of a brand-new day."

Hadrian's breathing leveled out into a hypnotic sound that lulled Liam into a shared slumber.

# Acknowledgements

A special heartfelt thanks to NineStar Press for giving this book & series new life. I love the care it's received in this new edition.

Thank you members, friends, & staff at Gay Authors.org. Without you all I might never have had the courage to take this ride.

And a special thanks and love for Tom, who may not have understood my muses (yes, plural) and creative needs, but put up with me and them anyway.

# About the Author

While spending years more focused on visual arts, J. Alan Veerkamp, never let go of his innate passion for storytelling, wanting to write and draw comic books when he grew up. Once he discovered M/M fiction, a whole new world opened filled with possibilities. Why couldn't you have fantastic and dynamic sexy tales with an M/M cast? He started reading the online tales of authors like, Night Tempest, Rob Colton, and Alicia Nordwell, which only fueled his need to create. Eventually he found GayAuthors.org, and with a little coercive nudge, started sharing his tales with an unexpected level of positive response. The experience and support gave him the courage to cross his fingers and aim for the world of M/M publishing.

Born and raised in Michigan, J. Alan continues to type away, wishing it was practical to use a noisy, old fashioned keyboard that clacks with each strike, if just to annoy his loving partner and spoiled miniature dachshund.

Facebook: www.facebook.com/jalanveerkamp

Twitter: @jalanveerkamp

Website: www.jalanveerkamp.wordpress.com

# Also Available from NineStar Press

# Connect with NineStar Press

www.ninestarpress.com

www.facebook.com/ninestarpress

www.facebook.com/groups/NineStarNiche

www.twitter.com/ninestarpress

www.tumblr.com/blog/ninestarpress